Rebel Yell

Cambrian Publications   San Jose, California
1998
Second Edition, 1999

A Cambrian Publications Book

First Edition
Second Edition, 1999

ISBN 1-878914-50-2

Cambrian Publications
www.cambrianpubs.com

Series Editor: Brian Clark

Cover design: Brian Clark; photo: Sarah Wichlacz; model: Brandon Hall.
Contents page image: Andi Olsen.
The publisher wishes to thank Eric Isaacson, Marlowe Johnson, Dawn Levy, Shawn Rider and Trish Thomas for their invaluable help in the process of editing and designing this book.

Rebel Yell

A Short Guide to Writing Fiction

Lance Olsen

For Andi,
Creative Righter Extraordinaire

Contents

Breakout

THE CHALLENGES OF WRITING FOR THE NEW MILLENNIUM

Carefully follow what most handbooks on writing fiction tell you, and chances are you'll end up producing a nice, tight, well-crafted story that could have been produced just as easily in 1830.

You'll end up producing a story where language is transparent and fictive focus falls on your protagonist's psychology. Your character will be rounded, resonant, believable, and usually middle or lower-middle class. Your setting will probably be urban or suburban and rendered with the precision of a photograph. The form of your story will be so predictable as to be virtually invisible: it will have a beginning, a muddle, and an ending through which your rounded resonant character will travel in a fairly limited amount of strictly structured chronological time in order to learn something about himself, herself, or his or her relationship to society or nature.

In a narratological nutshell, you'll end up producing a piece of *realism*, and realism is a genre of averages.

It's all about middle-of-the-road people living on Main Street in Middletown, Middle America.

It prefers the everyday in terms of style, shape, and content.

There's nothing fancy about it, nothing flashy.

And that's just the way realist writers like it. They strive to invent stories about ordinary folks living through the unexceptional moments that comprise diurnally dull and usually distantly unhappy life in breadbasket America: childhood, adolescence, love, marriage, parenthood, infidelity, paying the rent, buying the groceries, watching the TV, dropping by the 7-Eleven, getting sick, and eventually dying, usually of cancer.

Alain Robbe-Grillet, in his explosive collection of essays on experimental writing, *For a New Novel* (1963), calls this the *Balzacian mode of fiction* because in a very real sense its impulse stems from the early nineteenth-century novels of Honoré de Balzac, but it could just as well be called the *Defoean mode of fiction*—after Daniel Defoe, the first novelistic realist, and his 1719 puritanically detailed pseudo-reportage of Robinson Crusoe's daily accomplishments on an island in the middle of nowhere. Illuminatingly, Crusoe's first impulse after finding himself shipwrecked is to recreate as closely as possible a bourgeois European enclave—another Main Street.

A mode that appeared in the eighteenth century with the rise of the new middle class in England and on the Continent, rooted in the less-than-factual journalism, diaries, letters, and journals of the time, realism is the stuff of Richardson and Fielding, Dickens and Dreiser, William Dean Howells and Sinclair Lewis, Ernest Hemingway and Ann Beattie, John Updike and *The Bridges of Madison County*.

I mention that last tremendously bad best seller among all those pretty darn good realist writers because, as Samuel R. Delany once commented in an interview, those sorts of narratives aren't written for sharp, perspicacious readers in, say, New York, where all the major publishing houses and most of the major slick magazines in America reside, but for a certain imagined housewife living in a small, yet comfortable, house somewhere in Nebraska.

If there's nothing in your narrative that she can relate to, nothing and no one she wants to know something about, then as far as that mainstream market goes, well, you're plain out of luck.

"The housewife in Nebraska has, of course, a male counterpart," Delany continues. "In commercial terms, he's only about a third as important as she is. The basic model for the novel reader has traditionally been female since the time of Richardson. But his good opinion is considered far more prestigious. He's a high school English teacher in Montana who hikes for a hobby on weekends and has some military service behind him. He despises the housewife—though reputedly she wants to have an affair with him. . . . Between them, that Nebraska housewife and that Montana English teacher tyrannized mid-century American fiction."

One reason that virtual couple likes realist novels so much, Marxist theorist Fredric Jameson figures, is that that kind of book "persuades us in a concrete fashion that human actions, human life is somehow a complete, interlocking whole, a single formed, meaningful substance. . . . Our satisfaction with the completeness of plot is therefore a kind of satisfaction with society as well."

Every narrative strategy thereby suggests a metaphysical one.

Writing is nothing if not a series of choices, and to write one way rather than another is to imply a mode of thinking that privileges one perspective on the world over another.

The problem with the realist strategy—besides the obvious gaff that more and more of us these days are neither Nebraskan housewives nor Montanan teachers, figuratively speaking—is that many of us don't share its deep-structure assumptions at the turn of the millennium. Given the high-tech, increasingly global, hugely unstable, multi-cultural, multi-gendered, multi-genred pluriverse our fluid selves inhabit, the idea that life is somehow a complete, interlocking whole strikes a good number of us as out-of-step with our Age of Uncertainty, even a little quaint, perhaps naive, if not downright amusing.

We no longer intuit that existence is necessarily meaningful, if we ever did, and we're certainly not satisfied with society.

So why should we write as if we did and were?

Why should we pad along the cramped, homogeneous corridors of suburbia, or the cramped, homogeneous corridors of domestic fiction that reflects it?

Shouldn't our task as authors rather be (or perhaps *also* be) to explore ways to create that accurately reflect our sense of lived contemporary experience?

Shouldn't we be writing for the new millennium?

If the answer is yes, enter the alternative.

For the purposes of this guide, let's define the term as loosely and inclusively as possible: everything that is neither mainstream realism, nor the cookie-cutter pulp of something like romance, is alternative—both commercially and aesthetically, as seen from the dominant culture's point of view.

Many of the points we'll make through the course of our discussion, which intends to touch on everything from the current publishing climate in America, to the process of writing and undermining traditional components of narrative, to finding a publisher and even helping promote one's own book after publication, can be applied to poetry as well. In fact, one of the premises of this discussion, as with so many postmodern others over the last twenty years or so,

Steven Shaviro

Q. How would you define "alternative" fiction?

A. I think this can have only a negative definition: anything that is *not* part of the mainstream. The publishing industry, like other industries, is undergoing a process of economic "rationalization" (standardization, downsizing). As a result, the only books that get easily published and heavily promoted tend to be located within very narrow parameters as regards both form (short sentences, realist narrative, characters the reader can 'identify' with, etc.) and content (happy endings, affirmation of family values, etc.). Anything that doesn't fit these parameters, anything that attempts to be innovative, is "alternative."

Q. What do you expect alternative fiction to look like at the launch of the new millennium? What would you like it to look like?

A. One should never make predictions when it comes to art. What I hope for is something that surprises me.

Q. Why? What forces will help shape it?

A. I think the Internet and other new electronic media will certainly be important in terms of distribution, as a cheap alternative to the current stranglehold that a few multinational corporations currently have on the publishing industry. Independent publishers have been having a hard time recently, but the Internet should help cut distribution costs, and maybe production costs as well. As for the influence of electronic media (hypertext, CD-ROMs, etc.) on the form and content of new works of fiction themselves, I am hopeful this will happen but I would not venture to predict how.

Q. How will it function and what will it do?

A. Marshall McLuhan said that when a new medium comes into existence, it starts out by using content taken from an older medium. It takes a while for the new medium's own potential languages and usages to be discovered. Just as film started out mimicking theater, so the new electronic media are still in the stage of mimicking print. Nobody has really discovered yet what new forms of language they might produce.

Q. What advice would you have for an alternative writer sitting down to pen her or his first piece of fiction?

A.   I can't give any advice about the writing process itself. But once you have finished something, look into the possibilities of online publishing. It is a relatively cheap way of getting your work out into the world.

Q.   Given the economic realities you describe, why would someone want to write alternative fiction, or, in your case, critifiction?

A.   I have always liked Marguerite Duras's response to the question: *Why write?* She said, "I write because I do not have the strength of character to do nothing."

Steven Shaviro is the author of, among others, Doom Patrols (dhalgren.english. washington.edu/~steve/doom.html) and Stranded in the Jungle (dhalgren.english. washington.edu/~steve/Stranded/index.html). He teaches at the University of Washington.

is that the boundaries separating these once disparate genres—all genres, actually—have begun to dissolve.

This text doesn't intend to be a manifesto, a public declaration of aesthetic principles, policies, and rules. I'm aware that a guidebook about the alternative smacks of oxymoron. After all, if you can codify and systematize the alternative, then how alternative can it be, right?

But that's *not* what this text is trying to do.

ManiQuesto is more like it.

That is, this book intends to be an invitation to think about where we are in space and time, and to ask how each of us might most effectively capture that place and point in our prose. It doesn't intend to be a how-to text in the same way, for instance, that Janet Burroway's very helpful *Writing Fiction: A Guide to Narrative Craft* (1992) intends to be a how-to text. While her book and most of those like it are designed to nudge young authors toward writing mainstream realist narratives, this is designed to encourage young authors to investigate which mode of writing best nails down what they have to express.

It's an invitation to think about fictive possibilities rather than limitations, an opening up of perceptions and perspectives rather than a closing down of compositional options.

And it has one bottom-line thesis: taking chances with writing fiction is more engaging and more enjoyable than not taking chances.

It therefore assumes that every piece of writing should be a kind of experiment in narration, and that, as we all know, some experiments succeed while others don't. The excitement and fulfillment of the experiment exists in the process, not necessarily the product.

It also takes for granted that a collaborative paradigm for writing is usually more fruitful than an isolationist one. Romantic myths aside, writing isn't about solitaire and ego. It's about synergy and cooperation.

Every writer, my assumption goes, should make a good-spirited attempt to talk with and help out other writers in any way she or he can, from joining forces in the actual act of creation and post-creation critique, to offering support communities along the literary interstate, to assisting in getting out the word about other writers' manuscripts and published work.

Alternative writing's a big party, and everyone's invited.

Now Read This

Alternative Reading Lists: Mark Amerika and I put together a long list of alternative fiction recommendations at the end of the collection of essays we edited, *In Memoriam to Postmodernism: Essays on the Avant-Pop* (San Diego State University Press, 1995), which you can find for free online at <www.altx.com/memoriam/pomo.html>.

I also keep a regularly updated short-list of fresh new alternative fiction at <www.uidaho.edu/~lolsen/readings.html>.

Barth, John. "The Literature of Exhaustion" (1967) & "The Literature of Replenishment" (1979). Two cornerstone essays on the innovative by one of the most influential edge-writers of the second half of the twentieth century. The first focuses on the death of old forms of fiction, the second on fiction's postmodern reinvigoration.

Bookstore: If you don't live in a city with a good bookstore, fear not. You can shop digitally for alternative fare at the biggest bookstore in the world at <www.amazon.com>.

Federman, Raymond. "Surfiction: A Postmodern Position" (1973). "The only kind of fiction that still means something today," this key essay asserts, "is the kind of fiction that tries to explore the possibilities of fiction beyond its own limitations; the kind of fiction that challenges the tradition that governs it."

Robbe-Grillet, Alain. *For a New Novel* (1963). It's really hard to write mainstream realism again after reading these essays that demand a special fiction for the present.

Watt, Ian. *The Rise of the Novel* (1957). A superb study of the development of the realist novel and an assessment of its assumptions.

Stretching & Flexing

Bring in to your writing group a short passage from your favorite fiction of all time, and one from your least favorite, and be prepared to explain why each affects you the way it does, paying close attention to style, voice, ear, form, character, and imaginative flair. What would you like to steal from the first? What can you learn by negative example from the second? What does each tell you about your preferences?

Eat Your Elders

READ THE PAST TO WRITE THE FUTURE

Literary history is not only a series of ruptures, but also a complex network of continuities, re-presentations, re-evaluations, re-collections, an ongoing circus of minds in motion.

Writing, whether we acknowledge it or not, is not so much a monologue as a conversation across space and time.

Unfortunately, American culture has a flawed sense of memory at best. Our attention spans tend to be like Plexiglas cages of dexedrined flies in the nose cones of Tomahawk missiles strapped to Saturn rockets, nine million pounds of thrust behind us to get us the hell away from yesterday. Why? Ours is a pioneer consciousness that doesn't like to look over its shoulder, or check out the rear-view mirror, environmentally, culturally, emotionally, you name it, because objects back there are always larger than they appear.

Which is, in a certain sense, just dandy, so long as you don't want to be a writer with aspirations toward the innovative, the fringe, the alternative, because then an ahistorical sense will probably lead to the reinvention of the same anti-narratological wheel James Joyce discovered in 1922, Laurence Sterne in the eighteenth century, Rabelais in the sixteenth.

In other words, you need to know and understand the rules of mainstream writing and the canonical as well as alternative traditions in order to break those rules and extend those traditions.

How?

By making reading a daily addiction.

Q. Can you remember what originally got you interested in alternative fiction?

A. Having spent my (mis)formative years in SF fandom, the grandaddy of the small press scene, I was keenly aware of the Do-It-Yourself tradition in publishing. I always had the sense that there were plenty of outlets other than big New York publishers—and that if you didn't like even the small ones that existed, you could start your own! When *Factsheet Five* first appeared, I got excited all over again at the potential of the small press/alternative media scene. Mike Gunderloy deserves to have a monument erected to him— or a small shrine in every home.

Q. In what ways has it been helpful for you to be as richly familiar with the alternative and canonical traditions as you are?

A. I'm a big believer in lineage and history: as someone or other said, "It's not cool to be ignorant of your own culture." If you want to participate in something, it behooves you to immerse yourself deeply and get up to speed as fast as possible. Although everyone's learning curve will have a different degree of slope, there's no excuse for reinventing the wheel. Unless of course you can improve on it!

Q. What three or four alternative texts would you suggest to a writer just coming to that neighborhood for the first time?

A. I would recommend any of Don Webb's short-story collections as an example of what can be done fiction-wise in the small press venue. The Loompanics catalog might be a good place for browsers interested in the range of philosophies present in the underground, as would the huge compilation issued not too long ago by Amok Books. ReSearch books remain monumental testaments to ingenuity and accomplishment.

Paul Di Filippo's first published story, "Falling Expectations," appeared in the small press zine UnEarth in 1977. His novel, Ciphers, is from Cambrian/Permeable, and Joe's Liver is forthcoming from Cambrian.

Susannah Breslin and Lily James

Q. What is Postfeminist Playground and how did it come to be?

A. The Postfeminist Playground is an interactive, on-line magazine for women and men. We were both originally interested in the term "postfeminism," having seen women and men frustrated with the limitations of feminism. We wanted to create a place for these people to interact, publish, and develop outside of feminism's stiff ideologies and anti-male posturing. The Postfeminist Playground is about being female, getting laid, writing, and intellectually getting off. There was no other publication looking at the issues women really care about—and having fun with them—so we created our own venue.

Q. Why did you decide to set up alternative shop on the Web in the form of Postfeminist Playground, instead of, say, via a hard-copy zine or even small press?

A. The Web is an immediate, virtually free, interactive, and widely accessible forum. We wanted to go beyond attracting the usual group of zine and small press followers because we knew there was a bigger audience out there to reach that we didn't have to become commercial to draw. The people who read small press publications and zines represent a very small and specific portion of the population. If you want five people to read you, go ahead and keep targeting a small audience. But we felt postfeminism was alternative, but went beyond just that.

Q. What are the strengths of the Web as an outlet for alternative fiction? The weaknesses?

A. The Web is perfect for alternative fiction because it takes you out of the martyred position of I-am-alternative-and-I-live-in-a-studio-and-have-no-money and puts you in a world where you can create what you want, how you want, and obtain a huge and loyal readership. The fiction we publish is funny and smart, although by no means mainstream. The fiction is alternative not because we label ourselves as alternative, but because the fiction itself is raw, edgy, sexy, and fresh. Web surfers like what's new, things they can't see anywhere else, whereas someone looking for a book to read on the beach or in bed may not appreciate innovation in the same way.

Q. The paradigm you're employing for Postfeminist Playground is one of collaboration, community. Can you talk a little about that as a seemingly new paradigm in the arts?

A. The Internet offers direct and immediate contact, resulting in increased collaboration, and leading to community growth. If we see a writer we like on the Web, we can e-mail him or her (immediately), solicit a submission (immediately), and publish that piece (immediately). Collaboration in the arts is nothing new and neither is the concept of an artistic community. But the speed at which that community can collaborate and the scope to which it can grow as a community has increased exponentially because of the Web. Peter Sellars recently described our time as "Post-NEA" and asserted that it is through collaboration and community that artists and writers will now prosper. We embrace that. But we aren't interested in living on bread and water either. The community and collaboration provided by the Web is a great way to create a business.

Q. Given the current publishing climate in the United States, whose bottom line is the bottom line, can you articulate your motivation for pursuing the alternative in the arts?

A. The work we do, the tone we use, the art we present are all very, very alternative. It would not be published in any mainstream publication. And the alternative up until this point has been positioned very much in an anti-capitalist stance. We are not interested in embracing this (false) perception. Rather, we are interested in bringing the alternative into the mainstream, maintaining its alternative tone and content, but making its distribution widespread and its reception profitable.

Susannah Breslin and Lily James are co-creators of The Postfeminist Playground at www.pfplayground.com.

An ideal model for this approach to art is Pablo Picasso. Drop in on his development in 1891, when he's barely ten years old, and you find him producing exquisitely mimetic paintings, ingesting and digesting the academic tradition in art while perfecting his technique. Drop in on his development less than half a decade later, and you find him mimicking myriad styles, not only those of mimetic painters, but also everyone else's from Toulouse-Lautrec's to Gauguin's. In 1900 he journeys from Barcelona, where he received his early training, to Paris, where he next spends hour after year becoming conversant with the Old Masters in the Louvre, as well as with Classical and pre-Classical sculpture. In 1904, not yet twenty-five, he moves into a tenement in Montmartre and surrounds himself with an ever-growing circle of friends and fellow artists. There, through a complex pattern of imaginative collaboration, he erupts into one of the most remarkable phenomena of the twentieth-century, reinventing himself and his art continuously, continually renowned by critics and artists alike for his versatility, prolificness, creative energy, range, and technical mastery.

Picasso's work is marked by nothing if not uninterrupted surprise and renewal, a paroxysmal sense of the uncharted, even as it uses and abuses both the canonical and alternative traditions, although it was the Surrealist André Breton who put the core idea operating here into print: *Beauty must be convulsive,* he wrote, *or it will not be.*

Convulsive history is the history of ongoing alternatives, diverse voices that sing diverse indie counterpoint against the overly sweet dominant pop melody called The Mainstream, diamond-toothed Termite Art whose function is to gnaw away at the marble foundation of those conventional citadels which line the Madison Avenue of consciousness.

Convulsive history thinks itself back through a hypothetical trajectory of vanguard art, appropriating from the past while nibbling always forward, from the fifties, sixties, seventies, eighties, and nineties: through the Avant-Pop, Surfiction, Metafiction, Punk, Cyberpunk, RiboFunk, the Multimedia Moment, the Deconstructive Turn, the Novel of Excess & Regress & Digress, Language Poetry, Beat fiction, Faction, Magical Realism, the Nouveau Roman, the New Wave, and so on, back through Lettrism, Surrealism, Dadaism, Expressionism, Decadence, Imagism, Vorticism, Futurism, and Symbolism, and back again, finally, to the doorstep of that paradigmless paradigm of Romanticism (think of Blake's schizoid visions, or, better, of the presence of Frankenstein's monster—the latter an appro-priated, electrocuted, existentially and socially and epistemologically alien icon of the extreme instant in the arts) with its thematics and formalistics of trespass, revolution, Dionysian border-breaking, psy-chotic breach, brilliant rage, paranoid rant, with its exploration of the illogical, the unconscious, the inner-world, the drastic aesthetico-spiritual brink.

Convulsive beauty is the stuff that keeps you young at percep-tion and heart, makes your brain itch, wakes us all in the midst of our perpetual perceptual narcosis.

It's a history one should become familiar with before attempting to join it because, as Jorge Luis Borges points out, "the fact is that every writer *creates* his own precursors. His work modifies our con-ception of the past, as it will modify the future."

Now Read This

Borges, Jorge Luis. "Kafka and His Precursors" (1957). A magical essay about the relationship of the writer to tradition by one of the great metafictionists.

Eliot, T. S. "Tradition and the Individual Talent" (1919). Seminal (and provocative) essay on the subject by author of the poetic equivalent of Picasso's Cubism, *The Waste Land.*

Olsen, Lance. "Convulsive Beauty, or: Thirteen Ways of Looking at a ManiQuesto" (1997). For more on the idea and tradition of convulsive beauty. You can find the electronic version on-line at www.permeable.com.

Stretching & Flexing

James Joyce recasts *The Odyssey* (ca. 800 B.C.) in his magnum opus, *Ulysses* (1922). In his hilarious novel *Snow White* (1975), Donald Barthelme takes the traditional fairy tale and resets it in a pop New York City in the sixties. Robert Coover looks to the Bible for his inspiration for "The Brother" (1969), the myth of Noah and the Ark told from the point of view of the brother left behind to drown. And Stephen Wright in *Going Native* (1994) retells Conrad's *Heart of Darkness* (1902) by sending two affluent Ameri-cans from L.A. up a river in Borneo. Locate a traditional narra-tive you've always enjoyed, and retell it in a way that allows us to see it with new eyes. You might want to change setting, time, or point of view to attain the effect you're looking for.

Downsize This!

THE CORPORATIZATION OF THE
LITERARY MARKET PLACE

Many beginning writers believe that once they're done writing their story or novel, they're done with the hard part. The rest is finding the most comfortable place to vacation along with Stephen King and Michael Crichton while waiting for those royalty checks to start rolling in.

While that may have been more or less (actually, less) the case twenty or fifty years ago, it's certainly no longer the case for most writers—even some of the very best—today.

Michael Arnzen, the avant-horror writer, once pieced together a list of statistics from various sources for an introductory fiction-writing course we were team-teaching. He titled the thing "Some Interesting Facts/Thoughts about Writing as a Career," and here are some of the more sobering highlights:

- It seems that everyone's got a book in them. According to a survey by the American Council for the Arts, 38 million people in the U.S. are writing creatively.

- Nevertheless, less than 1% of the books submitted by writers each year to publishers actually get accepted and published.

- Most books are not fiction. 85% of the ones published in America each year are nonfiction.

Q. Why do you write, and, more interestingly, why do you choose to write alternative fiction?

A. Of all explanations for why artists create, critic Harold Bloom's feels to me the most accurate: Bloom sees creativity as a radical rebellion against the pervasive failure to create—a failure which, in some infantile part of the artist's mind, is equated with death itself. Creativity grows out of the fear, the terror of death.

Alternative fiction might be seen as fiction in which the pressure of observation and the complexity of organization are simply at a different level from where they're set in normative endeavors. But (or, better, therefore), save on the most contingent, provisional level, I don't see the fundamental enterprise of, say, Dickens, Joyce, and Kathy Acker to be particularly, meaningfully different.

The variables in all three cases are variables in observation and organization. In the work of each writer, observation is aimed in one direction or another, then adjusted up or down as one moves along through the text. Organization of the textual material in each case is either complex, or formal, or simple, or informal.

In much alternative fiction the observation and the organization are simpler than they are in normative fiction—the simplicity highlights and makes us aware of the observation and the organization *per se.* Because normative fiction still makes up most of what people read, for many of us it still seems somehow "natural." One thing that alternative fiction does is "denature" normative fiction and make us more aware of how it functions as artifice.

When I conscientiously choose to write something that might be more easily called alternative fiction than not, usually it's because somehow I want to highlight some aspect of process—either of its organization or of its observation.

Q. How has the marketplace changed since you arrived on it and why?

A. Marketplace questions are rarely, if ever, questions about alternative fiction. A novel of mine that many people consider to have some aspects of alternative fiction about it—*Dhalgren*—was published by Bantam Books in January 1975. Over a period of a dozen years, it sold quite well—somewhat over a million copies. What your question may be addressing is the situation that a publishing executive at Bantam Books was also addressing when he said to me in 1987, a few years before he left the company to work somewhere less constraining: "If *Dhalgren* came in today, Chip, we probably couldn't publish it."

Notice he was not an editor but a publishing executive. Nor did he say: "We couldn't accept it editorially." He said, specifically, "we…couldn't publish it." Publishing a book is a complex process in which an editor's acceptance is only the first step.

Publishing includes marketing, distribution, and promotion. And that's what the publisher would not be set up to do today. That has to do with the prevalence of what are called publishing "slots."

In the late sixties there were a hundred-plus sizable publishers in New York City. By 1980, there were only seventy-nine. By 1995, there were fifteen. And with the recent merger of HarperCollins and Bantam-Doubleday-Dell, that number has gone down to five.

In the five major companies, the first thing that must happen to a book today is that it must be fitted into a "slot." It must be put into an official category. And that category will determine everything from the kind of packaging it gets to the amount of money that will be spent on its advertising to the target number of copies the publisher hopes to sell, and is therefore willing to print.

Some slots have the possibility of best-sellerdom built into them. But most do not—which is to say, the assumption is that, with most categories of book, the book can only be but so successful, and thus there is no possibility that the book put in such and such a slot will break out and run away. The advantage to this system—and there *are* some advantages—is that books do not compete with one another. They only compete with books in the same slot—books that are already judged to be of the same type. A book only needs to do well in terms of its own category: a book of short stories by a new writer, say, only has to do well vis-à-vis other books of short stories by new writers. It will be spoken about within the company as a success if it does well in that context. It doesn't ha ve to outsell the newest best seller by Belva Plane to be considered a success. The disadvantages are, however, self-evident from the remainder of my story.

Here's how my editor, Fred Pohl, told me he was able to publish the book at Bantam:

Bantam had invited me to edit a line of books for them, to appear as 'Frederick Pohl Selections,' and they wanted to see what I could do. For starters, they were more or less letting me have my way. When I accepted *Dhalgren*, I told everybody in the company: 'I'm doing this big, solid novel by Delany. It's highly sexual, too. Real best seller material.' To some people I would say, 'You know, I'm doing this strange, mysterious, wacky kind of novel, very experimental, that personally I think is just wonderful . . .' But I went out of my way not to mention that the two books were the same—until finally, at the sales conference, it came out. Then, when everyone was a little confused and wondering what was supposed to happen next, I stood up and said, very forcefully, to the sales representatives: 'Look, if you get out there and place that book, it will sell. It will make money! People will buy it up like hotcakes.' Now while I was saying it, I was scared to death. They could have gone out there, pushed the book—and we could have had 90% returns! But because it was SF—because it was my line of books and I was being given my head—the sales force went out and did just what I told them. And the book sold. Within weeks we were back for a second printing. Then there was a third—even before the official publication date. Four months later, we'd gone through two more printings."

Without ever becoming a bona fide best seller, *Dhalgren* sold half a million copies in its first year and another half million or so over the next dozen. When the publishing executive told me, a decade later, that the book could not be published if it had come in today, what he meant specifically is that there was now no "publishing slot" that the book could be fit into.

Since (arbitrarily) 1976, with the Simplified Copyright Law, the Thor Power Tool Decision, and the host of economic changes that have restructured American mainstream publishing over the last twenty years, the first thing that happens to a book today once it's accepted (which was not true in 1973 when Pohl accepted *Dhalgren* at Bantam Books), is that the editor sends a memo around to the rest of the company telling what "slot" his newly accepted book goes into, which immediately triggers a set of marketing procedures, a certain sort of advertising, a certain type of sales approach, that is coordinated throughout the company for all books that go in that particular slot.

If there is no slot for the book, it is—by definition, today—unmarketable and therefore unpublishable.

And there is simply no "slot" today in any major publisher that is set out for 800-page-plus novels that are strange, mysterious, highly sexual, and experimental—which is what *Dhalgren* was. And that, in a nutshell, is how the market has changed.

Q. In what sense, if any, do you think writing can be taught?

A. I honestly don't know if writing on the level we are speaking about can be taught.

The mechanics of grammar and various rules of organization and style can be taught. Frankly, I would like to see them taught far more thoroughly than they are.

On the level we're discussing, however, when we speak of creative writing, writing presupposes a certain kind of reading. Now reading *can* be taught. When I teach reading, and point out various patterns in the text, be it at the level of the phrase, the sentence, the scene, or some larger structure, I feel I'm much closer to teaching writing than I am when I actually run a workshop and people hand in their attempts at stories, essays, or poems.

In one important respect, all there is to learn about writing is a number of patterns, on all those levels (phrase, sentence, scene . . .) that writing can conform to. New levels of observation and organization make us violate (or, indeed, conform to) some of these patterns. The existence of these previous patterns alone is what makes the new patterns (of alternative fiction, say) signify.

Well, you now know all I know *about* writing.

Anything else would be what I know *of* writing itself.

And the only way to learn that is by reading…

No, I wonder seriously if writing can be taught, in the usual sense: of explanation, practice, and repetition, leading to mastery.

To me, as I've written before, good writing (especially the more experimental) feels much more like submission than mastery. And that's why I think all the rhetoric that points to, that leads toward the notion of "mastery" in matters aesthetic is deeply misguided.

Q. Is there a difference between teaching how to write mainstream fiction and alternative fiction? If so, can you articulate the difference?

A. If we hold onto the provisionality and contingency of the differences between the two types of fiction, of course there are differences in teaching them.

Any exercise that urges us to observe in a different way becomes a route to new fictive material that will likely register as alternative; any exercise that suggests new ways of organizing the materials of writing—from words, to sentences, to scenes, to whole works—will also likely generate alternative fiction.

Spend a single day during which you write three descriptive sentences about every object you encounter (which you stop and look at closely for a minimum three minutes) that begins with the letter "b"—and *only* those that begin with the letter "b." (You might call it "Being and Time.") Fulfilling such a writerly task may well produce an interesting fiction.

Or—depending on the quality of your descriptive sentences—it may produce a very dull one. But until you try it, until you actually spend some time inhabiting such an Oulipo-esque schema, there's no way to know or to judge the results beforehand.

Q. You wrote a number of sentences in *Dhalgren*, the novel many (including myself) consider your magnum opus, on individual cards before inserting them into the text. Why craft so carefully when so few will notice?

A. Emily Dickinson once wrote: "Nothing survives except fine execution." I encountered that statement as a kid—and I bought it. Yes, I'd like my work to survive, if only a little longer than it might had I not worked on it as hard as I did.

In *Dhalgren*, by the by, more sentences were written at the head of notebook pages than on index cards—because I needed to rework each sentence to bring it in line with iron and crystal. I gave up on index cards fairly quickly (yes, an idea initially borrowed from Nabokov); there wasn't enough room.

And people do notice. I can tell the difference between writing that is carefully worked over and writing that is not. You only have to read a paragraph or page of Ethan Canin or Joanna Russ or Guy Davenport—three very different writers—to know that all three put real thought into which word is going to follow which; which also means not only does each make all sorts of wonderful verbal choices, but that each has forbidden him- or herself all sorts of commonplace choices. There are dozens of ways that ordinary writers allow themselves to negotiate sentences that Canin and Russ and Davenport are just not interested in using. The modes of mental organization they represent are too facile. The commonplace observations and received dogma they allow the writer to slip in are just not ones these writers want to promote. With a Gass or a Nabokov, recognizing the difference between their prose and the ordinary is like recognizing the difference between someone who gets up and walks across the room and someone who leaps up, to grab a trapeze hanging from the ceiling, vaults into the air and spins, balances, and flips. Most of the time, though, it's more like telling the difference between walking and dancing.

People recognize the difference, and they take pleasure in the dancing—even if they themselves can't execute such steps.

Q. Many of your characters—Hogg, for instance—are less than likable, even frightening and repulsive. Why choose to write about such social pariahs, and how do you ease the reader into coming along for the

narratological ride? In other words, what can we
learn about the nature of characterization from your
choices?

A. I don't like to talk about "teasing the reader." I'm not terribly interested in character the way it's usually conceived—that is, as a ground bodying forth certain psychological truths—or as a playing field to display the usual emotional pyrotechnics we associate with "good characters": sympathy, antipathy, identification. I'm interested in characters only as each is a locus for allowing certain sorts of sentences to be uttered—by the character or about the character.

But, as I've written elsewhere, I begin a sentence lover. It's at the level of the sentence you're more likely to *find* me, as a writer. Now I'm interested in the larger structures sentences can fit in and generate. Still, for me, writing *begins* as an excuse to put together certain sorts of particularly satisfying sentences.

Q. Is there a question along writing lines you always
wanted to ask?

A. Again, only of the practical and provisional sort. Goethe once remarked, in terms of his own writing, "Why, once a man accomplishes something admirable, does the entire universe conspire to see he never does it again?"

I want to write more books that I, personally, can be proud of.

So, yes, I spend a lot of time wondering why the very institutions that seem to be most appreciative of what I've done (the academy, the SF readership that enjoyed my earlier work, the publishers for whom my work has had its limited measure of success) are the very institutions that make it hardest for me to go on writing.

Samuel R. Delany, Professor of Comparative Literature at the University of
Massachusetts at Amherst, is author of many speculative and transgressive novels
and theoretical essays on fiction.

- Big corporations and conglomerates control the publishing world. Currently 2% of all U.S. publishing houses are putting out 75% of all books.

- The amount of the cover price of a book that actually goes to the writer (called *royalties*) ranges anywhere from 3% to 25%. The average is 6% to 12%.

- Most authors never receive even this, because their books don't earn out their *advances* (moneys paid to an author before the book goes on sale, which must be made up before the author gets further royalties).

- One doesn't fare much better at the level of consumer magazines. Each receives a conservative average of 1,000 submissions a year. The more popular the magazine, the more submissions it receives. In a typical year *Redbook*, for example, receives 25,000 short story submissions for only 5 spots. The chances are, therefore, 5,000 to 1 that a writer will be accepted.

- The average "successful" writer sends a story or article out about 12 times before it's accepted.

- The average income of a "successful" writer is less than $5,000 a year.

The bad news doesn't stop there, either.

Downsizing, beginning in the eighties, resulted in publishers cutting their lists, laying off editors, and trimming the fat. Publishing houses began to merge or become absorbed by larger media multinationals.

Meanwhile, mega-bookstores like Barnes & Noble and Borders began moving in next to (and sometimes literally across the street from) small independently owned bookstores, thereby slowly driving them out of business.

The result of both these trends has been to move the focus away from aesthetic quality in publishing and toward the fiscal brass tacks.

"Why should I publish books if they are not going to make money?" Sonny Mehta, head of Knopf, asked not too long ago.

Why indeed.

Today, in America alone, according to a recent article in *The Wall*

Larry McCaffrey

Q. You're someone with a close eye on the contemporary fiction scene and its marketplace. Can you sketch in what that marketplace looks like now from your vantage point, and why that is?

A. Right now the commercial scene for serious literature looks to me like one of the sets built for *Honey, I Shrunk the Literary Marketplace*, or *The Incredible Shrinking Serious Fiction Writer*. Everything looks normal enough until the camera pulls back to give you a perspective on how tiny your world has become.

Q. What space exists there for alternative fiction?

A. The space for alternative publishing is increasingly less literally a book space of printed pages. You hear a lot these days about the small presses and university presses taking up the slack created when the commercial houses abandoned any commitment to publishing serious books, but, frankly, I don't see that happening. I mean who is publishing truly radical books right now? The Fiction Collective 2 (and its Black Ice Books spin-off), Dalkey, Sun and Moon, Permeable Press, McPherson, with maybe a few marginal places like Four Walls, the University of Nebraska Press, and Coffee House. There's probably a few others I haven't heard of yet, but overall the list is depressingly small. There does seem to be an expanding *virtual* space for alternative fiction in fanzines and certain Net sites like Mark Amerika's Alt-X (which has recently posted several long-out-of-print classics like Ronald Sukenick's *Out* and Raymond Federman's *Voice in the Closet*); but this space is mainly clogged with junk—non-commercial, even alternative stuff, but junk nonetheless. For most serious readers, it's just not going to be worth the effort of trying to locate quality fiction in this space until more effective navigational tools become available.

Q. What sort of current trends and writers in and out of the alternative excite you these days?

A. What excites me these days definitely *isn't* picking up a book by another writer who wants to show how plugged in she is to the randomness and plurality and nihilism and hyperstimulation of our surface-laden post-millennial life, or somebody who offers up her work with the sense of "Here it is, make of it what you will," but finding something that makes real demands on readers, something that's been obviously *labored* over by someone capable of creating memorable sentences, someone who *hasn't* seen it all and is willing to risk being unhip enough to write a book that actually matters. I guess above all, I'm bored with irony. Some recent turn-ons: DeLillo's *Underworld*, Doug Rice's *The Blood of Mugwump*, Pynchon's *Mason & Dixon*, Stephen Wright's *Going Native* (which still gets my vote for the book of the decade), Eurudice's *f/32*, William Vollmann's *The Rifles*, Robert Coover's *The Briar Rose*, David Matlin's *How the Night is Divided.*

Larry McCaffery, Professor of English at San Diego State University, is author of numerous books on contemporary fiction, including Storming the Reality Studio: A Casebook of Cyberpunk and Postmodern Fiction and After Yesterday's Crash: The Avant-Pop Anthology.

Alan Wilde

Q. How can a critic of the contemporary like you get a handle on what's being published these days, both in terms of mainstream and alternative fiction, given the vast numbers of books that appear every year?

A. As for staying on top of what's going on in the literary precinct, forget it. Everything is so thoroughly splintered that there's nothing to be on top of. It seems to me that this is a time of total chaos both in literature and in criticism, and probably the best you can do is please yourself.

Q. What do you suppose contributed to the creation of this moment?

A. From the beginning of the century up to and including poststructuralism, one theoretical model or the other has been dominant. Sometimes the models were more or less "transparent" (literary history, intellectual history, New Criticism)—that is, people practiced the theory as often as not without realizing they were doing it. And still do. Witness all the people who do "close reading" of texts without necessarily realizing that they are New Critics. Sometimes the models have been very visible indeed, as in the case of structuralism, poststructuralism, phenomenology, and so on. The last major Theory that commanded widespread allegiance was, of course, poststructuralism; and there, I think, begins our tale. Its success, particularly under the guise of deconstruction, leads precisely to our current situation—that is, its emphasis on skepticism, relativism, margins, borders, and so on, eventually made any kind of "hegemonic" (excuse the term) theory all but impossible.

My point is that theory, transparent or visible, privileged certain texts or kinds of texts and therefore provided a framework within which to value novels, poems, and so on. With the disintegration of theory into a collection of small, discrete "isms," any kind of encompassing frame has melted away. What we have now is a literary ouroboros: small groups of writers are validated by small groups of critics who praise the writers that validate their theories.

Needless to say, this simplifies everything. There are, no doubt, endless sociological factors that enter into the picture: the shifting composition of the American population, which gives rise to, say, identity politics; the opening up of once closed doors, which gives rise to feminist studies, queer studies, and so on.

Q. If you were a betting sort of critic, what would you

imagine the literary landscape will look like in the
early twenty-first century? More of the same? Is it
possible, once this sort of multiverse has erupted,
to ever find our way back to more predictable liter-
ary-theoretical footing? Is it desirable?

A.   I'll try to grab just one strand of your question: what's likely to happen in
college and university English departments. My suspicion is that theory
will continue to rule the roost—not for intellectual but for economic reasons. We're all familiar by now with academe's emulation of corporate
models—and with its current corollary, downsizing. Continuing or return-
ing to the idea of centuries or periods would mean at least one teacher per
century/period. With theory in control, one could conceivably reduce a department to one person, who would choose whatever literary works were
convenient to illustrate this or that theory. You can easily enough extrapo-
late from that kind of training to the literary landscape in the early twenty-
first century. As you can tell by now, I don't find the situation "desirable";
but it does seem to me inevitable: little cells of like-minded people doing
their own thing without much awareness of or interest in what's happening
in other cells.

Given his current view of the profession, Alan Wilde, professor emeritus of English
at Temple University and author of Horizons of Assent: Modernism,
Postmodernism, and the Ironic Imagination, spends more of his time these
days working on computer painting than on criticism.

Bob Greene

Q. How has the situation for independent bookstores changed over the last ten or fifteen years?

A. The situation of independent bookstores has changed dramatically. For the small store, it's hard to tell what has hurt more—the development of chains or the superstore concept or the idea of entitlement to everything as a shopper's right. The average shopper feels that everything should be instantaneously available to them. Corporations feed this jones, as do so-called technological advances (if technology is so liberating why is everyone miserable?), so the average person expects instant gratification. A more insidious development has taken place among publishers, as well. They are enamored by the nontraditional sales place, i.e., locations other than bookstores. The publisher gives a bigger discount to the nontraditional outlet and feels little loyalty towards the bookstore as a concept.

Q. What accounts for the change?

A. Growth for growth's sake is the ideology of the cancer cell. This idea coupled with the cultural fetish of being Number One leads to a state where competiton is everything . . . and it's not competition to be the best you can be, but competiton to destroy everything else.

Q. How does that affect the kinds of books being sold?

A. The return-on-investment demands of the large stores are so high compared to independents (Tattered Cover in Denver has a one-percent profit) that books must sell large numbers to be profitable. Nothing wrong with that, but the large numbers must be generated within seven or ten days. Culture, the human heart, and imagination have become like bread—Wonderbread: all air and a cotton candy taste.

Q. What's your prognosis? Will a state of equilibrium be reached between mega-bookstores and independents, or is this the beginning of the end?

A. My prognosis is take two bottles of beer and see if the sky falls overnight. It's hard to say what's going to happen in bookselling. In the near future, you can only expect constant change. 👀

Bob Greene owns and operates BookPeople, an independent bookstore in Moscow, Idaho.

Street Journal, about 1.3 million titles are in print, 140,000 of which were first published in 1996. That sounds pretty good, until we realize only about 4,500 of them were novels, only 250 of them first novels, and that in many cases they are the literary analog of vanilla ice cream: homogeneous, unthreatening, and, in most cases, just plain uninteresting.

Philip Roth estimates the audience for "serious" fiction currently runs no more than a disheartening 120,000. Nan Talese, a major editor at Doubleday, puts it closer to 4,000.

So while it's true someone like John Grisham's law-firm novels sell more than 4.5 million copies in hardcover alone, the romance genre sells more than $1 billion worth of books (50 percent of all mass-market paperbacks), and much of what's popular is due to hype and luck, it's also true that most writers can't live from what they make off their writing, and that breaking into the New York publishing world is harder today than it's ever been before. Nor, given the sociological and economic realities, is this trend going to ease up in the foreseeable future. In five years, it will be harder still. In ten, virtually impossible.

In spite of such gloom and doom, though, there's still some very real cause for optimism.

And it's that sense of optimism that this guide will attempt to map.

For starters, against all odds, some wonderful writers are doing some wonderful things on the American scene. Names like Kathryn Dunn, Stephen Wright, and David Foster Wallace leap to mind. Second, due in large part to desktop publishing, there are more hardcopy alternative fiction outlets than ever before. *The International Directory of Little Magazines and Small Presses* lists more than 5,000 of them. Third, since the early nineties the World Wide Web has provided a low-cost arena in which to produce fiction, and a number of excellent e-zines are thriving, from *George Jr.* to *Pug*.

What Samuel Beckett once told Raymond Federman is truer now than it's ever been: "Whatever you write never compromise, never cheat, and if you plan to write for money or for fame, do something else."

It's also true that punk's Do-It-Yourself aesthetic is alive and well on the alternative publishing scene.

It all comes down to the David and Goliath myth: the individual's reaction time is fast, the corporation's reaction time is slow, and consequently alternative fiction has abundant opportunities to flourish,

Curtis White

Q. One of the alternatives to New York megapublishing is the small press, like FC2 and Black Ice, the latter which you co-direct. What does the state of the small press in America look like from within?

A. First, since presses like FC2, Dalkey Archive, Sun and Moon, and Coffee House publish so many more quality literary titles than any commercial publisher you can name, I don't know why anyone should think of us as small. Among the four, more than a hundred new literary titles and reprints were published last season alone. In terms of production, significance, visibility: these are the best of times.

Q. What sort of problems does a small press have to surmount to stay in business?

A. The biggest problem is: how to play in the same pool with Random House and Barnes & Noble and not get inundated. The rules of the game are written for giant organizations with lots of money to lose and cash flow resources. Last year, returns from Barnes & Nobel canceled out all sales for the fall season. If it hadn't been for our notorious N.E.A. grant, we'd be gone now.

Q. Will the small press continue to operate as it has-- as a viable alternative to the McDonaldization of the literary marketplace--in the twenty-first century?

A. Yes. This will mean at least three things: preservation of the literary past (Dalkey); discovery and maintenance of the literary present (Sun and Moon and FC2); polemical troublemaking pranksterism of Avant-Pop, cyber-mods, and chicklets everywhere (FC2, Semiotext[e], and a gadzillion more ephemeral zine-scenesters).

Curtis White is the author of five books of fiction, including Memories of My Father Watching T.V. He is co-director of FC2/Black Ice Books.

Q. You're a young writer just starting your career in alternative fiction. What sort of difficulties are you finding?

A. I've found that no matter how innovative and avant-smart you think you are with your writing—this is especially true for experimental fiction—there's always someone before you who's been there, done that. So a lot of the game depends on how well READ you are and how well you READ, with a Grand Chasm of difference between the two. I think too many young writers get lost in the act of creating their own worlds that they lose sight of the importance of being able to enter other ones, and once that happens, whatever's magical about fiction curls up and dies.

Q. Of those difficulties, which do you think might be particular to your generation?

A. My generation was weaned on Hong Kong Fooey, the birth of CNN and MTV, and the sad cartoon of Reaganomics/Iran-Contra, so the attention span gets pretty thin in these waters. A lot of the Iowa-flavored fiction workshops I've been in are largely an amalgamation of whatever-brand genre writers who want their fiction like their thermonuclear physics…that is, fried formulaic. They want to know the path of least resistance to becoming a writer—where to find the cheat codes, how to sell 70 kazillion copies on their first novel, and where they can reach Don King to promote the thing. Now, I'm not sure that's entirely generational, but it's certainly a symptom of the late twentieth century, where writers become rock stars (literally, à la Stephen King and his traveling wilbury act) and anyone famous gets a book deal because Market has overshadowed the actual process and WORK of writing. Let me put it this way: millions of people bought Ivana Trump's first (and hopefully last) novel, not because she's a great (or even mediocre) novelist, but because she's Ivana Trump.

Q. Why are you so tenacious about staying with fiction writing in general, and alternative fiction writing in particular, given all this?

A. I hate to talk about saving writing from extinction like it's some kind of albino marmoset or something, but the sentiment might be more true today than ever. Alternative writing is a way to comment on the countless droves of schlock that're being pumped into the market like so much cyanide without having to breathe it full strength—sorta like a gas mask I guess you could say. There are more people who don't read than do, and the majority of those who do stick to mainstream commercial tripe. But, where alternative fiction is concerned, you gotta think locally and act globally, utilizing the plethora of small presses and independent zines (print and electronic) out there to disseminate your wake-up call to the United State of Amnesia dominating the publication market.

Trevor Dodge has published interviews, reviews, and original pieces of experimental fiction in online and print journals such as Alt-X, House Organ, Puck, Rain Taxi, and Carbon 14.

which is exactly what it's doing right now, and in multifarious flavors.

Now Read This

Bolles, Richard Nelson. *What Color Is Your Parachute?* (1980; updated frequently). For writers (and everybody else) on how to create a career that fits your needs.

Olsen, Lance, ed. *Surfing Tomorrow: Essays on the Future of American Fiction* (1995). Twenty-three pieces by critics and writers on the current and future state of fiction, both in terms of publishing practicalities and aesthetic concerns.

Stretching & Flexing

Go to your campus or local library and follow *Publishers Weekly*, the primary gloss on the New York publishing world, for two months. What sort of trends, concerns, themes do you find? Do these corroborate what I've just talked about in this section, or do you perceive different ones? What do these tell you about the current state of fiction in the United States?

What Workshops and M.F.A. Programs Do and Don't Do

Flannery O'Connor, who attended the Iowa Writers Workshop, the oldest, most esteemed, and most paradigmatic graduate writing program in the country (each year, more than 750 aspiring writers apply for its 15 or 30 slots, while every other program in the U.S. and Canada—all approximately 330 of them—designs itself with Iowa in mind), wasn't especially fond of her alma mater. "I don't believe in classes where students criticize each other's manuscripts," she announces in her well-known essay, "The Nature and Aim of Fiction." "Such criticism is generally composed in equal parts of ignorance, flattery, and spite. It's the blind leading the blind, and it can be dangerous."

That's not all that can be dangerous about the workshop environment. Although many first-rate writers, alternative and otherwise, have graduated from them, including John Barth, Frederick Barthelme, T. C. Boyle, Louise Erdrich, Lauren Fairbanks, Barry Hannah, Michael Joyce, Rick Moody, and David Foster Wallace, it's also true that at their worst those workshops have become the aesthetic equivalent of a Ford assembly line. As the pseudonymous Chris Altacruise argues in his vitriolic attack on them, the stories generated within their hermetically sealed walls almost always "display the hallmarks of committee effort: emotional restraint and a lack of linguistic idiosyncrasy; no vision, just voice; no fictional world of substance and variety, just a smooth surface of diaristic, autobiographical, and confessional speech."

Or, to put it another way, most sound just like aspiring Raymond Carvers wrote them, eager to enter the institutional halls of *The New Yorker*.

"*The New Yorker* has thus become the reincarnation of the nineteenth-century French Academy, promoting one school of fiction to the exclusion of all others," Altacruise concludes.

And that's the good news.

Some workshops devolve from discussions of craft and aesthetics into psycho-drivel therapy sessions which might tell you something about yourself, but seldom about your fiction. Others are rife with the fetid air of political correctness, a leftist brand of McCarthyism for the new millennium. Most end up producing what Altacruise calls Groupthink, "an unspoken consensus on politics and aesthetics that completely controls student work—from the story genre, down deep into the psychic creation of character, and out into the writer's very ability to imagine and create a world."

Workshops frequently give rise to the eerie sensation of the bland leading the bland, while the bland desperately try to convince themselves that in the valley of the blind the one-eyed man is king.

That said, however, it's simply too easy to dismiss writing programs—especially graduate ones—out of hand. After all, a number of terrific alternative writers *have* come out of them, and most people, after being away from them for a decade or so, speak of them glowingly.

M.F.A. programs give you, if nothing else, between two and three subsidized years to do very little else except write and think about writing, and what more could any young writer ask for?

They also surround you with good readers. And even if you seldom agree with them, they will still serve as great sounding boards off of which to bounce your own ideas about what fiction should be. David Shields, the fiction and nonfiction author, and I argued aesthetics over outrageous ice-cream sundaes in his apartment almost nightly while we were at Iowa together. The result wasn't that we ever really swayed each other very far, but we definitely helped each other crystallize our own creative assumptions, goals, and visions.

Many other students there became some of my most influential teachers through what I perceived at the time to be their less-than-sterling examples.

Moreover, both undergraduate and graduate programs in creative writing give you the opportunity to take truckloads of lit courses, not to mention courses in many other areas that intrigue

Robert Coover

Q. You use the tradition to subvert the tradition in your fiction, retelling everything from fairy tales to biblical myths with a postmodern spin. How important do you suppose it is for young writers to acquaint themselves with both the canonical and alternative lineage in fiction?

A. Many writers read nothing at all and get by very nicely. Writers who wish to ride along on the tradition will likely find "alternative" fiction of little use or interest, and the canon may only intimidate them. Innovative writers, however, are by the very nature of their ambition engaged in an ongoing dialogue with the form itself and therefore must read it all. Not in any particular order, though. It's all contemporary. The Gilgamesh Epic was written yesterday.

Q. What sort of advice do you give your students at Brown University who are approaching the zone of alternative fiction for the first time?

A. For the most part, I only teach mainstream fiction; of course the mainstream is being recut from generation to generation, so my definition of "mainstream" is probably different from most. When I was young, for example, the mainstream writers were Beckett, Burroughs, Borges, and the like; of course that's obvious now, though at the time they had few readers. When students (or friends) approach so-called experimental writing, I suggest that they apply the same severity of judgment they would apply to the typical best seller, for novelty is not the same thing as quality (there's a lot of pretentious trivia published under the name of innovation, as we all know); but neither is imitation of conventional narrative, no matter how "pretty." Poor innovative writing is always more interesting than skillful conventional writing.

Q. In what sense, if any, can fiction writing--especially alternative fiction writing--be taught? In what sense can't it be taught?

A. The learning experience for writers is something of a mystery. Most writers learn only by writing. And reading, which is a kind of writing for them. Workshop dialogue can be useful to the writer with her ears open, but most student writers are deafened by their own egos and so frequently find workshop dialogue destructive. Expressing opinions sometimes helps, though. I often tell my workshoppers that on the day their stories are on the table they can absent themselves if they wish, for the comments will inevitably be aimed less at the story being discussed than at the failings of each of the speakers, who are working things out for themselves by way of critiquing the writing of another. I do try to break through conventional notions of form, and that can be done by example and challenge and exciting peer groups; I've found hyperfiction workshops especially useful in this regard, for conventional forms instantly vanish in hyperspace and, if wanted (why would they be?), must be reconstructed.

Robert Coover, one of the inimitable kings of the innovative in America, is author of many novels and short story collections, including Pricksongs & Descants and The Public Burning.

Thomas E. Kennedy

Q. You entered an M.F.A. program later than many in life. Why?

A. I was 38, had been trying to write fiction for twenty years, had just written my "breakthrough story"—i.e., the first time I felt I was close to "the source" of what I sought—and it suddenly seemed clear to me that now I was ready to be taught. So I applied to Vermont College. That was in 1982.

Q. How did you know you were ready for it?

A. Well, I didn't. I wanted a place where I could learn to grow as a writer, but my fear was I would show up and find the place full of 22-year-old Yalies who would know everything about literature except how to enjoy it. But, in fact, I was the median age and for the first time in my life, I was among people who knew exactly what I meant when I said something (and vice versa) and who wanted to spend all their time writing, talking writing, and having fun.

Q. The program you entered was a low-residency one. Can you talk a little about the setup and the pros and cons of those.

A. No cons, all pros. Two weeks of literary ecstasy followed by 5 months of planned hard work writing, reading, studying feedback from my mentor, repeated for two years. It was the time of my life, I loved it, best thing I ever did for myself as a writer.

Q. What, ultimately, did your time in an M.F.A. program teach you?

A. The main thing I won there was that I broke the strangle hold my mind had on my desire to write. I learned the difference, I guess, between thinking and imagining. I learned to fight and outdance the policemen of my mind.

Q. Do you have any advice for writers searching for ideas for their first stories?

A. Yes, my advice is not to search for ideas but to explore and discover, enter the unknown areas of consciousness or of the unconscious and follow the beam of your imagination into the darkness to see what is there and where it leads you, even if you get scared, especially if you get scared. Remember, as Jung said, we are no more responsible for the thoughts in our minds than for the beasts in the forest. Forget ideas, forget the mind, feel, see, hear, touch, smell! Good fiction is built on the senses. Do not think! At least not at first. Listen to the language around you and let it infect you with the germ of a story and then serve as an incubator to let that story grow. Allow your stories to happen rather than trying with your will or the power of thought to make them happen. Imagine! Write when you least expect it. Let your pen move. Tune in to the source inside where your dreams come from and do not censor (not at first). And remember, as Henry Miller said, "If you don't listen when the muse sings, you get excommunicated."

Thomas E. Kennedy has published a dozen books of fiction and literary criticism. He lives in Denmark.

you. They thereby give you an opportunity to delve into the canonical as well as alternative traditions. The graduate programs also usually give you an opportunity to sample teaching and/or editing to see if those might be careers you'd enjoy. (Since just after World War II, universities in a very real sense have begun fulfilling the role rich patrons used to in the Renaissance, providing succor and support to many talented writers.) And they all give you good friends as well as an apprentice support network—even in the most conservative program, like will seek out like—and those friends will see you through the rest of your career.

Education isn't something your professors make for you. It's something you make for yourself. If you do your homework, searching out classes and teachers that will help you, researching where and how your idols educated themselves, giving yourself time to follow your own interests and instincts, it is a pure plain pleasure.

Too, the best graduate programs in creative writing can serve as portals to jobs in teaching, publishing, editorial services, journalism, advertising and public relations, business and technical writing, educational writing, and book selling.

Sometimes, though not often by any means, those programs are even portals to publication and recognition.

I'm neither advocating such programs nor trying to discourage you from attending one. Each person is different, thank goodness, and certain people prosper in writing programs while others sink. Only you know, if anyone does, which you're likely to do.

But I *am* advocating that you do your research before you enter one, should you decide to, since each has a slightly different tone and course of study to it because of its unique faculty, and, if you do decide to enter, enter with your eyes open.

All of which, of course, begs a far more fundamental question: Can writing be taught?

"There are three rules for writing the novel," W. Somerset Maugham once observed. "Unfortunately, no one knows what they are." In a sense, this might be truer than most creative writing teachers would like to admit. We can easily teach the grammar. We can point to certain guiding principles that tend to work in lots of kinds of fiction writing. We can present the laundry list of clichés called craft. But every good writer writes differently from every other good writer. Each has a unique compositional process, a unique approach to the concept of fiction, a different style. And every good novel or story succeeds exactly to the extent that it *doesn't* quite follow the

Q. You've taken your fair share of writing workshops as an undergrad at Brown University and grad at Iowa, and you currently teach them at the University of Washington and elsewhere. What do you think the greatest benefits to taking them are?

A. The greatest benefit is being surrounded by writers who are as good or better than you are, and the catalyzing effect this may have on your work.

Q. Do you have any advice on when a young writer should begin taking workshops... at what stage in his or her development?

A. When you think you have no room to improve.

Q. Is an M.F.A. for everyone interested in becoming a writer? Why or why not?

A. Almost everyone can use a couple of years to concentrate on reading and writing; just find a program that is at least somewhat interested in the kind of writing you're interested in.

Q. What are the signs that you're ready to enter an M.F.A. program?

A. When you've wearied of the praise heaped upon your head by your mum and dad.

David Shields is the author of two novels, Dead Languages and Heroes; a collection of linked stories, A Handbook for Drowning; and a work of autobiographical nonfiction, Remote.

rules like every other good novel or story has before it. It's in the original interstices that we leave cookie-cutter narrative behind and move into genuine fictive surprise and delight.

So a key principle to follow: whatever works for you, works; you should treat the rest (including what doesn't work for you in these pages) as cosmic background radiation.

It's as simple as that.

At the same time, the *fundamentals* of writing can be taught in the same way the *fundamentals* of piano can be taught. We can teach you, metaphorically speaking, how to hold your hands and not arch your wrists. We can teach you the difference between grace notes and glissandos. We can teach you what constitutes a sonata or a sinfonia.

What we *can't* teach you is innate talent.

We can't make Barney into Beethoven. But give us a young Ludwig, and we can probably aid him in reaching his potential.

Plus we can help just about anyone write a little better by the time they leave our class than before they entered it, given another key principle, this one from Thomas Edison: *Genius is one percent inspiration and ninety-nine percent perspiration.*

It took even Beethoven years of practice to become a natural.

To change metaphors in midstream: being a writer, then, is like practicing to be an Olympic swimmer. No one in his or her right mind would ever think the latter could attain his or her goal without more than a decade's face-scrunching hard work, a rigorous daily regimen, and an almost sicko obsessive personality.

Why would anyone think it would be any different for a fictioneer?

Take a tip from Charles Dickens in this regard, at least at an allegoric level: every morning before he sat down to write he used a compass to assure himself his desk was aiming exactly the same direction it had been aiming the day before. And one from Thackery, who wrote exactly three hours every morning, rain or shine, pain or pine, and who, once, found he had just completed the novel he'd been working on for the last nine months, and still had fifteen minutes left—so began another one.

Whether or not you enter a writing program, make sure you develop a writing schedule and stick to it.

Practice, practice, practice.

Hemingway promised himself he wouldn't leave his writing studio until he'd written at least 500 words every morning. When I was a teenager, I upped the ante to 1,000.

What should you write about?

Well, you *shouldn't* write about what you know, despite what a lot of people will tell you.

No.

Write about what you *want* to know.

Write the piece you've always wanted to read but haven't been able to locate in any bookstore except the one that exists in your imagination.

Now Read This

Altacruise, Chris. "Stepford Writers: Undercover Inside the M.F.A. Creativity Boot Camp" in *Lingua Franca* (1990). Scathing—and usually accurate—indictment of the creative writing workshop.

AWP Official Guide to Writing Programs (Updated regularly). Found in most libraries, this indispensable guide lists all undergrad and grad programs in creative writing in the U.S. and Canada, outlines the various courses of study, and lists current faculty and contact addresses. There's also a section on 129 writers' conferences, colonies, and centers.

Career Associates. *Career Choices for the 90s for Students of English* (1990). Outlines what sort of day-jobs are open to us writer types.

Friedman, Bonnie. *Writing Past Dark: Envy, Fear, Distraction, and Other Dilemmas in the Writer's Life* (1993). How to transcend the dark side of being a grad student in a creative writing program, a creative writing teacher, and an aspiring fiction writer.

O'Connor, Flannery. "The Nature and Aim of Fiction" (1957). A fine examination of the writing process, with detours into the question of whether or not writing can be taught.

Wilbers, Stephen. *The Iowa Writers Workshop: Origins, Emergence, and Growth* (1980). Interesting for its history of America's oldest and most prestigious workshop.

Stretching & Flexing

1. If you decide not to go into an academic writing program, then the best thing to do is join a local community-based writing group or, better yet, start your own and stock it with creative minds on your wavelength. Build a Do-It-Yourself workshop. Hang up fliers around town, making sure to hit the independent bookstores, as well as cafés and venues that hold readings. Put a small ad in

the alternative papers. Circle your friends. Pass the news via word of mouth. Post on local computer bulletin boards.

2. If you decide you might be interested in entering an academic writing program, then begin your homework now. Go to your nearest campus or local library and look through *The AWP Official Guide to Writing Programs*. Make a list of programs that appeal to you in terms of faculty, course of study, and location. Then write away for catalogs and application forms.

Garbage Disposal Imagination

FUEL THE CREATIVE FIRE

There are probably as many reasons why people write as there are people who write and nanoseconds in the day.

Some put pen to paper or fingers to keyboard in order to pick scabs, and some to help wounds heal. Some write to search for some sort of truth, and some write to search for the surprising or the magical. Some write to find out why and how someone else ticks, or how and why they themselves tick, and some to change things, or keep things from changing, or reveal possibilities. Some write to dramatize an ideal, some to dramatize the real, some to warn us, some to entertain us, some to exorcise pity and fear, some to exercise them, some to discover our hearts, some to educate, some to call attention to the insignificant, some to get us to think about what's important, some to trick and trap outmoded ways of thinking, some to inform, replenish, enlighten, or relieve (or relive) a secret, or simply make a well-crafted euphonious *thing*. Some write to celebrate diversity, or record life, or understand ourselves, or breathe life into old forms, or invent new forms, or take the reader's breath away, or make others puzzle, or frighten, or disturb, or blow whistles, or escape, or predict, or test, or simply share. Some write to effect political change, make us stretch, push us, broaden us, or just have some cheap fun in the evenings when there's nothing on TV. Some write to imagine the impossible, or accomplish something, or take a moment to see what god feels like, while others do it to make money, or make fans, or get jobs, or build careers, or feel a little more human, or touch other humans, or forget humanity altogether, or maybe forget themselves for just a little while, or maybe remember who they really are, or maybe just be themselves, or maybe enter an alternate state, or taste what it feels like to be unutterably free.

Most of us do every one of those things all at once all the time.

So when you ask *How do I go about getting started on a story or novel?* you might expect to hear a chorus of just-as-various answers.

The best advice I can give is to conceive of your imagination as a humongous garbage disposal. Throw everything you can in there. Dead animals, weird utensils, snatches of interstellar void. Then, at some mystical instant you'll find you never, ever, have any control over, someone or something will hit the ON switch. Everything will commence grinding and churning and spitting and wheezing, and wham, you've got yourself the beginning of a short story or novel.

A writer is first and foremost a person who reads like his or her life depended on it, which, in a very real sense, it does. Throw loads of books into that garbage disposal. If you want to write horror, read every horror novel you can get your hands on. If you want to write fantasy or slipstream or Avant-Pop, ditto. In other words, read as deeply in the genre you're interested in as possible, and remember: everything, including realism and experimental writing, is a genre, meaning it has its own rules, meaning you can learn them. Know the major players. Know the minor players. Know the genre's history and its various contemporary manifestations.

And then *really* start reading.

You should know the general history of the novel, the general history of the short story, maybe even the general history of philosophy, science, art, music, drama, and critical theory.

"It is almost impossible to write a novel any better than the best novel you've read in the three-to-six months before you began your own," Samuel R. Delany asserts. "Thus, you *must* read excellent novels regularly."

"Read, read, read," William Faulkner chimes in. "Read everything—trash, classics, good and bad, and see how they do it. Just like a carpenter who works as an apprentice and studies the master."

Only that's just the beginning.

You should also read far afield. Read in different genres. Pick up *People* magazine. Pick up *Scientific American*. Pick up *Rolling Stone*. Pick up that strange book on Roswell conspiracy theories you saw in the bookstore yesterday, and, while you're at it, that one next to it on geothermal alternatives to energy production in Russia during the 1930s as seen through the post-Boolean algebra of C. Spencer Brown. Billboards, shampoo bottle ingredients…

Why?

Because ideas and techniques are almost always discovered serendipitously, and they are *every*where.

Once you've unearthed one of them, you should probably read some more.

Research your project.

Research it further.

My novel *Time Famine* (1996) carries a subplot that deals with the ill-fated Donner Party, which left Independence, Missouri, in the spring of 1846 for California only to bog down in the snowy Sierra Nevada late that fall and winter. Running low on provisions, they ultimately resorted to cannibalism to stay alive.

My initial fascination with the Donner Party derived from a roadtrip my wife and I took through Nevada and California pretty much on a whim. We pulled off the highway one day for a rest stop, and found ourselves looking up at the Donner Memorial. I read the plaque, and that was pretty much that.

As soon as I knew I wanted to write about their ordeal, I searched down newspaper accounts of the event that were published shortly after the rescue teams went in search of the Donner Party in 1847. Those made reference to a diary which one of the pioneers in the party wrote, so I read that. Then I looked up more recent histories of the incident, which made mention of a bad verse-novel written about it, which I read to get more details, and somehow that got me looking at several documentary films about survival in the nineteenth-century west, which got me reading about the pioneers in general, which for some reason got me reading various homo-erotic theories concerning cannibalism in American art, which…

Well, you get the daisy-chain picture.

I left out a lot of facts I discovered, and wholly rearranged and changed others, and invented still more to serve my narrative purposes.

But the point is I knew, when I was ready to write, what I was talking about.

Now Read This

Gheslin, Brester, ed. *The Creative Process* (1952). Artists, musicians, mathematicians, physicists, philosophers, and authors as varied as Einstein and Mozart, Nietzsche and Jung, write about

R
E
B
E
L

Y
E
L
L

Paul Di Filippo

Q. What sort of preparatory steps do you take before you begin a project?

A. I like to log a lot of library time when the fictional concept seems to demand it, as with my pseudohistorical project, *The Steampunk Trilogy*. That kind of prep work seems rather straightforward, an accumulation of a critical mass of facts, factoids, myths, and angles, all to be later twisted. But I also recall literally rolling around on the floor trying to wrap my mind around a nebulous shape that later materialized as my novel *Ciphers*. So both the conscious and the subconscious seem to have their roles to play.

Paul Di Filippo is a novelist, short story writer, reviewer, and saint. His novel, Ciphers, was published by Cambrian/Permeable.

their creative processes.

Kennedy, Thomas E., ed. *The Literary Review* (Fall 1998). "Stories and Sources" issue. A diverse collection of short stories followed by essays by those stories' authors explaining their generative methods.

Stretching & Flexing

1. Pick up an anthology of stories written in a genre you're not especially familiar with and read them.

2. Here's a hard one, and if you don't like it you should blame Truman Capote. He advised (and, by the way, listened to his own advise) that to really learn about the process of writing you should take your favorite novel and type it out word for word. That strikes me as both exhausting and vastly educational. Only how about we compromise a little: take your favorite short story and type *it* out word for word, noting how the author introduces and composes character, moves from scene to summary and back again, effects the transitions, constructs the dialogue, even uses punctuation to his or her advantage. It will take you a single afternoon, and teach you more than most semester-long creative-writing courses.

Rebel Without a Cause

FINDING IDEAS

So far we've been trying to establish the context in which we all write at the turn of the new millennium.

We've mentioned why mainstream realism still seems to be the preferred mode for most Americans and New York publishers, why we might be well-served if we exchange that model for other more timely ones (or at least attempt to visit some of those alternatives for a weekend or two), what the literary marketplace looks like these days and how that's changed from how it looked perhaps twenty or thirty years ago, the pros and cons of academic and non-academic writing programs which most contemporary writers have sampled at some stage in their careers, and why it's crucial to be aware of these things as well as of your literary heritage, whatever that heritage might be, even if it really turns out to be an anti-heritage heritage.

Now it's time to get into the thing itself. How do you get an idea for a story? How do you know it's a good one or not? How do you begin writing once you have one, and how do you continue writing once you've begun? What makes a story a story? What components shape a story? What do you do and where do you turn when you think you're done writing one?

Okay, so, first things first: Where do you go to get ideas?

As I've already suggested an embarrassing number of times, you read, and then you read some more.

You also travel, you listen, you look, you experience, you walk,

Q. The ideas for your stories are nothing if not dazzlingly inventive. Can you share your secret about how you come across them?

A. Nothing should ever be ruled out as a story idea. Nothing. If you have trouble getting started, take three things you see or thought of this morning during your walk. (All writers must walk.) Alien invasion, the shape of postal snorkel boxes, pennies in the dirt.

Q. What are your thoughts on keeping a journal and/or notebook? Do you do it, and, if so, does it help?

A. I believe in keeping one. But never, ever let anyone see it. That way you can write anything from essays on a relative's mole to your girlfriend's abilities to forbidden political thoughts. You can also write down lists of words you want to use and sentences you want to steal.

Q. Can you talk a little about your brainstorming process? What do you do to get a story rolling?

A. I must be willing to throw away anything. Some writers keep every little scrap. Most scraps are crap. Hell, most of what we write is crap, but go with it, because occasionally you'll get a gem—something that surprises you months later. Just have faith that the gem-to-crap ratio is low, so don't sweat false starts.

Q. What's your operating metaphor for the creative process?

A. I have never metaphorized my imagination. I assume that it is larger than any model I could produce of it. The subjective universe is always larger than the objective universe.

Q. Have you ever experienced writer's block? If so, do you have any tips on how to transcend it?

A. Yes, I have suffered writer's block for days at a time. I know of nothing more painful; this is from a man who had been attacked by a psycho with a razor blade, has shingles, and once had a nail driven through his foot. My cure for writer's block is to have some low-paying project that demands a certain number of words. Write five thousand words for game design or technical writing—and the mind will decide to cooperate to avoid boredom.

Q. Could you offer two or three ideas that might help others jump-start into stories?

A. An inferior artist kills a wealthy art collector, so that he may hang his second-rate canvas in a collection destined for a great museum. Let's see his mind. A virus from a mummy's tomb causes people to write in hieroglyphics. Let's see this from the point of view of the new Pharaoh of Burbank, California. Scientists announce that you can live longer watching TV commercials. Let's see the movement against this led by a fraudulent funeral director. Please dedicate the stories to me.

Don Webb has seen the publication of 250-plus short stories, essays, poems, comic books, rock songs, recipes. He has been in a movie. His latest books are The Double, Essential Salts, and The Explanation and Other Stories.

you drive, but most of all listen and look. If you can, fly to Europe, or, better, Asia. To travel is both to experience new sensations and *re*-view where you live with new eyes. Walk to your local bar. Go places you've never been before and do things you've never done. Try chainsawing down a tree. Hang glide. Try visiting an emergency room. Check out bizarre television shows and rent bizarre videos. Watch the Discovery Channel. Buy kooky CDs. Get in your car and just start going. Get on your bike and peddle a direction you've never peddled before. Trek to the nearest large city, throw away all your maps, and lose yourself for a day. If you live in a city, visit the smallest town you've ever visited. If you live in a town, go to the country. If you live in the woods, go to the desert. If you live in the desert, go to the mountains.

Along the way, notice details.

Details are imperative.

How are things different from what you're used to? Listen to how people talk. Look at how they dress, wear their hair, shave. How is *that* different? Is the texture of the air subtly unlike what you're used to? Of course it is. So the question is *how*. Describe what it smells like. How about the way the night comes on? The dawn? What are the dominant colors? The dominant textures?

Can you think about how some of the details might be put together into some sort of narrative?

Not to worry if you can't, but have a journal with you just in case. In fact, *always* have a journal with you. Or carry one of those little spiral-bound notebooks that fit with a pen in your back pocket. Carry one of them every second, because an idea might be waiting for you at the end of the next block, in the middle of a movie or the middle of a dream, and you'd hate to miss it. Don't even *try* to convince yourself you'll remember it when you get home—it just doesn't work that way.

Write it down, and write it down *now*.

Write down overheard lines at that local bar you visit, in the aisles of Wal-Mart, a booth in Burger King, the restroom in the art museum, the bench in the park. Write down descriptions of people, accessories they're sporting, nifty devices you hear about on the six o'clock news, items read about in the dentist's office, or passing comments your friend just dropped the day before yesterday that didn't seem important to you then but do now.

Write down your dreams.

Write down your best and worst memories.

Janice Eidus

Q. Your stories are rich with wacky ideas. Where do they come from, and where might young writers begin looking for theirs?

A. My ideas come from my own life: from real events and real people, as well as from my vision and my passionately-held, hard-earned worldview. My imagination allows me to transform the "real" things in my life, and to make them truer than fact, realer than real. Here are two examples of how I did this in my collection of short stories, *The Celibacy Club*: In "Nautilus," I transform my own love for physical exercise into a tale about a woman who falls madly and passionately in love with the leg-press machine at her gym; and in "Ladies with Long Hair," I turn my sorrow and rage over my own hairdresser's death from AIDS into a contemporary retelling of *Lysistrata*, as a group of women whose hairdressers have all died of an unnamed plague refuse to cut their Rapunzel-like long locks until a cure for AIDS is found. I urge beginning writers to explore their own lives, their passions, their political beliefs—and never to be afraid to bear witness in words to what they see, and know, and hold to be true, no matter how unusual or offbeat.

Q. What sort of work habits do you use to help you get started on a writing project?

A. I believe in "a sound mind in a sound body." That is, I integrate a lot of pure physical exercise, and a lot of quiet contemplation, into the manic, intellectual life of the writer. The more I live my life "in balance," the easier it is for me to be disciplined and focused as a writer. Letting these other kinds of "food for the soul" into my life on a regular basis allows me to be deeply engaged in writing—and to be fearless about tackling new books and stories.

Q. Have you ever had writer's block? If so, do you have any suggestions for how to surmount it?

A. Writer's block is another way of saying "fear." And yes, I have experienced fear, as have most writers I know (no matter how prolific and widely published they are). Most of us have, during times of vulnerability, feared not being able to write a perfectly brilliant book, or not getting published, or receiving bad reviews, or offending someone. Writing past these fears is an act of courage under both real and imagined fire (for undoubtedly at one time or another, each of these fears will be realized). I have always valued courage in others, and I look to those I admire to tap into it in myself.

Janice Eidus, twice winner of the O. Henry Prize for her short stories, as well as a Pushcart Prize, is author of the collections *The Celibacy Club* and *Vito Loves Geraldine*, and the novels *Urban Bliss* and *Faithful Rebecca*, and co-editor of *It's Only Rock'n'Roll: Rock'n'Roll Short Stories*.

Write down, word for word, the fight you had with your partner last week in a way that puts yourself in his or her sneakers.

Write down sentences from novels you wish you'd written, steal them, and prepare to tuck them in your own stories.

Write down the names of novels you plan to read.

The short-story writer Ron Carlson keeps a bag filled with little scraps of paper by his computer. Each paper has exactly that written on it: something appropriated from a supermarket tabloid, eavesdropped on the campus where he teaches, picked up on CNN. When he can't think of anything to write, he reaches into that packed bag of tricks, pulls something out, and begins a riff on it.

To a person with an imagination, the world is a story waiting to be told.

"For godsake, keep your eyes open," William Burroughs urged young writers. "Notice what's going on around you."

He couldn't be more dead on.

Writing is all about learning to see, hear, smell, taste, and touch more accurately than most people do. (Erza Pound called writers "the antennae of the species.") It's all about ferreting out the significant detail that makes a place a place, a person a person, a car a car.

Writing's all about *paying attention* to the universe around you at some profoundly deep level, always being awake, because the world is such an amazing place to exist in, and you don't want to let even a spore of it slip away from you.

Stretching & Flexing

Begin a journal or notebook, and get in the habit of writing in it frequently. While there are no rules for keeping either, you might want to recall that a journal or notebook isn't a diary. That is, it's not there just to record in a flat voice what you did on a particular day. Rather, it's a catalyst for starting to think about what you're thinking and feeling. It's a chronicle of your world and the geography of your imagination. It's a place to find your voice and writing rhythms, experiment, take risks, opine, draft stories, ponder books you're reading, jot down great quotes, compose letters you'll never send, record memories and expectations and snippets of overheard dialogue, explore sense impressions. It's a place, to put it simply, to practice paying attention. When working in your journal or notebook, make sure not to censor yourself, and make sure to keep it to yourself, so you always know you have an imaginative free zone there. If you're having trouble getting started or keeping going, try writing about one of these:

- Pen a letter to a dead president. Include a request, a regret, or an appreciation.

- Remember the best or worst moment from your childhood.

- Write down the dream you had last night.

- Write the letters of the alphabet down the lefthand margin of the page, then use each to create a sensible poem or story.

- In a full paragraph, answer the question: How does the weather taste today?

Rebel Without a Clause

SURVIVING WRITER'S BLOCK

Once you think you might have an idea, let yourself obsess on it.

Let it haunt you when it wants to haunt you: while you're trying to take notes in a class, watch a video, talk to someone or sleep or shower.

Sometimes you'll forget it for days at a stretch, and sometimes it simply won't give you a minute's rest.

That's a good thing.

Let it nag.

Write it down in your journal or notebook so you won't forget it, modify it every now and then, and maybe even sit at your computer screen and begin brainstorming on it. Don't think too hard, just let your imagination wander around the idea at will, and jot down whatever comes to mind in whatever order it appears.

One of the great things about word processors is that they instantly transform composition into perpetual process. You can fiddle, diddle, rearrange, copy, cut, paste, open separate files for separate chapters or separate story sections, open a window for notes, open another for your outline if you use an outline, and still another for a list of characters and their attributes, and have them all up there on your screen simultaneously so you can flip between them as needed.

Some writers don't feel comfortable talking to other people about their ideas until they have something written down. That's fine, and understandable. But if you *do* feel comfortable doing it, sit with a friend and your journal and start rambling. My wife and I do that with everything I write and every art project she launches into, and you'll be amazed by how much can come out of a good give-and-take session like that.

As I say, many people suggest you write what you know, and only what you know, and I'm here to tell you they're flat wrong. You should write what you want to know—and then embellish like mad. *That's* how to move into new and exciting narrative spaces. Dostoevsky didn't kill an old woman in order to write *Crime and Punishment*. He just possessed a profoundly impressive imagination. H. G. Wells didn't build a time machine. Shakespeare didn't meet King Lear, Homer Odysseus, Ovid the extraordinary characters inhabiting his *Metamorphoses*. Writing what you know is another myth from mainstream realism, which is, we would all do well to keep in mind, a terribly short-lived genre, barely a 200-year-old blip on the multi-millennia-wide radar screen of anti-realism.

Except what if, having done everything discussed above, you *still* don't get an idea?

Or, worse, what if you used to get ideas, but suddenly can't anymore?

What, that is, if writer's block descends upon you like an awful black piano out of a two-story window, along with that nauseating feeling that you just can't think creatively anymore, just can't produce?

First and foremost, don't sweat it.

You're in great company. Most authors experience writer's block at one time or another in their lives. Many have to struggle with it almost every day.

The more you think about it, the worse it'll get.

"Every writer I know has trouble writing," Joseph Heller said, and Joan Didion affirmed that "there is always a point in the writing of a piece when I sit in a room literally papered with false starts and cannot put one word after another and imagine that I have suffered a small stroke, leaving me apparently undamaged but actually aphasic."

There are several things you can do about it that'll really help.

- Back off. Give your mind a rest. Get out of the house for a while. See a movie. Go somewhere new. Maybe take your journal or notebook along, and practice observing. If that feels intimidating, bag it. Wait. Relax. Breathe deeply. Lie on the floor. Don't panic. Play Sonic Youth or atonal Schönberg, loud. Let your unconscious do some work behind your back. Chances are, given a day, a week or two, perhaps even a month or six weeks, you'll wake up one morning psyched to hit the fictive pavement running again.

- Visit the Surrealists. They knew what they were doing. Their first manifesto appeared in France in 1924 and advocated the expression of the imagination as realized in dreams and presented without conscious control. They have gobs of exercises for hotwiring creativity. Three of my favorite Surrealist "games" are:

The Exquisite Corpse. Assemble three players around a table. Have each write a definite or indefinite article and an adjective on a sheet of paper. Fold the sheets so no one can see the words. Everyone pass their sheet to the left. Repeat the process with a noun, then a verb, another definite or indefinite article, adjective, then another noun. Unfold the sheets and share. Now (this is an Olsen addition) use the resulting lines as the first of a paragraph-long story or thirteen-line poem.

Leapfrog. Assemble three players around a table. Give the first a sheet of paper. Tell him or her to write for a specified amount of time (one to three minutes is usually enough; if everyone's feeling fiery, go for five). Stop him or her (in mid-sentence, if necessary) and pass to the next player, who must take up where the first player left off. Repeat till story is complete or an hour transpires.

Automatic Writing. Put on some music that fits your mood (the fewer lyrics, the better) and get out your journal or notebook. Then listen to André Breton in his 1934 manifesto, "What is Surrealism?": "Let your state of mind be as passive and receptive as possible. Forget your genius, talents, as well as the genius and talents of others. Repeat to yourself that literature is pretty well the sorriest road that leads to everywhere. Write quickly without any previously chosen subjects, quickly enough not to dwell on, and not to be tempted to read over, what you have written…. Punctuation of course necessarily hinders the stream of absolute continuity which preoccupies us. But you should particularly distrust the prompting whisper. If through a fault ever so trifling there is a forewarning of silence to come … break off unhesitatingly the line that has become too lucid. After the word whose origin seems suspect you should place a letter, any letter, l for example, always the letter l, and restore the arbitrary flux by making that letter the initial of the word to come."

- Conversely, don't take *No* from your unconscious. Write every day regardless of how you feel. Gail Godwin once admitted she went into her writing room and simply sat there every morning, whether she thought she had something to say or not, just so if the muse happened to visit she'd be home. Tell yourself that a writer is a person who writes. Establish a work schedule (most professional writers seldom write more than three or four hours a day, and many choose to do so in the morning, but, again, you'll soon find what works best for you) and, if at all possible, a work space (a writing room, a writing niche). Stick to the schedule you devise. Give yourself deadlines. If the Pope calls while you're writing, tell him you're busy and you'll call back. Better yet, just leave the answering machine on. Whenever you can't think of anything to write, choose from one of the following and plunge in:

1. Go to a bar or diner and practice short, medium, and long descriptions. Describe one patron in language that will single her/him out from all the others.

2. Visit your family and practice seeing, hearing, smelling, and feeling. Then go back to your writing space and put down everything you can remember—setting, dialogue, appearance of people, everything.

3. Take your all-time favorite short story and imitate it as closely as you can in terms of tone, characterization, dialogue, plot, etc., without actually copying it. All young writers (just like Picasso) learn through imitation. No one is born original. You have to learn originality.

4. Read a story by Y, then ask yourself: How would X tell it differently? What about S and M? Write the various versions.

5. Read the newspaper or a deliciously seamy tabloid, paying particular attention to the crime sections, and base a story on what

you find there. It worked for Dostoevsky and Flaubert, as well as for Judith Rossner in *Looking for Mr. Goodbar.*

6. Take a published story and edit it to half its original length without losing its essential meaning, paying attention to the kind of things you cut.

7. Imagine the moments just before your own birth or just after your own death. Base a story on them.

8. Write your own epitaph as though you died yesterday, in the year 2070.

9. Write a story about nothing for three pages. This is a challenging one, but Samuel Beckett, Alain Robbe-Grillet, and Raymond Federman have written whole novels using this principle.

10. If everything else fails, write a story about someone who can't write a story. This person, oddly enough, looks and feels a lot like you.

Now Read This

Breton, André. "What is Surrealism?" (1934). Terrific introduction to thinking beyond what Breton calls "the reign of logic."

Brotchie, Alastair and Mel Gooding, eds. *Surrealist Games* (1993). A delightful compilation of communal exercises guaranteed to get you writing.

Nelson, Victoria. *On Writer's Block* (1993). What it is and how to survive it.

Is it
Ripe Yet?

CULTIVATING AND DEVELOPING IDEAS

Or, on the other hand, let's say you have a ton of ideas. How do you know which one's right for a good story?

The honest answer is you don't.

Ideas don't necessarily make the story. A killer idea presented in a dreary or fumbled fashion isn't worth the price of an 800-number phone call. On the other hand, a fairly commonplace idea can start shouting and jumping up and down on the page and waving its tiny arms over its tiny head because of the language used to present it, or the characters who accrue around it, or the fresh formal approach through which you articulate it.

Moreover, writing is discovery. As E. L. Doctorow commented, he rarely knows what he believes until he's written about it. Many times it's only through the act of composition that we locate what we really think and feel about something. Dostoevsky would begin authoring a scene in which he reckoned he understood exactly what he believed, only to find his characters would convince him otherwise by the end and leave him in a quandary.

Many times we don't have an idea for a story so much as a vague sense of some character we want to probe, or an issue we'd like to ponder, or maybe the dimmest sketch of a scene in our heads, or maybe little more than an image, a group of words that may or may not be a full sentence, the foggy outlines of a place or an action or a sound or a smell.

But if you intuit you're ready to start writing, then you're ready to start writing.

If you're pretty new to this stuff, or just want a stronger sense of purpose before you begin, there are three questions you can ask yourself to find whether you're driving up the right on-ramp:

- *Does your protagonist (a word from the Greek meaning "first actor," or chief player in your narrative) want something he or she can't have?*

Stories are all about the thwarting of desire. Create a character who needs something more than anything else in the world—to be loved, to get away with murder, to remove that annoying sirloin gristle stuck between his or her front teeth—and refuse to let him or her have it for a while.

If there's a person preventing your *protagonist* from getting what he or she wants, then you've got yourself an *antagonist*.

- *Do you have a sense of your story's plot, of how its action is shaped and where it's heading?*

It's okay if you don't. Some authors barely know the opening of their narratives, and some only have an unformed sense of something that's going to happen in the middle, and some can sort of see the end point but not how to get there.

Half the fun in writing is surprising yourself with how you're able to travel to Z from B.

The other half is your characters surprising you.

But—particularly when you're just starting out—it sometimes helps to know where you're beginning and where you're ending and why, even if the middle is unformed and blobbish. If nothing else, it will almost surely save you several drafts of narratological hunting and pecking.

- *Has it been said before in the same way?*

Here's a little secret: Ecclesiastes botched it—there are all *sorts* of new things under the sun.

Granted: there are a limited number of human emotions, a limited number of tastes and smells, a limited number of core plots (the journey, the love story, the education, the revenge story, the heist, etc.), even a limited number of words in the English language.

And yet there are also an infinite number of ways to discuss those emotions, to capture those tastes and smells, to retell those core plots, to combine those words. Mutate the world and thrive.

Think about this: You can hear a sentence today, and then listen for that sentence to be repeated just once more for the rest of your life in just the same order, and chances are you'll be disappointed.

Now *that's* sorcery.

Early in the twentieth century, Ezra Pound advised young Imagist poets to MAKE IT NEW. At the beginning of the new millennium, that's still splendid advice for all authors.

If you're saying the same old things in the same old ways, well, why bother?

Find a new angle.

Imagine telling your narrative from a strikingly different point of view from how it's usually told, or employing an innovative structure you've never come across before, or breaking up traditional chronology in a method that both interests you and puts a new twist on your story, or recasting your sentences in an inventive form, or twidgling with tense or metaphor, or throwing a fictive wrench into how a certain kind of story unfolds (if it's a tale of education, maybe your protagonist doesn't ultimately learn anything; if a murder mystery, maybe the bad guy doesn't get caught, or maybe the murderer is really the good guy, or maybe there hasn't been a murder after all), or…or…or…the possibilities, you can begin to tell, are mind boggling.

Now Read This

Barthelme, Donald. *Forty Stories* (1987). One of the masters of making it new in contemporary fiction.

Beckett, Samuel. *Molloy, Malone Dies, The Unnamable* (1955, 1956, 1958). Tremendously important and blackly funny Irish anti-novellas.

Borges, Jorge-Luis. *Ficciones* (1956). You've never read stories quite like these. By the guy who in many ways began both the Latin American magical realist and the global metafictional traditions.

Calvino, Italo. *If on a Winter's Night a Traveler…* (1979). The detective story as epistemological fable.

McCaffery, Larry, and Sinda Gregory, eds. *Alive and Writing: Interviews with American Authors of the 1980s* (1987). Interviews with Walter Abish, Samuel R. Delany, Ursula Le Guin, Tom Robbins and many more on the how's and why's of edge writing in America.

McCaffery, Larry, ed. *Across the Wounded Galaxies: Interviews with Contemporary American Science Fiction Writers* (1990). The title's a little misleading, but super idea-generating interviews with the likes of William Burroughs, Octavia Butler, and William Gibson.

McHale, Brian. *Postmodernist Fiction* (1987). The finest overview of techniques and approaches used in pomo anti-narrative. Sure to get the ideas boiling.

Pynchon, Thomas. *Gravity's Rainbow* (1973). The most important post-war American novel, with a new technique on every page.

Sterne, Laurence. *Tristram Shandy* (1759-1767). The side-splittingly funny proto-pomo British novel.

Ready for Prime-Time

THE REBEL'S FIRST PAGE

L et's play a game.

You're a tongue-lollingly overworked editor of a small alternative zine. If you don't run the whole thing yourself, it sure usually feels that way. You make no money. You hold down two day jobs just to make frayed ends meet. You get ninety manuscripts a month. You seldom have space for more than one or two of them. You haven't read anything good for what feels like a year. The guy who's done layout for you for the last half decade quit yesterday. Distributors owe you money. You had a fight with your partner this morning. And you've drunk way, *way* too much coffee.

You open and read the first paragraphs of the following five stories, paying no attention to the cover letter that accompanies each or the by-line.

Which are you going to want to read more of?

Why?

> 1. Jim and Irene Westcott were the kind of people who seem to strike that satisfactory average of income, endeavor, and respectability that is reached by the statistical reports in college alumni bulletins. They were the parents of two young children, they had been married nine years, they lived on the twelfth floor of an apartment house near Sutton Place, they went to the theater on an average of 10.3 times a year, and they hoped someday to live in Westchester.

Q. Can you sketch in a little about the zine you work on and your role in its production?

A. When guest-editing issues of the *Fringeware Review* (www.fringeware. com), I elaborate a theme for the issue, then take submissions, make assignments, and generally gather the issue's material (fiction, nonfiction, reviews, etc.). The final product, with artwork, comes about as a result of collaboration with art directors, editors, writers, and artists. When working for Portland's monthly magazine, *Anodyne* (www.teleport.com/~anodyne), as a Senior Editor and later Editor-in-Chief, I worked closely with section editors to select and assign material. I still worked personally with many writers, particularly where feature articles were concerned, and kept a close eye on the visual presentation and article order of the publication as a whole.

For my zine, *Hot Geeks!* (www.magdalen.com), I do everything from editing to layout to distribution, and take my sweet time about it.

Q. As an editor, what catches your eye in a piece coming over the transom?

A. A cover letter or friendly e-mail note plus a few clips from publications (even unpublished writing samples) get my attention more than unsolicited manuscripts. At least introduce yourself and ask what we're looking for prior to submitting material out of the blue; this improves your chances of submitting something we can actually use. In situations where reading "slush" is inevitable (calls for fiction, etc.), I need the writer's style and choice of subject matter to grab my attention within two paragraphs (one is even better). Humor, personal writing voice, and the ability to self-edit get gold stars.

Don't go overboard trying to shock me or pick "wild" subject matter; some editors are party to all kinds of crazy goings-on in the world. We get jaded. Something interesting and sincere will capture my attention more than something that's trying to be really cool, far out, shocking, or neophilic.

Q. How far do you read before deciding to go on or putting the piece aside?

A. It depends. Generally, the first two paragraphs will determine whether I keep reading or skip to the end in search of a well-written sentence.

Q. What should young writers do when sending out their work for the first time?

A. I'm probably not the best person to ask about this; the uptight, "professional" style of old-school publishing rituals seems absurd to me. In the land of Way New, Way Weird, Way Small media that I prefer, establishing a personal rapport (often via e-mail) can be an important and enjoyable first step for both parties. If I wanted to read boring, straight-up cover letters all day, I'd be working in the Human Resources department of some faceless multinational corporation.

Q. What shouldn't young writers do when sending out their work for the first time?

A. Don't send long, unsolicited manuscripts. If I didn't ask you to write the thing, and I'm spending my time looking at it, it had best stay under 1,000 words.

Tiffany Lee Brown's editorial experience covers an eclectic array of subjects including culture, technology, fashion, music, and art, for small press publications like Anodyne, Chicane, and Future Sex.

2. The first children who saw the dark and slinky bulge approaching through the sea let themselves think it was an enemy ship. Then they saw it had no flags or masts and they thought it was a whale. But when it washed up on the beach, they removed the clumps of seaweed, the jellyfish tentacles, and the remains of fish and flotsam, and only then did they see that it was a drowned man.

3. Leroy Moffitt's wife, Norma Jean, is working on her pectorals. She lifts three-pound dumbbells to warm up, then progresses to a twenty-pound barbell. Standing with her legs apart, she reminds Leroy of Wonder Woman.

4. Wilgus found his Uncle Delmer sitting on the couch in the living room, staring at the wavy lines and falling snow on the silent television screen. Delmer held an open Bible in his lap and a king-size beer in his hand.
   "Delmer old buddy, how you doing?" Wilgus asked as he sat down next to his uncle.
   Delmer waited a long time before he answered. Without taking his eyes off the TV screen he said, "I ain't doing no good."

5. Boys are playing basketball around a telephone pole with a backboard bolted to it. Legs, shouts. The scrape and snap of Keds on loose alley pebbles seems to catapult their voices high into the moist March air blue above the wires. Rabbit Angstrom, coming up the alley in a business suit, stops and watches, though he's twenty-six and six three. So tall, he seems an unlikely rabbit, but the breadth of white face, the pallor of his blue irises, and a nervous flutter under his brief nose as he stabs a cigarette into his mouth partially explain the nickname, which was given to him when he too was a boy. He stands there thinking, the kids keep coming, they keep crowding you up.

There's no right answer here.

Truth is, they're all really strong passages, even if most are fairly conventional in their tone and perspective.

So your response, in certain ways, is going to tell you more about your own aesthetic tastes than about some Platonic narrative ideal.

We're talking Rorschach here.

Still, there's oodles to learn from these openings—particularly about beginnings.

For starters, notice how much *work* they're each doing in just a couple of lines.

Your first sentence or three establishes a tremendous amount of things: the tone of your story (is it serious, playful, ironic, sad, joyous?), the genre (you're setting up a contract with your reader that raises certain expectations on his or her part about what *kind* of story you're writing), your voice (word choice, sentence length, diction level, rhythms, etc.), your setting (where is the story taking place, exactly, and in what sort of world?), your main character (stories almost always begin with the point of view of the protagonist, and begin in a few quick strokes to give us a sense of who she or he is, and what she or he wants but can't have), the socioeconomic realities of your fictive universe (through subtle clues you're beginning to answer the questions: *how does my character make his or her living? how does she or he dress, eat, exist?*), your conflict (it's frequently not spelled out right away, but hinted at to generate what's called a narrative hook, something that draws the reader into the story), your tense (is the story supposed to be happening as we read it, or in the past, or perhaps even in the future?), authorial distance from your main character (are we dealing with, say, an unreliable first-person narrator, or a godlike omniscient one?), and probably even theme (many times a careful reader can tell what a story is about by the end of the first full paragraph).

Put this together with what you can learn from a story's *title*, which should somehow function to guide you into the narrative's concerns (either poetically, as in Pynchon's gorgeous *Gravity's Rainbow*, which describes the arc of a V-2's trajectory, and hence alludes to the subject of that novel, World War II, or more prosaically, as in a title that names the main character [Fielding's *Tom Jones*] or focal point [Barthelme's "The Balloon"] or the primary theme [Updike's "Departures"]), and you know a cruise-ship more than you think you do by the time you've gotten near the bottom of page one.

No wonder, then, that those first few lines are so hard to compose. For many, they're the most difficult part of the whole story. And why shouldn't they be, given all the decisions an author has to make as he or she invents them? It's like juggling forty knives, some of which are on fire.

And no wonder few editors read much beyond the first page of manuscripts that come across the transom. Usually they can tell ev-

Q. Can you sketch in a little about the zine you work on and your role in its production?

A. I started publishing *The Spitting Image* primarily to unveil dioramas that possess a strange and eerie beauty, with a preference for fiction that is stylistically exquisite and yet steeped in emotional perversion. I try to fit the grimy shoes of an archeologist who sifts through vast and perilous deserts in order to haul an unknown treasure into the public eye. This is why much of *The Spitting Image* revolves around my translations of obscure German writers; it's often my only means of sharing a momentous literary discovery with American friends. The aesthetics, choice of contents, and especially the handcrafted covers are very personal, but the magazine has found great resonance in readers from Alaska to Japan.

Q. As an editor, what catches your eye in a piece coming across the transom?

A. The best pieces are those in which nothing catches my eye, those that make me look away from the act of reading. A clear, harmonious style, unpredictable mannerisms, an unusual image lurking in my peripheral vision—these are some of the things I look for.

Q. How far do you read before deciding to go on or putting the piece aside?

A. If there are more than a couple of grammatical or spelling errors, I stop, since the writer obviously doesn't care about the manuscript. English is my second language; I expect American writers to speak it at least as well as I do. Unfortunately, many of the stories I receive seem to be written without real dedication. Potential contributors should know that I receive close to 2000 manuscripts per issue; they should not bother if they aren't serious about being published.

Q. What should young writers do when sending out their work for the first time?

A. They should take the time to find out what the editor is looking for; editors often spend a lot of time publicizing guidelines. *The Spitting Image* is very receptive to new writers, so they shouldn't worry about being honest in their cover letters. It's a great pleasure to publish someone whose writing is polished, yet too outlandish for other markets.

Q. What shouldn't young writers do when sending out their work for the first time?

A. Don't summarize and praise your story in the cover letter; don't include photos of yourself or your house; don't use large, red fonts; don't try to make me feel sorry for your cat; don't make me suspect you're an avid reader of *Writer's Digest*; don't include your measurements in your bio; don't praise the magazine and get the name wrong; don't praise the magazine before the first issue appears; don't use the words "busty babe" more than once per sentence; don't outline which parts of the story actually happened and how they really turned out; and please! don't send cover letters in rhymed verse.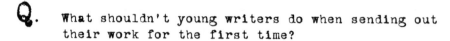

Julia Solis lives in New York City.

Q. Can you sketch in a little about the zine you work on and your role in its production?

A. *FlashPoint* is both a print and an on-line (webdelsol.com/FLASHPOINT/) 'journal of the arts and politics,' featuring poetry, graphics, essays, criticism, interviews—and, stingily but more and more, fiction. The founding editors (Joe Brennan and Carlo Parcelli) are poets; I write fiction, so I screen the fiction submissions. But so far I've been the primary editor of the on-line journal, which incorporates pieces from the print issue, but also new things.

Q. As an editor, what catches your eye in a submission?

A. Language. Is the writer's tongue master of what he/she wants to tell? Genre, subject, plot if any (and I like a good story, well-plotted), are secondary. I like a variety of approaches to story, from mainstream to Avant-Pop and beyond, and try to lay out a smorgasboard in each *FlashPoint*.

Q. How far do you read before deciding to go on or putting the piece aside?

A. So far, the whole piece; but, as a new magazine, most of our submissions have been solicited. We have not yet advertised for unsolicited, but if and when we do, and we get inundated, I'm sure I'll eyeball the first page for language (the A pile), then character or situation (the B pile)—and anything that doesn't make the A or B will get the "Sorry!" note. The B's will be given two or three pages minimum to make the next cut, the A's every page. Language! Language!

Q. What should young writers do when sending out their work for the first time?

A. Observe the courtesies, of course (neat, clean copy; SASE; etc.). Ask for a critical comment if rejected. If you get a rejection-with-comment, say thanks (taking exception, if appropriate). A writer's essential relation to criticism is the dialectical discipline: listen-and-not-listen/not-listen-and-listen. Remember that rejection is at least nine-tenths of any writer's career: i.e., the norm. When you get a rejection slip without comment, curse it, throw it, and move on.

Q. What shouldn't young writers do when sending out their work for the first time?

A. Don't fly blind—check out magazines in *Novel & Short Story Writers Market*, buy samples of the likelier ones, and at least scan them. Doesn't save time or money, but saves and educates brain . . . at the very least increasing market savvy. Above all, don't give up. Never give up. As a writer, you don't live and die for this story or that novel—you live and die for writing. When you die, give up—until then, write and breathe.

J. R. Foley writes and breathes in the Washington, D.C. area.

erything they need to from that much prose, and usually the rest of the story simply confirms the impression established there. If you don't get their attention right away, you probably won't get it at all.

That's why it's so essential to spend lots of time up front.

Let's return to those five openings and discuss some of their more salient features.

1. Most of my students don't give this one much of a chance. When asked to vote for their favorite of the five, they almost never choose it. The language is flat and uninteresting as Jim and Irene Westcott seem to be. It exudes averageness even at a statistical level, and no one reads for averageness. So it tends to come as a shock that this one's by one of the great American short story writers, John Cheever, and that it's flat averageness is really a kind of joke, setting the stage as it does for the opposite later on. Titled "The Enormous Radio," this is a slipstream tale about how Jim and Irene unwittingly buy a radio that can pick up conversations in other rooms in the apartment building they live in, giving us an aural window into what "average" America is *really* all about, and it's all about weirdness. This piece thus subverts the conventions of a traditional opening, and serves as a good caveat to editors (and readers) everywhere about why we might want to read to page two.

2. A favorite among my students, and for good reason: it's by Nobel Laureate Gabriel García Márquez, a natural storyteller if ever there was one. The language is a little faded because it's a translation from the Spanish, but the narrative momentum and sense of wonder are evident from the get-go, and the last line demands that you read into the next paragraph to find out what happens. Just as the fundamental structure of this paragraph is the fracturing of expectation (how can a dead man be mistaken for a ship?), so too the fundamental structure of the magical realist story as a whole—it's called "The Handsomest Drowned Man in the World"—turns out to be a rich surprise.

3. It's not so much the language, which is very polished, even sparse, that catches readers' attention in Bobbie Ann Mason's story "Shiloh," but the slightly unfamiliar use of present tense,

which creates a photographic immediacy to the scene; the slightly unfamiliar presentation of gender, where Leroy's wife (whose name echoes Marilyn Monroe's original) is the one who's working out to attain that sexy superhero physique; and the perfectly offbeat monikers—all of which point to a scrumptiously understated sense of humor based on incongruity. No doubt it's a workshop piece, a late outrider of Carvermania, but it's Carveresque with an engaging pop perspective.

4. People who like perfect-pitch dialogue and lovable characters respond positively to this passage, which initiates a story by the less-well-known southern writer Gurney Norman entitled "The Revival." (Norman is better known, by the way, for his uproarious 1972 countercultural novel, *Divine Right's Trip*.) It obviously lays out its mythic theme, underlined by the title itself, and sets its conflict in motion by putting the open Bible in one of Delmer's hands and that king-size beer in the other, while making Delmer's mind blank and receptive as that dead television he's ogling. What most people *don't* know about this piece, which runs for a brief nine pages, is that in draft form it ran a full fifty, and took Norman nearly six months to compose; till, that is, he realized the first forty-one pages were extraneous warm-up before his *real* story, the one we read here, lurched to life. While an excessive example, it's nonetheless a good one to remind us that the first few pages of most first drafts are little more than stretching exercises that can be cut during revision.

5. This isn't the opening to a short story, but a novel—and a famous one at that: John Updike's *Rabbit Run* (1960). Not as many students pick this one as do numbers two and four, and I suspect this is because language is foregrounded here almost to the point of becoming a second protagonist, and many students raised on mainstream fiction just don't appreciate that move on Updike's part. But that's the very reason I adore it. The language leaps to consciousness like those kids playing basketball: in the two-word sensory-charged second sentence ("Legs, shouts."), in the repeated choice of active verbs (Rabbit doesn't "stick" a cigarette into his mouth; he "stabs" it in), in the perfect poetically alliterative use of

significant detail ("the moist March air blue above the wires"), and in the striking metaphors ("he seems an unlikely rabbit, but the breadth of white face, the pallor of his blue irises, and a nervous flutter under his brief nose . . ."). And the distance between twenty-six-year-old Rabbit (his last name riddled with rabbitoidal angst) and the young kids announces just how isolated this protagonist feels from his own past, which in turn announces the novel's central theme and conflict.

And all in five sentences.
Not bad, huh?

Stretching & Flexing

1. Pick up an anthology of short fiction—Eric Rabkin's *Stories: An Anthology and Introduction* is a good place to start—and read as many first pages as you can, looking at them just like we did in this section for what works, what doesn't, and why. This is a great exercise to do with friends.

2. Using what we've just discussed, write a knockout opener which begins: "I was listening to Y when I first X." Replace Y with the title of a song. Replace X with an action. If your imagination needs a tweak, just think back on your own life and use a memory to provide the basic info.

Jasmine Sailing

Q. Can you sketch in a little about the zine you work on and your role in its production?

A. Magazine: *Cyber-Psychos AOD*, "The Magazine of Mental Aberrations." Distribution: Thousands and thousands internationally, but they all really get destroyed and used to line cat boxes. Role: God. Publisher, editor, conceptualizer, writer, fibber, sniggler.

Q. As an editor, what snags your attention in a story that comes across your desk?

A. Pure unmitigated insanity. Cover letters that don't reek of boring dropped names and pretentions, that actually say something interesting. Eye-catching experimentalism that isn't useless or cluttering. Genuine passion glaring from the page.

Q. How far do you read before deciding to go on or putting the piece aside?

A. Generally I'll read the entire thing, once I've started it, no matter how painful it is. There have been a few exceptions that became forgotten after flying out the window (to the sounds of my loud screams). The first few pages tend to be more than enough to clue you in on your happiness levels though.

Q. What should young writers do when sending out their work for the first time?

A. Refrain from saying "I know this is perfect for your magazine and you'll agree," despite it being obvious that you've never laid eyes on the magazine. Insincere flattery BACKFIRES (at least with me). Read the magazines first, put some actual thought into which ones would be appropriate for you. Read the guidelines.

Q. What shouldn't young writers do when sending out their work for the first time?

A. Don't get discouraged by a rejection. I can't even begin to count how many "too dark" and "too cerebral" rejections I've gotten over the years, but I know people still love me despite my morbid insanity. Use good advice for improving your style, but always remain honest with yourself in writing. Eventually you'll find a niche that appreciates the honesty.

Jasmine Sailing is the editor/publisher of the Cyber-Psychos AOD books and magazine.

What Comes after Page One?

STRATEGIES FOR DEVELOPING YOUR STORY

A writer again is a person who writes.

A writer *isn't* a person who wears a black beret and sits around in dingy bars or cafés *talking* about writing.

Once you've got that opening to your story, whatever you do, don't stop. There are a million reasons why you can't write today. There is only one why you can: because you want to.

"When my horse is running good," William Faulkner said, "I don't stop to give him sugar."

"I'm only really alive when I'm working," said Tennessee Williams.

Develop that work schedule, and stick to it. How many days a week will you write? What time of the day? For how long? The answer doesn't need to be every morning or night, but it does need to be regularly. If you can't write seven days a week, write five. If you can't write five, write three. If you can't write in the morning, write in the afternoon. If you can't write in the afternoon, write in the evening. If you can't write for four hours, write at least for two. But be consistent. Mean it. Show language you care.

Try listening to music when you write, and try listening to silence. Try keeping the blinds open so lots of visual stimulation cascades in, and try keeping the blinds shut. Some writers swear by chocolate bonbons or jelly beans within arm's reach, and most swear by a pot of coffee that can kick you if you're not looking, and a very few will tell you that a glass of wine or stronger will loosen up the creative impulse, though the truth is most (including everyone from Maxim Gorky to James Jones, Robert Stone, W.H. Auden, and Ring Lardner) will tell you, along with Samuel Johnson, that "one of the disadvantages of wine is that it makes a man mistake words for thoughts," and with John Cheever that "even a glass of sherry shows in a sentence."

A parable:

Once upon a time there was a young guy who wanted to be a writer, but he was a busy college student, and there was just too much work to do for his classes, and there were all those experiences he needed to have that were called Growing Up, and he was working for the campus paper, and trying hold down a part-time job, and he helped build sets for the plays the drama department put on, and so he figured he'd wait till summer.

Then he'd *really* get into all that creative expression business.

Only summer came, and he realized he was still short of cash. He needed a full-time job. So he found something at a lumber mill, except it required vast amounts of physical exertion, and he was so beat at the end of every day all he wanted to do was watch TV and drink beer.

"Fine," he thought. "I'll get through my degree, and then just watch me. I'll write like wildfire."

So he put his creative enterprise aside again, and he set his nose to the grindstone, and he finished his B.A., at which point it dawned on him that to enter a good-paying career he needed an M.A., and in another field. No English major ever landed a lucrative position (despite what his advisor had told him).

"No sweat," he said. "I'm young. I've got fifty years ahead of me. All the time in the world."

So he got that M.B.A. and entered the work force, promising he'd donate every weekend and every vacation to his world of words. Except then he met a young woman, and they fell in love, and they married, and they had 2.3 children, and she had a job, too, it being tough economically speaking, so he stayed home sometimes and played with the kids, and his work was a lot more demanding than he'd ever thought it would be, and the years, well, the years just skidded by like a bad accident.

"Hey," he said. "That's okay. I'm happy. I have a good life. I'll work hard now and then retire early, and the rest of my life will be one long fictive festival."

Only obviously the kids needed to go to college, and that cost money, and he didn't really expect his wife to get sick like that and grow those doctor bills like green peas in a well-watered garden, and so he never quite got around to retiring early, only, heck, he did retire right on time, and that had to say something, and it was the happiest day of his life.

This was it.

He had arrived.

For the next twenty years he'd do nothing but bask in plot and language and watch his characters astonish him. He could hardly wait to see what they'd do. He had so much to write about. So much to tell about the life he'd led.

He bought himself a state-of-the-art computer and the latest word-processing program and spent six months learning how to use them.

He remodeled the kids' room—they'd gone off to start a life of their own, having all 2.3 graduated college with honors—and bought a spiffy ergonomic desk.

Then, one morning, he was finally ready.

He woke up early, ate a light breakfast, poured himself a cup of coffee, and padded into his writing room, where he sat down in front of the phosphorescent screen, put his fingers on the keyboard, and died of a heart attack.

His name, by the way, was Ralph Feinstein.

And no one's ever heard of Ralph Feinstein, have they?

That's because he never got around to writing a word. He mainstreamed his life, spiced it up with alibis, and wiled it away.

"Everyone who does not *need* to be a writer, who thinks he can do something else, ought to do something else," Georges Simenon wrote.

And Georges is right.

So you have your opening, and you have your desire, and you have your schedule. What now?

Authors tend to go one of two ways from here on out. They either improvise or they outline. Both have risks and benefits, so you'll have to see which works best for you.

Improvisation. Though I had written one unpublished novella, two unpublished novels, and a lot of published stories by the time I sat down to begin work on what turned out to be my first published novel, *Live from Earth*, I really hadn't a clue what I was doing.

In a lot of ways, you learn how to write a good novel by writing a couple of bad ones.

So I decided to have some fun.

I'd follow my own narrative rhythms and intuitions, improvise, and see where things took me. I had a hazy sense of the overall story, but every scene, every paragraph, every line came pretty much as a surprise to me. For a while, for instance, some cute aliens who were green and three inches tall and looked a little like broccoli entered my story for no particular reason. Once, some people stopped talking in the middle of a serious conversation, music came on from nowhere, and they began dancing a softshoe and singing a fairly ribald ditty called "The Bovine Duet."

It was terrific horseplay.

I woke up each morning without a hint where I was going to tour that day or why. As a result, I felt rich with freedom and danger.

Two years later, I had completed my first full draft. It was 450 pages long.

Then I went back and started editing it, giving it narrative muscle and forward momentum, cutting what didn't help advance plot or character, trimming the narratological adipose.

A year more, and I was done with my fourth draft. It was 225 pages long.

And that's both the benefit and the risk of improvisation in a succinct, not-so-easy-to-swallow capsule.

It's simply a blast to enter a state of continuous improvisation, following your own biochemical rhythms, shooting off exit ramps into parts of the novelistic city you didn't even know existed, finding hidden neighborhoods, seeing characters walk on you didn't expect to walk on in order to deliver lines you didn't think they were capable of delivering. It's liberating business which can take you in directions you just didn't believe you could go. Plus it allows you to compose quickly, even effortlessly, getting down gobs of prose in the wink of a cursor and blink of a synapse.

On the other hand, by its very nature improvisation is a method that will doom you to unnecessary detours that may be a pleasure to take at the moment, but will in the long run also waste a whole bunch of time, trees, and ink.

Hence there's always…

Outlining. After *Live from Earth*, I wrote a novel called *Burnt*, an academic satire in which a professor kills a student because of that student's awful prose style. *Burnt* became—through a string of un-

Q. Many moons ago you told me you tried to barrel through a first draft, get anything down you could, and *then* go back and craft. Is that still how you go about things?

A. Yes, pretty much. Rather than do a detailed outline, I prefer to let the characters and situations develop organically within a very rough structure. From this "finished" product I can finally figure out what the story's really about and who the people really are. The second draft then involves digging a lot more deeply into motivation and moment-to-moment events. That leaves the third (and subsequent) drafts to work on the language.

Q. Have you ever tried outlining? If so, what did you discover?

A. I did a lot of outlining early on, but really it's too left-brained an activity for me. It tends to lead me more toward contrivance than toward honesty.

Q. What sort of advice would you give a young writer about the actual writing process?

A. Retype. It's the best advice I know. I write on a computer, but when I finish a draft I go back and retype the entire thing, then (in the case of novels) retype it again. It gives me a chance to get tired of the sound of my own voice, and forces me to keep the writing as fresh as I can to keep my own interest alive. When people tell me it sounds like too much work, I wonder what they think writing is supposed to be.

Lewis Shiner's novels include *Glimpses*, which won the World Fantasy Award, and *Slam*.

Kathy Acker

Q. Can you talk a little bit about your writing process. My sense from reading your work is that it grows organically... as Robert Coover once said of Donald Barthelme's, like barnacles on a hull. Is that right?

A. That's right. It grows organically. That is, I have to listen to it in the same way that I have to listen to whatever I'm reading. And seeing, experiencing, the whole bit. My sense is that I write by listening, by reading, etc. Which is to say—with a leap—that I write by being written.

Q. Have you ever tried outlining? Would you ever recommend it to others?

A. I only outline writing that's done for money. (I used to say: writing that's not much fun.) Only when the article is too complicated to write directly. When I have outlined, I have always, in subsequent drafts, neglected the outline. So the outline is just a device to get from point *a* to point *b* (in forgetting point a). I'm more interested in the forgotten than in facts.

Q. What sort of advice would you give a young writer about the actual writing process?

A. Well, when I taught, I tried to listen to each student. Where he or she was at. Tried to say: you have to listen to yourself. Not to that screaming ego self, but all the rest. If it's human, it's not formulaic. And then there's (the problem of) writing in the world. Money, publishing, etc. I've never been great about those babies, but it still seems to me that patience or endurance and some extremely thick duck feathers are necessities.

Before her death in 1997, Kathy Acker was at the forefront of literary inventiveness for years with works like Blood & Guts in High School and Pussy, King of the Pirates.

expected publishing twists and turns—my third instead of my second published novel. With it, I improvised to get the first draft, then immediately switched to outline to pull it together and give it a tight shape.

That, I discovered, worked like a charm for me.

Then everything changed.

I wrote *Tonguing the Zeitgeist* next, a science fictional retelling of the Faust myth that explores the commodification of the arts in a rock'n'roll near-future world, and for that one I outlined from soup to crisis, and the scales fell from my eyes.

What I did was take a week or two to block out a very general sense of storyline, something that could be put down in a single paragraph. Over the following three weeks, I broke that paragraph up, usually making each sentence into its own chapter (I knew I wanted twenty-one chapters, that number being the numerological equivalent of coming into adulthood), which I then teased out into its own paragraph.

Meanwhile, my characters started to develop in the recesses of my imagination, and so I opened a separate file and began to keep notes on each of them—everything from descriptions of their appearance to discussions of their motivations.

Too, I began coming up with loads of SF details, names, and other atmospheric data, so I opened yet another file for these.

When I actually started writing, I often found myself veering from the outline, or needing to go back and re-direct it slightly here, not-so-slightly there. Nonetheless, the composition went infinitely more smoothly than it ever had before: it took just over a year and a half from concept to completion, and this time I came in with only about 50 fatty pages that needed editorial liposuction.

A number of people will tell you outlining makes the writing process more mechanical and rigid than improvisation.

I'm here to tell you that's not necessarily as evil as it sounds.

Knowing where you're going and how you're going to get there not only saves you plenty of time and energy, it's also extremely helpful when you're preparing what's called a partial (the first 50 pages or so and an outline) for an agent or publisher, writing nonfiction, or trying to collaborate on a project with others.

My point, then, isn't that you ought to decide between improvisation and outline. There's most likely a little of the former in the latter, and vice versa.

Michael Arnzen

Q. What was your writing process like on your avant-horror novel, *Grave Markings*?

A. Total immersion. I began with a rough concept, and just started obsessively writing. It was mostly an experiment (as all acts of writing are)—I wanted to see if I could sustain a plot for more than 4,000 words. I'd sit at the keyboard until I felt I'd written as much as I could each day. Nonstop. All of it was "on the fly"—I'd set characters with a goal, and throw obstacles in their way if I felt I was rushing toward the ending. And when I was exhausted at the end of each day, I'd jot down an outline for the following series of events, usually the next three chapters or so. New ideas would occur to me in my sleep, and so I'd wake up and jot those down, too, revising my plans along the way. I didn't know what I was doing, and I didn't know how the book would end, but when I reached about 50,000 words, something clicked and the ending joyously wrote itself in one marathon session. It only took me somewhere between three and four weeks to get a first draft done. The revisions took two years!

Q. If you had it to write again, would you approach it differently?

A. Oh yeah. I don't have the same energy level I had back then, and I've unfortunately built up a strong tolerance for coffee. I try to write "plot treatments" in bursts now… something like an outline that takes a concept and exhausts its possibilities. Then I go back and write the chapters, afterwards—cautiously, meticulously, based not only on my mad ideas (after all, those are always handy), but also on research and a dire care for the patterns of language.

Q. What sort of advice would you give a young writer about the actual writing process?

A. You should be writing the sort of books and stories you like to read. Chances are, you haven't read a "perfect" book. So get furious that no one's written one yet, and show 'em how it oughta be done. Get furious about it every day. Beat the keys like a boxing bag, day after day after day. Get addicted to your writing schedule and stick to it. You don't need a trainer— you just need the will to get up and fight. And when you're not writing, read. Especially the awful hackneyed kind of books. They'll keep you mean.

Michael Arnzen is the author of *Grave Markings*, winner of the Bram Stoker Award for Best First Novel.

Nor is it that one approach to writing is intrinsically better than the other.

Rather, I'm suggesting you try both, even flip-flop between the two, in order to discover what balance best brings out your best, and in order to get you to think about the pros and cons of each within the context of your own fiction.

So write on.

Stretching & Flexing

1. If you haven't already done so, take time to sit down and work out the most productive weekly writing schedule for yourself. What days? What time of day? How long? Then plock that schedule on your refrigerator with a magnet and keep to it. Remember, it usually takes about three weeks to change an old behavior or start a new one, so get going!

2. Next time you sit down to write, try an outline if you've never tried one before, or, if that's the way you normally work, try a round of improvisation. Begin playing with both, fine-tuning, finding what approach to writing you feel most comfortable with, but don't be too fast to judge: give both some real time and effort. You'll ultimately be a more productive writer.

Ch-Ch-Changes

THE ELEMENTS OF A STORY

Stories are about change.

Working on yours, you should continuously ask yourself: *How are things undergoing transformation?*

Is my character growing, learning, slowly gaining control of his or her environment, slowly losing his or her grip on reality, reaching his or her goal, losing his or her path, getting the girl or boy, finding what he or she wants, succeeding or failing?

Is she or he in some way different at the end of the action than at the beginning?

Character exists in plot, so a corollary to those questions is this: *Is the plot moving quickly and evenly enough to keep up a feeling of forward momentum in my reader?*

If the answer's no, you ought to ask yourself why someone might want to experience your story. It's possible you'll come up with a thousand rejoinders. People don't read *exclusively* for change, after all. They read, too, for pure emotional charge, linguistic music, sensuous sentence rhythms, plain old surprise, beautiful descriptions, perfect-pitch dialogue, impressive formal innovation, a sense of place, the sheer simple gratification of tracing various motifs, startling juxtapositions, the act of a powerful imagination in motion.

But if there's no change in your central character, and thus no real movement of plot forward, you should be aware you're treading on some exceptionally thin narrative ice.

That doesn't mean something should blow up in every sentence.

It just means that it's exceedingly difficult to write a story about nothing happening to a character who doesn't change, and it's exceedingly difficult to write a story in which every scene—even every sentence—doesn't in some way move plot forward.

What's the point?

The idea that change is an integral part of narrative structure became so second-nature to most people that in 1863 a critic named Gustav Freytag even drew a diagram of the basic mechanics of a five-act tragedy in his book on the subject, *Technik des Dramas*. Those mechanics perfectly describe the workings of a typical piece of fiction—story or novel—as well. The result has come to be known as Freytag's Pyramid, and it's still extremely useful in providing a sense of how most fictions develop in five fairly distinct—though frequently overlapping—stages.

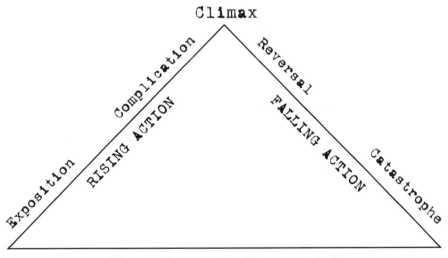

First, you need to present the *exposition*—that is, introduce your main character(s), sketch in setting, display your dominant tone, and provide any other necessary background facts your reader ought to know in order to understand what will happen in the course of your narration. After that, introduce your story's *complication*, an entanglement caused by the clash of opposing forces (somebody wants something and for some reason can't have it, or can't have it just yet). The complication generates a sense of forward momentum that carries your story toward the *climax* or *crisis*, where the decisive action on which the plot will hinge occurs (traditionally the metaphorical showdown, a physical or psychological battle). Once the crisis has occurred, the action of your story begins to fall through what's called a *rever-sal*, or change in your protagonist's fortune (he or she usually gets what he or she wants in comedy, and doesn't in tragedy), toward what used to be called the *catastrophe* (because in tragedy, which Freytag was describing, it almost always involves the death of the hero), but is now more regularly referred to as the *dénouement* (literally "unknotting") or *resolution*, where the solution, explanation, or outcome of the story takes place.

How would this function in practice?

Let's take a quick look.

Heather (our *protagonist*, or main character), a thirteen-year-old who is almost six-feet tall and so tends to stand with a height-correcting stoop, is walking down a tree-lined avenue in Greenwich Village one summer afternoon (*exposition*). Little does Heather know, at that very second a Persian cat called Tweedles (our *antagonist*, the character preventing our protagonist from getting what he or she wants), who's had just a rotten life at the hands of his abusive owner, Igor Smurf, decides to commit suicide and leaps out a fourth-story window above her (*complication*). Tweedles plummets toward Heather's unsuspecting-yet-pretty-thin cranium, every yard picking up speed and hence impact potential; except at the last moment the grenade Igor Smurf forced down Tweedles's throat five seconds before detonates, disintegrating the feline in a cloud of burned fur and a suddenly stifled yip (*crisis*). Heather flinches, and stoops some more, as a light pink mist begins to descend around her like a surreal autumn drizzle, except somewhere deep inside she knows everything's going to be okay (*reversal*). And so she continues down that tree-lined street, admiring the dappling sun among the leaves, on her way to murder her mother's pet Chihuahua (*dénouement*, with just a hint of further complication for good luck, or maybe a possible sequel).

Notice, while you're at it, how much conflict will be a part of nearly every story. That's because trouble is more interesting to read about than its lack. Put your protagonist in danger, and everyone will want to know what happens next. That doesn't mean you need to have detonating cats in every scene. In fact, subtle psychological danger is usually more appealing to readers—at least grownup readers—than the overt physical kind.

Notice, too, that while Freytag's Pyramid suggests there's only one complication per story, there are more times than not a number of them (especially in novels), each a little more complicated than the one before it, and that while Freytag situates crisis at the precise midpoint in a tale, it often occurs much closer to the end than the beginning. Nowadays, reversal and dénouement are regularly tantamount to epilogue.

Last, keep in mind that *story* and *plot* are two different things, if you want to get technical about it. In his groundbreaking discourse on fiction writing, *Aspects of the Novel* (1927), E. M. Forster defines story as "a narrative of events in their time-sequence" and plot as "a narrative of events, the emphasis falling on causality." That's a little fuzzy until you think about it a bit. Story is the stuff of the world. Plot is the stuff of fiction. Story is event. Plot is event shaped. Junk happens in the universe, and people talk about it, but a fiction writer rearranges that junk into carefully crafted episodes which have an aesthetic and clear cause-and-effect relationship among themselves.

In life, put simply, cats are always falling out of windows in Greenwich Village.

In fiction, they fall because they're trying to kill themselves because they've been abused by people named things like Igor Smurf and because they're about to explode because a grenade has been jammed down their throats while a teenager named Heather moves obliviously below them on her ironic way to animal abuses of a different register.

Now Read This

Aristotle. *The Poetics* (ca. 330 B.C.). In a sense, all other criticism about fiction is a footnote to this, the first extant critical work.

Booth, Wayne. *The Rhetoric of Fiction* (1961). A beautifully lucid and intelligent analysis of the components that comprise fiction.

Braine, John. *Writing a Novel* (1975). Hard to find these days, this is a superlative practical guide to (mostly conventional) novel writing.

Burroughs, William S. *Naked Lunch* (1959). Perhaps the most subversive novel ever published in America, *Naked Lunch* breaks every one of Freytag's suppositions.

Forster, E. M. *Aspects of the Novel* (1927). Still one of the best texts on how to write fiction by one of the modern masters, with much on story and plot.

Hersey, John, ed. *The Writer's Craft* (1974). A splendid collection of essays, interviews, and journal entries on various aspects of writing (including, but not at all limited to, story and plot) by many nineteenth- and twentieth-century giants from

Conrad, James, and Thomas Mann, to Robbe-Grillet, Gertrude Stein, and William S. Burroughs.

Stretching & Flexing

1. Use Freytag's Pyramid to compose a number of very, very short stories—each no more than a paragraph long—to familiarize yourself with the components that make up most fiction and to practice concision. Maybe each story can form part of a longer narrative mosaic.

2. How can you subvert the elements in Freytag's Pyramid to interesting effect without compromising the aesthetic coherence of a story? Try writing a number of very, very short stories— again, each no more than a paragraph long—that do this. Is it possible to switch components, delete some, reconfigure them in alluring ways?

12 Genre Jive

DABBLING IN DIFFERENT FORMS

Every fiction, from the most stock piece of mainstream realism or pulp to the most head-bangingly weird piece of experimentation, is more or less a subset of some *genre* or combination of genres—part, in other words, of a larger system of conventions and expectations about how we're supposed to read and make sense of a specific work.

When you pick up a story or novel and begin running your eyes over its words, you instantaneously enter into a contract with its author about what type of fiction it will be, what sort of things can and can't happen within it, even in many cases the shape of its plot, the feel of its language, the qualities of its setting, the richness of its characters, and the nature of its conclusion. If the author violates that contract too abruptly or too forcefully, changing, say, an apparently realistic story into an experimental science fiction on the sixteenth of seventeen pages for no particular reason, most readers feel cheated rather than surprised and delighted, the same way you would if your publisher violated your publishing contract.

Most if not all professional writers know that they're composing within the perimeters of a particular genre with a particular tradition, and most novices who don't will labor thrice as long to accomplish half as much, since they'll need to reinvent protocols that have already existed for ages about how to write what they're writing.

It's definitely worth your while, then, to know a little about each genre before you begin writing, and to read deeply in the ones that fascinate you the most.

Writing is a series of decisions, and what genre or genres you decide to use or abuse will have a profound influence on the form and content of the story you author.

Every genre has its own strengths and weaknesses. Each can do certain things very well that other genres can't do, and each can't do certain things very well that other genres can. If you know this before you choose one to work within or against, you'll save yourself 400 major headaches.

Before discussing the chief features of a handful of major contemporary genres, a caveat is in order: no single one is intrinsically better or worse than any other. Each is simply as good or bad as the writer generating within it. The idea that's perpetuated—usually subtextually and subvocally—in most creative writing workshops, stating that mainstream realism is somehow the Really Serious Literary Genre and all others intellectually lower-class cousins to the Real Thing, is therefore patently absurd, as everyone from Homer to Shakespeare, James Joyce to George Orwell, and Salman Rushdie to Toni Morrison knew or knows.

Instead, genre's all about the ability of each piece of fiction to function in certain ways, do certain kinds of narratological work.

Nor should you think of writing within a specific genre as some sort of claustrophobic constraint or creative limitation. Rather, imagine each genre as part of your possible palette for expressing your ideas and emotions. Use them the same way an artist might the color blue or the techniques of a Cubist collage to get across what he or she needs to get across. Ultimately, the best mature writers of vision will learn to write against simplistic genres, explore ways to transcend them in engaging modes. But emerging writers can't do so effectively (we're back to Picasso again) without first studying and achieving an inside-out understanding of several target ones.

So, at first glance, it may seem like I'm wanting things both ways: espousing the importance of understanding the borders that define and constrain writing in a genre context, *and* castigating publishers for categorizing a submission when considering it for publication.

In fact I'm suggesting that, as in politics, so in literature: those ignorant of history will be doomed to repeat it to no purpose.

Those writers who haven't taken the time and mental effort to learn what genre is, how it functions, what the assumptions are of various ones, where they came from and where they might be going, will have to do much greater creative legwork to arrive at the same point as those writers who *have* taken the time and mental effort.

And, while you're reading what follows, keep tucked in a corner of your brain what's come to be known as Sturgeon's Law. Theodore Sturgeon, one of the twentieth century's truly fine science fiction writers, declares:

> Ninety percent of everything is crud.
>
> Corollary 1: The existence of immense quantities of trash in science fiction is admitted and it is regretted; but it is no more unnatural than the existence of trash anywhere.
>
> Corollary 2: The best science fiction is as good as the best fiction in any field.

The same, it almost (but not quite) goes without saying, is true of any genre.

Again, a genre's only as good as the person who's using, abusing, and extending its conventions. If you follow them too closely, you get cookie-cutter fiction. If you don't follow them closely enough, you get narrative goo. Science fiction can be the equivalent of bugged-eyed monsters, spark-spitting rayguns, and bad dubbing, or it can be Mary Shelley's *Frankenstein*, Philip K. Dick's *The Man in the High Castle*, and Richard Kadrey's *Metrophage*. Experimentation can be the equivalent of murky ideas, mucked-up language, and black berets in smoky cafés, or it can be William Faulkner's *As I Lay Dying*, Kathy Acker's *Blood and Guts in High School*, and David Foster Wallace's *Infinite Jest*.

Know the genres you'll be working within and without. Think about their suppositions concerning the world and about how to pull those into line with your own.

Then take a deep breath and step beyond them.

Some Market-Driven Genres

L et's quickly look at some—though by no means all—of the most prevalent contemporary genres and subgenres that are marketable, i. e., money-propelled.

Because we dealt with the assumptions of realism at some length in the introduction to this guide, let's take for granted a certain understanding of its behavior and move on to some other possibilities:

Fantasy. A helpful way to understand each genre is to ask: What is its relationship to the world? Each, you will thereby discover, makes certain suppositions about what Samuel R. Delany calls *subjunctivity*, the tension between the words on the page and their referents.

If, as critic Brooks Landon points out, the reader of reportage or non-fiction presupposes that its language refers to what *has happened*, and the reader of realism that its language refers to what *could have happened*, then the reader of the elder statesman of genres, fantasy, which dates back to the earliest recorded fictions, presupposes its language refers to what *could not have happened*. Hence we enter the realm of the supernatural, the marvelous, of fairy tales, romances, horror stories, and utopias in which narrative events are usually backed by a coherent ideology (often Christian in romance, for instance, humanist in utopia). The tone is frequently impersonal, authoritative, certain, confident. Goodness and nobility frequently triumph in its supraworld (*Yvain*, *The Divine Comedy*, Tolkien, contemporary Sword&Sorcery, even the novelizations of *Star Wars*). Often the narrative situation has been set long ago and far away where times and places have ceased to disturb us, and often the conclusion is comic to the extent it implies an ultimate gathering together, reconciliation, and benevolent universe which is theological in nature.

In this way, fantasy is a compensatory genre, looking back to a lost, beautiful, and often aristocratic moral and social hierarchy that was communally and teleologically meaningful.

What fantasy is good at, then, is the exploration of the Large Human Questions concerning good and evil, life and death, this world and the next. Consequently, its characters tend to represent types rather than individuals, and narrative surprise often gives way to narrative ritual—retellings of the same core story (the battle, say, between the forces of lightness and darkness) recloaked in subtly different guises.

The greatest difficulty with this genre is making it new.

Romance, Western, Horror, Erotica, Pornography. Each of these is a subgenre of fantasy in the sense that each tends to be compensatory in nature, occupied with types rather than individuals, and often devoted to retelling certain core stories. In the case of the first three, those stories often revolve around the conflict between good and evil.

In most cases, each also revolves around what could not in all probability have happened. From one perspective, then, each exists somewhere on a continuum arced between myth, on the one hand, and mimesis, on the other.

The chivalric medieval *romance* appeared in French literature in the twelfth century and in English in the thirteenth, replacing the weightier, more serious *epic* as dominant narrative form. If heroism and action reign supreme in epic, then love and a pervasive sense of mystery come to join them in romance. At the center of both subgenres is the *quest story*, in which a protagonist sets out on a journey to accomplish some moral goal. He—and it is almost always a he, since these subgenres tend to be products of deeply patriarchal cultures—moves through remote and exotic spaces in a semi-magical world of larger-than-life characters whose powers exceed those of normal humans but fall short of those of the gods. Almost invariably, a passionate love interest imbues the plot with much of its forward momentum.

Change chivalric romance's knights into frontiersmen, scouts, and cowboys, change the evil forces into Indians and bandits, and change the terrain from a quasi-mythical Europe to quasi-mythical U.S. West, and you have the essence of the classic *western*, a subgenre that has consumed the American psyche since its inception in the early nineteenth century in the narratives of writers like James Fenimore Cooper and the advent of the *dime novels*, cheaply printed paperbound tales of adventure, lurid crime, and detection.

Change those knights into tall, dark, and handsome lovers, change the point of view from masculine to feminine, change the evil forces into human passions, and change the terrain from the fierce battlefield to the frilly bedroom, and you have the essence of the contemporary *romance novel*.

Change the emphasis of the romance novel from love to sensuality, and you have the essence of contemporary *erotica*, which employs sexual elements as one part of a larger aesthetic or thematic aspect of a work and which has a tradition that tracks back to some of the earliest literature in both eastern and western culture.

Change the emphasis of erotica from sensuality to sexuality as an end in itself—what Vladimir Nabokov referred to as a "copulation of clichés"—and you have the essence of *pornography*.

Put a psychologically sinister spin on chivalric romance's narrative universe, transplant the setting from battlefield to shadowy subterranean labyrinths that stand for the human unconscious, manifest those evil forces as monsters, devils, psychokillers, and ghosts, embrace the ideal of social trespass that is ultimately righted, and you have the essence of the modern *horror tale*, a subgenre that grows out of the *gothic novel* from the eighteenth and nineteenth centuries. There, in works like Horace Walpole's *Castle of Otranto* (1764), William Beckford's *Vathek* (1786), and Edgar Allan Poe's stories, long underground passageways, dark stairwells, frightening mysteries, and minds-in-extremis abound. While such settings have tended to fall away in contemporary versions of the subgenre, such as those constructed by Stephen King and Clive Barker, the same atmosphere of unknown terror continues in full force, as does the essential battle between good and evil.

Or, in an aesthetic quantum leap, charge those same features of action, moral quest, and characterological stylization with a serious philosophical dimension, and you have, as Richard Chase argues in *The American Novel and Its Tradition* (1957), the essence of some of the most important narratives produced in this country, from Hawthorne's *Scarlet Letter* (1850), Melville's *Moby-Dick* (1851), and Henry James's *Portrait of a Lady* (1881), to Twain's *Huck Finn* (1884),

Fitzgerald's *Great Gatsby* (1925), and Faulkner's *As I Lay Dying* (1930).

It's never the core story that makes or breaks a narrative, then. It's what you do with it, how you extend it, subvert it, revise it, complicate it, present it, or blend it with others, that counts.

Detective, Mystery, Thriller. Each of these subgenres of fantasy fall much closer to mimesis than myth on our hypothetical continuum, but each exists in a world that still isn't quite ours.

They persist, that is, in being compensatory in nature, occupied with larger-than-life types rather than individuals, devoted to retelling certain core stories that revolve around the quest and concepts of good and evil, and dedicated to action rather than depth psychology. Yet in each case the narrative world is much more concerned with epistemology—what we know, how we know, and what we can know—than the previous market-driven subgenres I've mentioned. Each, in other words, centers around some kind of sleuth (a police official, a spy, etc.) who attempts to solve a conundrum (more personal in the detective and mystery stories, more political in the thriller) through the logical assembling and interpretation of evidence. Reason always triumphs in the end.

While the first detective of them all was probably Oedipus, whose job it was to piece together various clues in order to discover why his kingdom was suffering, most critics date the emergence of the classical *detective story* with the publication of Edgar Allan Poe's "The Murders in the Rue Morgue" (1841). British versions by such writers as Sir Arthur Conan Doyle tend to place emphasis on style, a few specific locales, and logic. American versions, which flourished from the twenties onward, carry with them a pulpier prose, a larger scope, and a heavy charge of sensationalism.

Although the terms *detective story* and *mystery* are frequently used interchangeably, the latter tends to be associated with those tales in which the conventional detective story is disrupted slightly—say, for instance, when no literal detective exists, or when the identity of the criminal is known from the start.

A *courtroom novel* is just a detective novel told, as it were, after the fact.

Change the detective to a double agent, counter-terrorist, or person in the employment of some other arm of government, change the setting from fairly local to global, and change the key characters' motivation from subjective to political, and you have the essence of the *thriller*.

Science Fiction. You can easily see how this genre has its roots in fantasy as well—in its fascination with journeys into strange foreign lands (or, in this case, solar systems and alternate dimensions), for instance, its love of adventure, and its emphasis on The Big Questions. But if readers of fantasy presuppose its language refers to what *could not have happened*, readers of science fiction presuppose its language refers to what *has not happened—yet.*

Many scholars trace the beginnings of this genre back to the Industrial Revolution in England during the middle of the eighteenth century that depended on the development of such devices as James Watt's steam engine. Not only did the Industrial Revolution bring on a sense of rapid cultural acceleration, a concentration of people in urban areas, and a change in the very nature of work for many, it also gave rise to a highly ambivalent reaction to technology which suddenly flourished throughout Europe and, soon after, America.

This reaction was first fully articulated by Mary Shelley in what many consider the first true SF novel: *Frankenstein* (1818). What that novel does, like so much SF, is to defamiliarize our world by means of extended metaphor and re-present it to us so we can see and contemplate it anew. So Victor Frankenstein's monster is less about a horrific creation than it is about the modern condition—one filled with an overwhelming feeling of isolation, alienation, and divorce from the natural world. Selfhood in Shelley's story has become a patchwork affair, the human a teratoidal fragmentation at the hands of technology.

Science fiction, then, often concentrates on large, serious philosophical questions rather than small, serious psychological ones, and this places it light years away from domestic realism. Much of it (though by no means all) concentrates on action and gadgets. Accordingly, its characters tend not to be as fully formed as those in realism, their relationships less complex.

While SF's strength tends to be found in its philosophical speculations (that brand of the genre more interested in epistemological and ontological investigations than in those neat gadgets goes by the name of *speculative fiction*) into what might happen if we're not careful (*dystopia*), and what might happen if we are (*utopia*), its challenge to the writer is not to sacrifice rich characterization and narrative surprise in the interests of action and glitzy toys.

Alternative Genres

The wide spectrum of viable market-driven genres from realism to fantasy and its subsets is always going to be a little predictable around the narrative edges, then.

I can only hint at that predictability here, but it should be clear by now that the risk of working within the nuts-and-bolts confines of such assembly-line fiction is a sort of imaginative tedium, a creative petrifaction, the nagging sense any writer doing so must have that she or he has already been there and done that. Many readers, on the other hand, tend to find an almost ritualistic comfort in the repetition of familiar forms, the nostalgic sense that one horror story or western or thriller is going to read pretty much like another. Hence the incredible success of those subgenres, which tap into a culture's need for feelings of completion, wholeness, and reliability.

For me, interesting fiction begins when those familiar forms begin to dissolve or reconfigure in unexpected ways; when simple romance tropes fracture into Melville's *Moby-Dick*, when the gothic novel shudders into *Frankenstein*. That's the moment when possibility, surprise, and re-vision enter the generative system, when, in a word, beauty becomes convulsive. In terms of socio-literary history, that moment occurred (I'm grossly oversimplifying here, of course, because of space limitations, but the essence of my point remains valid) with the rise of modernism in the nineteenth century when for many writers the idea of stable genre and the stable society and worldview it suggests became radically problematized.

Let's take a quick look at why and how this happened, then glance at some of the fictional responses to that problematization.

If *pre-modern* consciousness frames its world in terms of *master-narratives*, or grand fictions that lend shape and substance to people's lives (the idea of humanism within the Renaissance, or those of symmetry, order, and reason within Neoclassicism or the Enlightenment), then *modern* consciousness senses a potential loss of master-narratives.

By the late nineteenth century, many people felt that developments in geology had begun to shrink humankind's position in time, while developments in astronomy had begun to shrink its position in space. Darwinian biology underscored this sense of existential displacement, dislodging our privileged position in the Great Chain of Being. Reinforcing this reconfiguration at the turn of the century was the horrible dimensions of destruction wrought by World War I, and the emergence of Freud's immensely dark view of the human psyche, with his emphasis upon a language of desire, irrationality, and repressed violence. Add to these a poignant feeling of rootlessness brought on by the proliferation of the automobile and airplane, of a contracting globe and increasing sense of cultural relativism brought on by the invention of photography, film, the telephone, and radio— and the striking feeling of dislocation and disorder pervading literary, artistic, and musical projects becomes intelligible. The predictability of Newtonian physics bursts into Einsteinian spatiotemporal relativity in more than just the laboratory.

A hunger for the cohesion and coherence that customs and conventions once provided thereby arises side by side with an energetic and even at times optimistic avant-garde attempt to make it new. Amid the geography of modern literature we locate Joyce, Woolf, and Faulkner rethinking narrative, and e. e. cummings, Stevens, and Williams rethinking poetry, but we also locate Yeats on a lifelong pilgrimage for a unified private mythology, Hemingway for the Code, Eliot for the great gift of Tradition itself. We locate, to put it slightly differently, a group of creators who saw their work, not only as an artistic revolution, but also as an existential last stand against encroaching cosmic chaos, as a way (to paraphrase Eliot in the final section of *The Waste Land*) to shore up their culture's fragments against its ruins.

Through the development of elaborate symbolic structures, these creative pioneers attempted to encircle and tame what they perceived as a frenzied universe. No doubt their texts at first glance appear almost as confusing as the chaotic cosmos aswarm beyond them, but upon closer study they yield a deep sense of order and meaning beneath their seeming voids of meaninglessness. Beneath the sometimes bewildering shards of *The Waste Land* (1922), for instance, we discern the ordering principle of Jessie Weston's scholarly work on ritual and romance, and beneath the sometimes confounding stream-of-consciousness and linguistic hoopla that comprises Joyce's *Ulysses* (1922), we make out Homeric myth, oldest icon of European heritage.

If modern consciousness develops a number of responses to the turbulent situation in which it finds itself by seeking to generate a sense of underlying aesthetic and philosophical design in the artifacts it produces, *postmodern* consciousness can't find any response adequate to the mind-bending situation in which it finds *itself*. The idea of the master-narrative hence detonates into a series of highly relativized micro-narratives, one just as valid (or invalid) as another.

We come across many who, in the wake of World War II, sense a new series of scientific, philosophical, political, and aesthetic shockwaves rolling through the culture. Postmodern consciousness, then, to employ theorist Jean-François Lyotard's point of view, tries to present the unpresentable, whether it be in the gray half-world of Beckett's aptly named novella *The Unnamable* (1953), where the protagonist is not sure where he/it is, who he/it is, or even *if* he/it is, or video artist Nam June Paik's vast walls of television screens playing unpredictable and random sets of images in a kind of cyberblitz. Postmodern consciousness skeptically problematizes all our culture once took for granted about language and experience—*and* generally basks in doing so. It becomes unclear exactly what the relationship of words to their referents is. The universe morphs into pluriverse; the world mutates from (as theorist Roland Barthes would have it) a *work* into a *text*.

That is, the postmodern creates a space where there is no longer an Author-God creating a single meaning, but a multidimensional area of ludic activity where a diversity of micro-narratives, none better or worse than any other, clash, blend, and reform in stimulating and challenging ways. We detect a group of artists who see their art as a celebration of decentralization, diversification, and demassification, whose works display little tolerance for borders of any kind—including those of rigid genre distinctions. In reaction to modern notions of desperate purpose, experimental design, mastery, synthesis, and a sense of tradition, the postmodern enjoys festive play, experimental designlessness, anarchy, deconstruction, and a devilish appropriation and demythologization of tradition.

While it's true that formulaic market-driven genres thrive today, and that experimentation in fiction has a long and distinguished tradition, finding early expression in such works as Rabelais's *Gargantua and Pantagruel* (1567) and Laurence Sterne's *Tristram Shandy* (1759-1567), and while it's equally true, as Vladimir Nabokov asserts, that every piece of fiction except the pulpiest is at least in some sense experimental, it's true as well that during the postmodern moment the idea of experimentalism has flourished and branched in a multitude of directions:

Magical Realism. Franz Roh first used this term in 1925 to describe tendencies in then-contemporary German artists. Since its first use, however, it has come to refer to certain Latin American authors and their literary descendants in North America and Europe who treat the everyday with fantastic awe and the fantastic with realistic understatement. Hence the unbelievable unexpectedly erupts within the commonplace. *One Hundred Years of Solitude* (1967), by Gabriel García Márquez, is the paradigmatic example.

Cyberpunk. Arising with resounding shockwaves in 1984 with the publication of William Gibson's *Neuromancer*, cyberpunk is a postmodern subset of science fiction that weds an investigative obsession into the universe of cybernetics and other cutting-edge technologies with a gritty, street-savvy punk aesthetic. Unlike most earlier SF, with the exception of the British and American New Wave of the sixties, cyberpunk is marked by stylistic pyrotechnics and literary ingenuity.

Slipstream. Bruce Sterling coined this term in a 1989 essay in *Science Fiction Eye*, a premier alternative zine, to refer to fiction that fell between two or more genres. Slipstream fiction is not quite fantasy, and not quite realism, and not quite something else either—but somehow all three at once. The intent of this sort of fiction (a good example is Ted Mooney's *Easy Travel to Other Planets* [1981]) is to make the reader feel slightly uncomfortable, slightly disconcerted and off balance, like living at the turn of the new millennium makes him or her feel.

Avant-Pop. A term appropriated by critic Larry McCaffery and surfictionist Ron Sukenick from Lester Bowie's jazz album, *Avant Pop: Brass Fantasy* (1986), and applied to fiction (as well as other arts) in the early nineties, this subgenre of postmodernism marries the avant-garde's dedication to innovative form with a radically ambivalent pop sensibility. The outcome is a kind of writing that looks back to the work of artists like Andy Warhol, musicians like the Beatles, and authors like William Burroughs who perform a dazzling tightrope dance that simultaneously embraces and deconstructs the mediascape's technosphere. A prime example among many is Harold Jaffe's short story collection *Eros Anti-Eros* (1990).

Transgressive Fiction. A catch-all term for that kind of postmodern fiction which challenges the dominant culture's fundamental assumptions about sex, gender, violence, social and pharmaceutical revolution, and sanity by creating extreme characters in extreme situations. This is the one that tends to catch Jesse Helms's eye in Congress, and is best represented by a furiously pornographic novel like Samuel R. Delany's *Hogg* (1996), which took nearly twenty years to find a publisher.

Each of these micro-genres, challenging their own assumptions and borders with other genres as they proceed, is not only a subspecies of postmodernism, but also of that longer tradition I referred to in the second section of this guide as Convulsive Beauty.

The strengths of this sort of writing are obvious: it's a mode that, as Gertrude Stein once said, releases our heads from the perceptual clamps they're usually stuck in. It gets us to see ourselves, our worlds, and even the essence of fiction in refreshingly new ways.

Its weaknesses, however, are just as obvious. Each of these subsets of postmodernism runs the risk of solidifying into its own petrified, rigid, predictable genre. Moreover, how long can we crank up the artistic volume, reconfigure the countercultural map, ratchet up the cerebral distortion, tiptoe around on the Convulsive Edge before we trip off, fall over, parachuteless, end up producing nothing but perpetual perceptual white noise, unreadable geographies, self-obliterating feedback? How long, in other words, can the New really be reNewed before it is: a) no longer New; or b) New but Untransformative? Is there an inevitable intractable vanguard horizon? An aesthetically terminal beach?

Of course, trying to find the answer to these questions is precisely the fun in composing alternative fiction and recreating the concept of genre every day of your writing life.

Now Read This

Le Guin, Ursula K. and Brian Attebery, eds. *The Norton Book of Science Fiction* (1993). With a stronger-than-usual offering of writers that foreground character and social concerns.

McCaffery, Larry, ed. *After Yesterday's Crash: The Avant-Pop Anthology* (1995). Fine intro, reading list, and collection of authors.

Rabkin, Eric, ed. *Stories: An Anthology and an Introduction* (1995). An excellent selection of fictions ranging over time and genres, plus a helpful essay on narrative and a glossary. Just the thing to help you meet many writers and varieties of writing.

Sterling, Bruce, ed. *Mirrorshades: The Cyberpunk Anthology* (1986). Manifesto and definitive collection of fiction.

Williamson, J. N., ed. *How to Write Tales of Horror Fantasy & Science Fiction* (1987). This one comes dangerously close to being a how-to-write-pulp guide, but take what it has with a grain of salt and you'll find some helpful brainfood here.

Stretching & Flexing

1. Reread the above section, paying close attention to genre definitions and distinctions, and then try to write a story in a genre you've never written in before. Don't forget ones I didn't discuss here such as noir and comix.

2. Write a slipstream fiction blending two or more genres described above, careful to keep some sense of aesthetic coherence and met expectation in your story.

15 Geography of Form

CHOOSING HOW TO
TELL YOUR STORY

Once you've decided on a genre within which to compose, or which to compose against, you need to decide the form that genre will take.

You can, obviously, simply tell your fifteen-to-eighteen-page story (the manuscript length of most published ones) from beginning to end, following chronology's arrow, using a conventional first- or third-person point of view, and modulating between summary and scene in fully formed paragraph blocks. Most writers work this way most of the time, and it's a modus operandi that yields some fine prose products.

But you should also remember that writing is possibility, and a lot of the enjoyment involved in it has to do with searching out fresh perspectives.

Sit at your desk and look around you. Now climb on top of it and turn around.

Alice slips through the silvery mist and peers, from the looking-glass chamber, back at where she left.

See how different your room looks?

Same thing with fiction, only more so.

"Everything has been thought of before," Goethe said, "but the problem is to think of it again."

I would add *think of it again in captivating ways.*

You should never feel constrained by genre, style, form, or whatever. Everything should feel like it's just about to happen.

So, fine, you can tell your fifteen-to-eighteen-page story from be-

Q. What is the relationship of thematics to formal innovation in *Blood of Mugwump*?

A. I can only say that the formal innovation that is a part of my writing has evolved out of the impossibility to speak otherwise. I try to write as clearly as possible but I live inside the nightmare of a body driven into schizophrenic indeterminate behavior by God and James Joyce. Through my desire to speak body, I have discovered cunt as language. Granted, between my soft lips, cunt is dyslexic by its very nature. And because I am cunt, genres have always failed me or at least genres have been fucked by the desires for speech. It is important, not to ever write "about" or "of" anything; rather, to write the body, to write flesh. Hence, the need for innovation. Body has always been dumb.

Q. *Blood of Mugwump* came under some major political fire when it appeared. What sort, and why?

A. *Mugwump* was attacked by Rep. Hoekstra (R., MI) as part of his campaign to de-fund the N.E.A. I cannot fully blame Hoekstra for his reading habit, for his addiction to the word as word. In part "we" (and my implication in this *we* terrifies me) are responsible for having produced such a reading machine. Hoekstra, like so many others, is simply illiterate because he cannot "travel" as a reader; he cannot, that is, be nomadic. Instead readers like him come to the text always already knowing how to read. Confronted by confusion, such a reader retires to his (and it is his, since this is a male-determined way of reading) reading chair and repeats "same as it ever was" as a sort of mantric lullabye. Even readers who "like" and "support" *Mugwump* have read the book in this way. This is more true of chromosomally male readers than it is of others. These readers celebrate the book on exactly the same terms that Hoekstra condemns the book. You see? No language. No grammar.

Q. What's the appeal, then, of formal and thematic innovation in a larger socio-literary context that tends to disparage it?

A. There is no actual "appeal to formal and thematic innovation." I do not ever, ever, set out to be innovative. Anyone who sets out to be innovative or plans to be experimental is silly. Writers who consciously attempt to "transgress" do not spend enough time thinking. Instead, they invent boundaries of the acceptable and then, lo and behold, "go beyond" the boundaries. Such behavior (as a writer) is ridiculous. My work only becomes innovative because I have been and am forced by the limits of language, grammar, and form to write *writing* in this specific way. Because my body is always in transit my language needs to never be settled. And while I do not have faith in the nostalgic return to making an "impact" on larger contexts, I do think it is important to discover ways for representing experiences that have not been trapped by existing paradigms. Much of my own living takes place inside the spaces between binary gender. There is no language already "in place" there; just look at what is being "passed" off as transgendered writing. Nearly all of it relies on familiar forms/representations that prevent the speaking of body.

Q. Who should young writers approaching the notion of formal and thematic innovation for the first time read?

A. Young writers should read as much classic literature as possible (i.e. Homer, Aeschylus, Dante, Virgil). Reading such work creates greater possibilities for writers to re-imagine language and form. Read all of Faulkner (even those lousy, sniveling, drunk novels, but especially the Quentin episode of *The Sound and the Fury*). Writers should avoid like the plague contemporary American writing. It is a hall of mirrors. An evil place. Avoid all writing that claims to be innovative (such writing is an echo and probably uses the word *fuck* too often). Writers who become addicted to contemporary writing are doomed to stand at the photo-copying machine, duplicating endless originals. Writers should read the camera movement of Orson Welles and then read how Jean-Luc Godard takes such style apart and then re-assembles it. Writers should listen to old, really old people (I'm not referring to Burroughs here) trying to talk about the first time they ever ate ice cream or figured out an ice cube. Writers should always force themselves to remember the very first time they had ever heard a word before they use the word.

Doug Rice, living against her schizophrenic flesh, is editor of Nobodaddies: A Journal of Pirated Flesh and Texts, author of Blood of Mugwump, and teaches at Kent State University-Salem.

ginning to end, following chronology's arrow, using a conventional first- or third-person point of view, and modulating between summary and scene in fully formed paragraph blocks—but how about instead presenting it as a sudden or flash fiction, condensing it down to its three- or five-page essence, televisually fast and poetically dense?

Charles Baxter: "The novel is, spatially, like an estate; the very short story is like an efficiency on the twenty-third floor. As it happens, more people these days live in efficiencies than on estates."

Is there a more engaging way to tell it than from beginning to end? Most epics, after all, begin *in medias res* . . . in the middle of things. And why follow chronology's arrow? Perhaps flashbacks are in order, or hallucinatory spatio-temporal disruptions. And have you thought about using the second-person point of view (*you* instead of *s/he* or *I*), or multiple viewpoints? Or the present tense, instead of the staid past?

How about framing your story as a series of journal entries, a confessional, a piece of reportage, an oratory, a diary, an epistolary interchange, a channel-surfing extravaganza, or some strange combination of all these? What sort of effects might that have on the way you present your information and your reader interprets it? Is one of these forms somehow more appropriate for getting across your protagonist's character, the narrative's action, your theme?

If, as Louis Sullivan, proponent of the International Style in architecture, suggested, form follows function (he meant that the design of a building should be derived from the purposes it will serve), then what form will best serve your story's function?

If your main character is especially introverted and his or her mind is especially fertile ground, you might want to dump your first-person point of view (which creates the illusion your character is *talking* to the reader) and try *interior monologue* or *stream-of-consciousness* (which create the illusion your character is *thinking* to him- or herself).

Interior monologue produces the impression of recording the associational and often illogical workings of a particular mind in motion in one of two ways. First, *directly*, it generates the sense of an absent author. A good example of this can be found in Faulkner's *As I Lay Dying* (1930):

> The trees look like chickens when they ruffle out into the
> cool dust on the hot days. If I jump off the porch I will be

Raymond Federman

Q. What originally led you to the kind of formal experiments that appear in a novel like *Double or Nothing* or novella like *Voice in the Closet*?

A. When I wrote *DoN* I had no idea I was experimenting. I was just trying to learn how to write a novel that could accommodate the kind of chaos the kind of incoherence the kind of doubt the kind of discontinuity the kind of fragmentation that my life was then and still is. I did not begin with formal experimentation. I began the way everybody begins a novel. By writing sentences more or less correctly. But then the sentences started to fall apart because what I was trying to say/write refused to let itself be said/written the normal way. And this because the language I was using was not mine. It was borrowed language. A second-hand language. And as you know second-hand things—let's say like a second-hand car—soon after you begin using them they fall apart. Basically the formal experimentation in *DoN* is fucked up language. I try to rectify that in *The Voice* by making neat little squares with words but that too did not work. It became an unreadable book. At least that's what people tell me.

Q. What's the appeal, from a writer's point of view, of formal innovation in a larger socio-literary context that tends not to value it?

A. The appeal is that you feel free from all socio-economic pressures because you know that you will not become rich and famous writing formal innovation. Or as my friend Sam Beckett said to me when I told him back in 1966 that I was writing a novel called *DoN*—he said: Raymond if you write for money do something else. And he added: never compromise your work. To answer your question more directly: I write because I have to write, and whether or not what I write is valued or devalued, I don't give a shit.

Q. What sort of advice would you have to young writers approaching the concept of formal innovation for the first time?

A Do something else. It does not pay. But if you insist on doing formal innovation go all the way. If you're going to innovate innnovate and don't fuck around. But remember whatever you do eventually your innovations will be recuperated into the mainstream and you will have innovated for nothing. My advice. Sell out to the establishment as soon as possible. It's a hopeless situation. Or as Sam Beckett once put it (sorry for mentioning him so often but I suffer from beckettmania) we are all born mad only a few remain so.

Raymond Federman, one of the grand innovators of fiction, is a bilingual novelist, poet, critic, and translator who has published over twenty books.

Derek Pell

Q. Can you talk a little about the shapes your formal innovations tend to take?

A. My "innovations" are amorphodytes. They are quite large at first. I quickly place them on a diet. During the long, often dreary editing process, a distinct shape appears. Only then does this shape look in the mirror and declare itself "trim."

Q. How has it changed since you began writing?

A. My prose is no longer obese. Not quite Beckett, mind you, but edging toward "lessness." I am more interested in working with self-imposed constraints than wallowing in a sense of total "freedom." After the sixties, I learned discipline.

Q. What got you interested in formal innovation in the first place?

A. I enjoy wearing a tux. Actually, it was my discovery (ca. 1967) of Alfred Jarry's pataphysics. This eventually lead me to Oulipo. Oulipo suggested a truly rigorous (scientific) approach to innovation that was very inspiring.

Q. Who should young writers approaching the notion of formal and thematic innovation for the first time read?

A. Alfred Jarry, certainly. The great Alphonse Allais. And Stefan Themerson. The holy trinity that has guided me through a very rocky life.

Derek Pell has published over twenty books, including Assassination Rhapsody, X-Texts, and Doktor Bey's Book of the Dead.

Q. Alt-X, which you help oversee, is the premier alternative Web site and *Grammatron* your latest hypertext Web project. How did each begin?

A. Alt-X started out as an experiment in electronic writing and publishing with an emphasis on Avant-Pop writing and theory which, when Alt-X started, in early 1994, was still in development. It has since grown into a full-blown multi-media art site with contributions from some of the most radical composers of our time.

It ends up that the pre-cyberspace narrative scripting of *Grammatron* prophesized the development of Alt-X. I started conceptualizing the network-narrative environment in early 1993, way before the development of Netscape, Real Audio, animated gifs, etc., and by having my lead avatar, Abe Golam, look back at a past that was clearly in *my* future, I was able to use the narrative itself as an R&D platform to help accelerate my own networked-writing practice forward.

Q. What is your sense of the strengths of the Web as a literary form?

A. I think its main strength is its ability to move beyond "the literary" while morphing our notion of how a narrative is distributed. Network, or distributed narrative form, is reconfiguring the writer into a kind of cyborg-narrator whose hyper-rhetorical performance is intimately connected to an internationally-distributed community of social beings interested in challenging our old-fashioned ideas about what a writer is. My recent trip to Mainz, home of Gutenberg and his press, was not the least bit nostalgic. Instead, I felt very relieved that I am part of a shift in the history of consciousness where narrative form can safely depart the cage of book-centered literary media and enter a more fluid, performative, hypermedia space.

Q. What are its weaknesses?

A. Dependency on non-standardized technology (everyone *gets* the way a book is supposed to work), Web-surfing impatience with complex forms that require a serious investment of time and mental energy (what are the long-term effects of instant gratification?), lack of commitment from educational institutions to teach people how to become sophisticated co-conspirators in the Web's reading/writing process....

Q. What sort of advice would you have to young writers approaching the notion of Web and webbed fiction for the first time?

A. Don't expect to get rich, don't expect to become famous, don't expect to tear the world to shreds with your unique vision. The key is in evolving a network of artist-associates who you can trust and whose work challenges you to greater narrative-building. Read poets from Black Mountain and Beat Generation, read startling meta- and surfiction from the sixties and seventies, dabble in cyberpunk for useful ideas (but only after having developed many new ones yourself), use the distributive power of the new media to create an interventionist practice and poetics and the let the rest take care of itself.

Mark Amerika lives in Boulder, Colorado. His hard-copy novels include Sexual Blood.

where the fish was, and it all cut up into not-fish now. I can hear the bed and her face and them and I can feel the floor shake when he walks on it that came and did it. That came and did it when she was all right but he came and did it.

Second, *indirectly*, in a manner whereby the author's voice intrudes every now and then to select, present, and guide. A good example of this can be found in Virginia Woolf's *Mrs. Dalloway* (1925):

> For having lived in Westminster—how many years now? over twenty,—one feels even in the midst of the traffic, or waking at night, Clarissa was positive, a particular hush, or solemnity; an indescribable pause; a suspense (but that might be her heart, affected, they said, by influenza) before Big Ben strikes. There! Out it boomed. First a warning, musical; then the hour, irrevocable.

While both direct and indirect interior monologue still embrace grammatical, articulate thought, associational and illogical as that thought might appear, *stream-of-consciousness* (the term originated with Alexander Bain in 1855, though it is usually associated with the philosopher and psychologist William James, novelist Henry James's brother) removes conventional grammatical structure, quotation marks, hyphens in compounds, and even commas and periods to more accurately reflect the machinations of fluid thought processes. One of the best examples of this is Molly Bloom's soliloquy in Joyce's *Ulysses* (1922):

> …I was a Flower of the mountain yes when I put the rose in my hair like the Andalusian girls used or shall I wear a red yes and how he kissed me under the Moorish wall and I thought well as well him as another and then I asked him with my eyes to ask again yes and then he asked me would I yes to say yes my mountain flower and first I put my arms around him yes and drew him down to me so he could feel my breasts all perfume yes and his heart was going like mad and yes I said yes I will Yes.

Ironically, even though both interior monologue and stream-of-consciousness give the appearance of creative chaos, they in truth take much longer to craft than conventional discourse.

Or what about experimenting with typography itself, the layout of the page and the use of white space and font style and size, as someone like Raymond Federman does in his *tour de force*, *Double or Nothing* (1971), a 259-page "novel" in which each page is laid out completely differently from every other page, the result being the fictional equivalent of concrete poetry that exploits the visual aspects of writing while paying homage to Apollinaire's *Calligrammes* (1918)?

Or is it possible to tell your story in a form that combines disparate media, as does, say, *graphic fiction*? Postmodern analog of the medieval illuminated manuscript, graphic fiction brings together highly skilled comic-book art with elements of the (often SF) novel. Alan Moore and Dave Gibbons's *Watchmen* (1986), one of the most popular and representative examples, is a tale of misplaced superheroes inhabiting a cyberpunkish alternate universe. It hearkens back to such Surrealist collage-novels as Max Ernst's *La Femme 100 Têtes* (1929), as well as the countercultural comix from the sixties, while playfully fusing and confusing magnificent drawings with a fake autobiography, a pseudo-history of one of the superheroes, a novel within a novel, notes, police reports, ornithological articles, letters, reviews, interviews, toy brochures, photos, advertisements, and more, all along alluding to everything from Francis Bacon's paintings to William Burroughs's novels.

Or what about moving off the printed page altogether and into the digital beyond?

Hypertext fiction, a nonlinear computer-based mode of writing which came to the literary foreground in 1987 with the appearance of Michael Joyce's *afternoon: a story*, and which currently also exists in the forms of the World Wide Web and diverse CD-ROMs, does away with a hard or stable copy of narrative. In its place, the reader uses a computer to explore an interlinking web of lexia, or story spaces, in an interactive way, literally developing his or her own version of the text, which may even include music and graphics as well as typographical play, contradicting plot elements, and opportunities for the reader to contribute character names, descriptions, and shards of action. After each reading experience, the reader can choose to save or abandon the forking paths he or she has just chosen to follow.

The outcome is a mode of narration that proposes, as George P. Landow claims in *Hypertext: The Convergence of Contemporary Critical Theory and Technology* (1992), that "we must abandon conceptual systems founded upon ideas of center, margin, hierarchy, and linearity

Q. When did you first become aware of the possibilties of hypertext fiction?

A. The first time I used a word processor I became dimly aware that its ability to move things that "should" be on page 60 from where they appeared, say on page 220, suggested the possibility of writing a story that changed each time you read it. A story where what should be appears in different places under different circumstances. We had built a system for writing these kinds of fiction (Storyspace) before I heard the word *hypertext*.

Q. What are its strengths as a literary form?

A. I'm tempted to say its realism, how truly it lets us render the shifting consciousness and shimmering coherences and transitory closures of the day-to-day beauty of the world around us. Hypertext is equal to the complexity and sweetness of living in a world populated by other, equally uncertain, human beings, their dreams, and their memories.

Q. What are its weaknesses?

A. Oh, the chief weakness is that it is thus far anchored to a slab of plastic and some sort of power source (all puns intended). But that's not a weakness of the literary form, I guess. In my mind all literary forms are composed in and of our weaknesses. This one has the weaknesses of poetry, which it is most similar to.

Q. Is it possible that it's an intermediate step to something else, and, if so, what might that something be?

A. There's a question fit for philosophy. All our steps are intermediate. This one seems to be veering toward television, god help us, perhaps even television imprinted on your eyeballs. I put my trust in words. Propellor heads talk about how we won't need stories, we'll have new, virtual worlds, but soon those new worlds, too, will have stories which we won't think we need and we will need words to put them into.

Q. What sort of advice would you have to young writers approaching hypertext fiction for the first time?

A. Avoid links, look to music. Hyperfiction isn't a matter of branches but rather of the different textures of experience into which language (and image) leads us. Hyperfiction is like sitting in a restaurant in the murmur of stories, some fully known, some only half-heard, among people with whom you share the briefest span of life and the certainty of death.

Michael Joyce's hypertext fictions include the novels, afternoon and Twilight, A Symphony, and shorter fictions including WOE, Lucy's Sister and the Web fiction Twelve Blue.

and replace them with ones of multilinearity, nodes, links, and net-works." Consequently, as Landow and others have argued, hypertext fiction enacts the deconstructive turn in a very tangible manner.

But, all this said, the *really* intriguing formal innovations are the ones you'll invent the day after tomorrow.

Now Read This

Abrams, M. H. *A Glossary of Literary Terms* (1957; updated regularly). You should always keep this around to thumb through. Great bathroom reading, it will not only provide useful definitions of fiction's components, but it will also act as a critical adrenalin rush into story ideas.

Coover, Robert. "The Babysitter" (1969). A proto-hypertext fiction, this one begins as a work of suburban domestic realism only to glide into an experimental investigation that offers contra-dicting plot elements that may be actual events or the imaginings of the characters or author himself.

Cortázar, Julio. *Hopscotch* (1963). A jazz-like 155-chaptered novel that can be read in different orders.

Eastgate Systems. www.eastgate.com The home of hypertext on the Web, and a must-see.

Jackson, Shelley. *Patchwork Girl* (1995). A hypertextual retelling of *Frankenstein* that collapses graphic novels, feminist theory, and gothic romance into something wholly new.

Pell, Derek. *Assassination Rhapsody* (1989). A terribly imaginative col-lage-text based on the unlikely subject of the Kennedy assas-sination.

Shapard, Robert and James Thomas. *Sudden Fiction International* (1989). Sixty short-shorts by writers from around the world.

Spiegelman, Art. *Maus: A Survivor's Tale* (1986). Powerful graphic novel about the holocaust where the Nazis are cats and the Jews mice.

Stretching & Flexing

Take a story you've already written, put it up on your computer screen, and begin to play with its formal characteristics, from sen-tence structure through presentation on the page, and see what for-mal breakthroughs you might be able to come up with that contrib-ute to its meaning.

16 Conurbation of the Mind

SETTING AS CHARACTER

At the end of the day, fiction writing is not only about the presentation of opulent, multivalent emotion, or even sharp, alluring intelligence.

It's about sleights of hand.

Fiction is, at base, a linguistic illusionist's bag of tricks for creating certain feelings and thoughts in readers without those readers ever perceiving (let alone even thinking about) the hole under the inverted top hat of narrative through which the white rabbit will spring.

Without spiritual and /or intellectual depth, writing is little more than word processing . . . yet without the legerdemain, it's little more than thick therapy session—and therapy sessions are good for the soul and psyche, but not necessarily for genuine art.

So now, having discussed some of the larger questions of genre and form involved in fiction writing, it's time to turn to some of the trade's tricks.

Let's begin with setting, and a passage from Gwyneth Jones's *White Queen* (1991), a postfeminist science fiction novel set primarily in near-future London that retells the first-contact story from a new angle accentuating gender concerns:

> Johnny's room had a window. It looked into the airwell between his building and a buried nineteenth-century façade. There was another window opposite, barely a meter away, grimy glass intact under a lintel of blurred stone flowers. It

was closed off inside by a partition wall. There was a trompe l'oeil effect: Johnny's lit room was reflected there at an oddly convincing angle. He had often caught himself thinking he had a neighbor.

Most people would read through this passage pretty quickly, paying it scant attention.

But look at how much information it's providing under the guise of casually describing Johnny's room, and how much data the reader is taking in unconsciously.

First, notice that Johnny's room only has one window. That means it's quite small. Next notice that that window looks into an airwell. That means that Johnny's living in anything but choice real estate—and *that* already begins to give us some insight into Johnny's socio-economic status (which, we've learned earlier, used to be much more upscale). The buried nineteenth-century façade plus the airwell spawn a certain shadowy, used-up, even claustrophobic atmosphere, and that atmosphere tells us not only about Johnny's world but about Johnny's perception of that world.

These are the *significant details* the reader's given, and at some level he or she is already analyzing them with respect to Johnny's state of mind—a state of mind, we discover in the remainder of the paragraph, that isn't as stable as Johnny would probably like it. Across the cramped airwell (notice in passing the use of the word "meter" instead of "yard," subtly cuing us to a European metric standard, and hence location) is another window, this one closed off in a way that causes it to mirror Johnny's room and from time to time dupe him into believing he has a neighbor. Johnny, in other words, is wont to confuse illusion and reality, and this confusion between what's authentic and what masquerades as authentic is a key theme in the novel as a whole as well as one of Johnny's primary character traits.

Johnny's emotional life, it turns out, is as hermetically sealed as that window and cramped airwell. His universe, which earlier had been expansive and alive (he worked as a kind of futuristic television journalist), has shrunk and clouded over like that grimy glass.

Now the only flowers—the only sign of life and hence hope—in reach are the blurred stone ones of the lintel, a fact which doesn't bode well for Johnny's narrative prognosis.

We could most likely go on, except the point's already been made. Most readers think of setting as an expendable background item, hardly worth mention, but most serious writers know better. Setting is a technique for bringing out fictive atmosphere, character, and theme. It helps provide the prevailing tone or mood of the story, as well as situating it in time and space for us. It usually exists in harmony with the protagonist and thus sheds light on his or her personality and disposition. It can even hint at things to come.

As an author, you need to know your setting inside out. Close your eyes and imagine every item in it before you begin composing. Take notes on it. What does it smell like? Feel like? What are the significant details you can use to capture it?

What, to put it slightly differently, makes it unique? If it's a corner of the city, how is that corner different from all other corners of all other cities? If it's a forest, what will make us see *that* forest rather than its generic brother?

Realize that setting almost always functions as a minor character in narrative, and sometimes—as in stories by Stephen Crane and Jack London, for instance, which pit humans against nature—it can become the story's primary antagonist.

So you must at the drop of a pen be able to answer all sorts of questions to yourself about it, even if you don't finally use all the answers in the piece you're composing: what season is it? what's the weather like? what time of day is it? what, precisely, is the texture of the light? the air? what does the geography look like? the architecture? what are the socio-economics of the place?

And, perhaps most consequential, what do your characters think about each of these things?

Now Read This

Delany, Samuel R. *Dhalgren* (1975). In this slipstream magnum opus, Delany makes his setting—the city of Bellona in which some unnamed catastrophe has transpired—one of his major (amorphous) characters.

Gibson, William. *Neuromancer* (1984). Gibson continually creates vivid settings in this Cyberpunk near-future classic.

Pynchon, Thomas. *Gravity's Rainbow* (1973). Pynchon's mind becomes the real setting in one of the twentieth century's masterworks.

Stretching & Flexing

1. Write a sudden fiction in which your character is somehow drastically out of sync with his or her setting. Perhaps she or he feels underdressed, socially inept, psychologically unhinged. Don't introduce any other characters—keep the conflict between your

Richard Kadrey

Q. What makes a story a story for you?

A. It's a question of compulsion. Like most writers, I have a million ideas, but the ones that get written are the ones that won't get out of my head. These stories have some juice, some twisted extra-literary element that I can never identify until I've written them.

Q. Do you have any tips on how to keep going on a writing project once you've begun? Do you keep some sort of writing schedule? Would you recommend it?

A. If you can keep to a schedule, it's the best thing you can do. Make starting to write ordinary, commonplace. If you have rituals around writing, do them (sharpening pencils, writing a letter beforehand, whatever). Schedules and rituals will help get you past the hyper-critical, self-conscious part of your mind.

Q. In a novel like *Kamikaze L'Amour*, you create a rich interaction between character and setting, using one to bring out the other. Could you talk about how and why you did that?

A. I'm an absolutist in this: setting is character. This works in two ways. One, considering the setting itself as another character who walks, talks and has desires. Letting the setting have its own opinions will allow the story to surprise you.

Two, setting is a key to the human characters. There's a reason everyone ends up where they are, whether it's a rainforest, sneaking into a girls dorm, scaling the walls of Versailles on Xmas Eve or creeping along a collapsing road in the Himalayan foothills (I've been all those places and there were always reasons, though some were better than others . . .).

Q. What sort of advice do you wish someone had given you when you were just starting out as a writer?

A. Getting published is only a tiny part of the process. Writing is something you'll do for the rest of your life. A career will take longer, much longer than you think, to establish. Keep your day job. Write what you want. Few people are going to pay you enough to make it worth your time to write shit.

Q. Your style is crisp, clean, yet richly metaphoric. Can you talk a little about your sentence-writing process?

A. I'm obsessive about my fiction prose and never, never satisfied with it. I want every word to do several jobs: to carry information and images, to convey poetry/rhythm and to kick the whole damned mess forward. I rewrite obsessively on a sentence level. Turn sentences around, inside out and backwards. But I try to keep my word choices simple. The thesaurus is not your friend. It can be useful, but like a snake you milk for its medicinal venom, you'd better approach the thesaurus with thick gloves and a stick.

Richard Kadrey is a columnist for The Site and the author of several books, including the Covert Culture Sourcebook series and the novel Kamikaze L'Amour.

single character and the narrative space he or she inhabits.

2. Your protagonist is an alien who's just landed on earth. He/she/it enters a setting we earthlings feel wholly comfortable in—Wal-Mart, maybe, or Pizza Hut, or your student union—but for him/her/it it spells nothing but nightmare. Why? Write a sudden fiction based on this premise.

3. Is it possible to write a sudden fiction in which setting is *not* important, perhaps doesn't even exist? Or where it is *exclusively* important, and where character completely ceases to be? Or where setting is radically redefined, maybe always in transition, or something other than we as readers might anticipate?

Desire
of Mire

MAKING THE MOST OF YOUR FLAT AND ROUND CHARACTERS

In *Aspects of the Novel* (1927), E. M. Forster distinguishes between two kinds of *character*, flat and round.

Simply put, *flat* ones function as background in your narrative. They're there to help out your main characters. So if your protagonist needs to get from Long Beach to West Hollywood to see the woman she's falling in love with for dinner via taxi, a flat character will be the cab driver behind the wheel. If your alien protagonist needs to cross Main Street in Anywhere, U.S.A., to reach the Wal-Mart to pick up a gadget for his flying saucer while noticing some of the indigenous peoples around him to give the reader a sense of this strange planet on which he's crashed, he'll probably notice some pretty flat characters.

They're the ones who don't change, won't surprise you, and are constructed around a single idea or quality—the sponge-nosed street person in the water-logged refrigerator box on the corner between Avenues C and D in Manhattan, the jesters in Renaissance drama, the red-faced laughing fat woman eating four Big Macs at the table behind where the action is really taking place.

If flat characters lack depth, then *round* characters are bursting with it. They're your leads. They're the ones to keep your narrative camera on. They're sufficiently complex to change over time. Rich with conflicting emotions, they surprise us by their actions without losing credibility, intrigue us, shock us, bore holes in our hearts. Hamlet, obviously, is one of the most wonderful round characters in literature. Raskolnikov in Dostoevsky's *Crime and Punishment* (1866) is

Cris Mazza

Q. What sort of advice can you give to young writers trying to peg down this concept of character for the first time?

A. The character isn't you; but, while writing, you must become the character. It's like a virtual reality experience, except without machines to give it to you. You create it for yourself. And of course, the whole time, your fingers are going as fast as they can to record the experience your mind is having.

Q. How do you go about generating characters in your own work?

A. It's almost like method acting. I become the character. I allow surprising things (behavior, dialogue, etc.) to arrive on the page without preplanning. It's that old surprising-and-inevitable-at-the-same-time cliché—because I am the character (but the character is not me), I can react almost as quickly as he or she will, but sometimes that inevitable/ appropriate reaction surprises me!

Q. Which writers should readers turn to for a good sense of literary characterization?

A. Almost anyone. Every writer I can think of achieves characterization with a different balance of techniques—dialogue or POV or through plot developments, narrative style, etc. Look for these different ways, don't just assume vivid characterization comes only with a first person narrator.

Cris Mazza is the author of four novels and four collections of short fiction.
including the PEN/Nelson Algren Award-winning How to Leave a Country.
She teaches in the Program for Writers at the University of Illinois at Chicago.

Greg Herriges

Q. What sort of steps do you take to create your characters?

A. I imagine the situation I will write about and fill the surrounding characters with qualities I've observed in acquaintances. Since most of my stories and novels are told in the first person (from a male point of view; I don't pretend to be able to tell a story as a female would, though I wish I could)—the protagonist is the most difficult character to pin down. I live with him a while, dream about him—and at last, when the suchness of the character is familiar—I give him a name, a name that sounds right, that fits. After that, I have to let him run free and do what he will. He usually knows where to go.

Q. What sort of advice can you give to young writers trying to peg down this notion of character for the first time?

A. Don't worry about your characters taking wrong turns. There is a synergistic action that takes place when they hit the page. You may wince at a bungled move or piece of dialogue later, but then you fix it in the mix, when you revise. The writer does a fair degree of role playing, living inside the characters, and so they begin to feel more genuine as you go along. Welcome the challenge of changing the masks.

Q. What do you never want to see another writer do with character again?

A. I never want to see a character "jeer" or look "crestfallen" again. Christ—the narrative lexicon of the commercial novel appalls me.

Q. What do you want to see more of, character-wise?

A. Three dimensions, please. I feel at home with and respect characters that worry the details of every day life, like Raymond Carver's characters. Yes—there is a story to be told, but not to the exclusion of the quotidian realities we all face: broken parking meters; mornings when you forget to use the anti-perspirant; unwanted or unexpected mental flashbacks; resurfacing desires or memories from childhood. Characters have pasts and lives. Use them, and make those characters real people. Your readers will then feel as if they know them.

Greg Herriges is a professor of English at a midwestern college, and the author of three novels, the latest of which is The Winter Dance Party Murders.

standing right behind him. Humbert Humbert in Nabokov's *Lolita* (1955) is walking up the block to join the round crowd.

Make a flat character into a round one, then, by giving him or her narrative backbeat: a past, a strength, and a weakness. The sponge-nosed street person in the water-logged refrigerator box fills up like a balloon as soon as we know that his name's Byron Penumbra, and he used to be a successful stock broker on Wall Street—till, that is, three weeks ago, when he just got sick of his nice pat suburban life, and so decided simply to walk out of it, which he did one night after dinner without warning and without fanfare, right through the front door and down the green-lawned avenue, sprinklers ticking, leaving behind his wife Joan and their two kids, June and Jedd, and has never felt more liberated and shameful than this very minute.

And that red-faced laughing fat woman eating four Big Macs at that table? Well, look at her move to the narrative foreground as soon as we know her happiness thing (her name, by the way, is Betty Fink, and her muumuu is from Sears) is a charade to the extent that she's now going to shuffle home to her tiny apartment behind the dry goods store and regurgitate all that food she just ate before she dresses in leather and lace (she picked the outfit up from a nice little boutique in London's Soho on her way back from Paris last month), and her next trick shows up, an ex-stock broker named Byron Penumbra ready to pay more than a thou for an hour of painful bliss at the pointy heels of this hefty dominatrix, who sincerely, deeply, profoundly loves her work like Bill Gates loves Microsoft.

What makes a round character interesting?

Surely that sense of complex motives and conflicting emotions. And surely her ability to change during the course of the narrative—to grow, wither, learn, forget, escape, fall, go insane, attain a brief *epiphany* (a term James Joyce used to refer to that sudden manifestation of meaning that slams into some characters at a climactic moment in life) and, in the final analysis, startle us in ways that never veer from who we feel she is and can be.

No psychological change, no story.

A character often becomes interesting at the distance he exists from goodness. Blake knew this when he fell hook, line, and sinker, not for Milton's God or Christ, but for Milton's Satan in *Paradise Lost* (1667)—the one, in other words, filled with rage and hurt and pride and vengeance and the recognition that wherever he flew, there was hell—kind of like some of us. *There* was a guy who could change in dramatic ways, *had* changed in dramatic ways.

Or Nabokov's Humbert Humbert, that child molester and aesthete who almost never saw himself as anything but a sweet gentle lover of nymphets, yet came to despise himself, yet relished his memories of Lolita as the one true love of his life, and was brilliantly funny, and a gorgeous stylist, and impressively educated, and a terrific gamester, and ready to provide an excuse for his actions in the wink of an eye, and profoundly in love, and profoundly in lust, and a murderer who didn't really think the murder he committed was so terribly bad after all.

Remember: your character doesn't need to be especially likable to be especially powerful. Frequently just the opposite is even more successful in snagging a reader's interest.

She doesn't even need to be honest with herself—or with the reader. Some of the most pleasing characters in literature (among them Huck Finn in Twain's novel [1884], Benjy in Faulkner's *The Sound and the Fury* [1929], and Holden Caulfield in J. D. Salinger's *The Catcher in the Rye* [1951]) are in fact *unreliable narrators*—narrators, that is, who err in their understanding of themselves and their worlds, and who sometimes carefully attempt to mislead the reader. They may simply be innocent (Holden) or retarded (Benjy), or they may be purposefully devious (Huck).

To develop these characters, authors often rely on the use of *verbal irony* (the distance between what's said and what's meant) and *dramatic irony* (the distance between what a character knows and the author/reader knows).

You might not want Odysseus over to dinner, but you just can't read enough about him.

A character needs to be someone who wants something very badly and can't have it. Pair that with making him or her the central point-of-view of the story, and you've probably worked the magic in terms of getting a reader to want to learn about him or her. In addition, he or she needs to be believable (i.e., consistent in his or her actions), and usually needs to possess *some* sympathetic qualities with which the reader can identify (Satan's horrible sense of loss, Humbert's intelligence, artistry, and pain). And no matter what else you do, he or she needs to be an individual rather than a type, or, worse, a *stereotype*, a mere oversimplification of an idea or sketchy trait or three.

All of these aspects—along with everything else about the writing process—are a lot easier to talk about than accomplish when you're hunched in front of your computer, listening to the hard drive hum in anticipation of the next stroke of the keyboard.

So how do you go about inventing a character, nuts-and-bolts-wise?

Think, initially, about giving him or her several defining physical characteristics—a unique speech pattern, a trademark gesture, a particularly revealing cut of hair or turn of lip or stoop of shoulder.

Close your eyes and picture him or her in your mind's eye.

Okay. Now give him or her a few memories of events that account for who he or she is. These will allow us to witness the way his or her mind processes the universe, put us inside his or her psyche. Humbert, for instance, returns to his beatific relationship with another nymphet, Anabel Lee, when he was an adolescent, and suggests that that relationship informs all the others he has with young girls.

Okay. Now expose him or her to various facets of life, and have him or her react. How does he or she wake up in the morning, for instance? Fall asleep at night? Deal with rain, snow, sunshine? Eat alone? Eat with others? Walk down the street? Walk down a narrow hallway in a government building? Each time you confront him or her with new stimuli and force him or her to interact with them, you're going to discover a different part of his or her character.

What next?

There are two large methods for presenting character, as Janet Burroway points out in *Writing Fiction* (1992): *indirect* and *direct*.

Indirect presentation means the author does the telling. He or she intrudes into the narrative to give us the character's history, motives, and beliefs in an abstract summary mode: "Byron Penumbra was a good man locked in a dull life until he one day looked up from his peach melba and realized his wife, Joan, a thick-brained ex-cheerleader with flaky skin and very white teeth, and his children, Joan and Jedd, whom he couldn't really tell apart, frightened him by their utter Aryan blandness…"

Indirect presentation tends to sound a little like Charles Dickens wrote it. That is, it sounds vaguely nineteenth century in its rhythms and omniscient perspective. Why? Because it relies primarily on telling and on summary, and at the turn of a millennium acutely influenced by filmic and televisual narration, showing and scene have become the privileged vehicles for relaying information in fiction.

That *doesn't* mean you should avoid indirect presentation at all costs. It just means that you should know what you're doing and

Brian Evenson

Q. What's been the most difficult narrative technique for you to master, and why?

A. Probably portrayal of interior feelings or thoughts. All of the techniques that people use—from interior monologue to the narrator simply telling you to a more disconnected approach—seem to me too artificial and unconvincing. They end up assuming a lot about what goes on in someone's head, and I find what they assume doesn't really equate to how my head works. I'm convinced that people have a lot less of an internal life and a lot less of what has been called consciousness—at least coherent consciousness—than has been believed.

Q. What sort of advice can you give young writers about mastering it?

A. I'd say restraint and experiment are equally important. You have to find a balance between saying too much and saying not enough. If just enough is given, the reader will fill it in with his or her own natural processes. Use a little as a catalyst to get the reader to do the rest.

Q. What should a young writer never do?

A. Never end a story with the words "And then I woke up."
Never only read contemporary American realism.
Never believe someone who tells you "it has to be done this way."
Be aware of the problems and prejudices of workshops, treat with suspicion people who say you should read more Raymond Carver, and do everything you can to avoid writing workshop fiction.

Q. What should a young writer always try to do more of?

A. More reading. The most important thing you can do is to read the best work from many different national traditions and to read a lot of very different things. It's the best way of seeing all the options, opening yourself up to new possibilities.

Brian Evenson is the author of two story collections, Altmann's Tongue and The Din of Celestial Birds, and a novel, Father of Lies.

why you're doing it if you decide to employ it.

More often than not, however, you'll discover a little of that stuff goes a very long way.

If you prefer, you can use four immediate kinds of *direct presentation* instead—or most likely in addition to—that indirect one. Actually, narrative is an act of mixing and matching all of these (I'm just distilling each so you can examine it more closely).

Appearance. First, you can describe what a person looks like. Aim for the unique details that create a unique personality—the worried vein squiggling like a blue worm across the left temple's hairline, the blurred purple-green tattoo of the naked girl on the inner right forearm. And don't forget, we live in a highly visual culture. People love to *see,* and they tend to see very well. So appearance should convey lots of news: socio-economic status, degree of emphasis your character puts on tidiness and cleanliness, whether she reads a lot (does she wear glasses?), how fashion-conscious she is, his or her age, race, gender, and so on.

What aspects of a person's appearance does your character focus on? What does he notice when first meeting someone—the stray hair clinging to the woman's black blouse, or the dime-gray of his eyes, or the fact that his shoes are Birkenstocks?

Speech. The debut impression produced by appearance can be in harmony or in conflict with this next mode of direct presentation. Does your character lisp, stutter, use pet words, employ malapropisms, speak in incomplete sentences, possess an accent? What sort of diction does he manifest? What sort of grasp on metaphor does he have? Does he speak in self-absorbed monologues, balanced sentences, shy single words? What's his syntax like—clear as an unmuddied stream or cat's-cradled with convolution? Does he respond to questions asked or mishear incoming data and respond to the questions of his psyche? Does he say what he means?

Action. How does your character move when she enters a crowded room? Is that different from the way she moves down a busy street? An empty street? In front of her mother or lover? What gestures define who she is? Does she scratch at her wattles, tug at her earlobe, surreptitiously pinch at the right knee of her torn prewashed jeans? Every story involves action, but ordinarily that action is a lot less obvious than guns blasting, planes cartwheeling, and people duck-ing and covering. And it's in the subtle action—whether that action is in sync with appearance and speech or in opposition to it—that character is announced.

Thought. Thought, like feeling, is an interior mode of experience, and no art form does interior better than fiction.

Film and visual art are all about surface presentation, from which the viewer can infer certain internal states. Fiction can create interior states for thousands of pages on end, teasing out nuances, exploring the shape and feel and formation and progression of thoughts and emotions, as Proust did in his seven-volume magnum opus, *Remembrance of Things Past* (1913–1927), or Joyce in *Ulysses* (1922).

Fiction can, as it were, turn the world inside out, allowing you to perceive external reality *solely* through the interior perambulations of mind.

So, to thought: does your character think a lot, or does he prefer feats to philosophy? If he does contemplate his world, then what sort of things does he think about, and how does he undertake that cognitive process? Does he obsess on detail, the sign of the slightly unhinged mind, or over and over again relive a crucial event from childhood or a year or two ago that helped make him who he is today? Does he think logically or associatively? Is he the kind of ex-trovert who's always thinking *and* talking, or the kind of introvert who's paralyzed by self-conscious reflection, or something in be-tween, or something else altogether?

Many young writers base characters on people they know, which can be a ball—and a sneakily delicious way to punish those who've done you dirty, reward those who've done you good, understand those whom you can't fathom on the day to day, and live out your desires or help others live out theirs.

But that sort of highly autobiographical approach almost always begins to wear thin before long. At the risk of repetition, it's prob-ably more productive to write about what you want to know and then embellish like mad than just report about the world around you. If you're committed to reportage, after all, why not simply write journalism or memoir?

Plus invention is enjoyable business.

Let your characters develop organically to serve your story rather than trying to pound your enemy's square stereotype into a round

Ed McClanahan

Q. Your characters have this trademark quality of the quirky and the genuinely moving. What sort of steps do you take to create them?

A. I write what I like to call "redemptive fiction," wherein I lead my characters to the brink of beyond-the-pale unacceptability, trusting that I'll find something in them—or better yet, that they will find something in themselves—that draws them back from the abyss. In *A Congress of Wonders*, the heroes are those characters who somehow find grace or strength in their own suffering (never mind that it's usually *comic* suffering) and thereby rise above the reader's expectations for them: In "Juanita and the Frog Prince," Juanita Sparks puts her fate in the hands of a most unpromising protector, and is richly rewarded for her faith; in the other two stories, Wanda Pearl Ratliff and Finch Fronk (respectively) transcend their joyless, barren lives when Wanda Pearl reveals her capacity for maternal love and Finch discovers that celibacy has not excluded him from fatherhood.

Q. What sort of advice can you give to young writers approaching character for the first time?

A. Remember that character is *fluid*, not static or rigid; like water, it seeks its own level. Writers make a terrible mistake when they pre-conceive their characters in such a way as to constrict the possibility of change, of growth—or, for that matter, of diminution. A character who can't surprise the writer can't surprise the reader either. Or, to put it another way, characters need to get *out* of character once in a while, just like regular folks; it keeps the old juices flowing.

Q. What do you never want to see another writer do with character again?

A. The least interesting characters are the ones you can't see into, the opaque ones who don't seem to have any inner life. A good character has more facets than a fly's eyeball. May the ghost of Flannery O'Connor smack the hand of any writer who forgets that.

Ed McClanahan, Merry Prankster extraordinaire, is author of The Natural Man, Famous People I Have Known, and A Congress of Wonders. He lives with his wife Hilda in Lexington, Kentucky.

character's plot position.

But if you *do* decide to base your character on someone you know—do just that: *base* them. And then do your fictive magic. If she's tall in real life, make her short and dumpy in your narrative. If she's popular, make her unpopular. If she is thirteen and thin and scared then make her thirty and chunky and self-assured.

And always find a corner of her psyche that matches a corner of yours, because if you can't find something in her with which to sympathize and empathize, no one else will be able to, either.

After you begin to get the hang of characterization, you might want to think about how to push the boundaries of the concept a little. Is it possible, for instance, to write a first-person fiction in which it's impossible to tell the gender or race of your protagonist? How would you go about writing a story that challenges the nineteenth-century notion of a unified self? How would this process of characterization be different for an alien from another galaxy or dimension, since presumably thought, language, and custom would be completely other? Can you tell a story about a wholly disagreeable person that will make someone want to read it—if so, how? How can you write about a good character in a good situation in a way that isn't deadly dull? Is it possible to write about a boring character in an interesting way? Although most fiction centers on character, is it possible to write an entertaining story that doesn't? Can you write a narrative that has no characters in it, or no human ones, or no animate ones, and sustain a reader's attention?

All of what I've said in this section carries with it an assumption about character that most writers make and most readers repress: characters aren't people—they're a series of fictive techniques on the page.

Hence it's helpful for a writer to recall that the myth of characters going off and doing things behind the author's back is nine times out of ten just that: a myth.

"Each writer is born with a repertory company in his head," Gore Vidal once commented, "and as you get older, you become more skillful in casting them." Characterization, in other words, usually isn't about characteroidal freedom but authorial control. Nabokov used to refer to his characters as "galley slaves," and John Cheever quipped: "The legend that characters run away from their authors—taking up drugs, having sex operations, and becoming president—implies that the writer is a fool with no knowledge or mastery of his craft. The idea of authors running around helplessly behind their cretinous inventions is contemptible."

That's probably too strongly said by half, and on occasion wrong (Dickens used to weep when writing about the death of his favorite characters), but it remains a fine reminder that writing is a conscious as well as unconscious choice and an education into who's really sitting behind that curtain in the grand narratological city of Oz.

Now Read This

Dickens, Charles. *Great Expectations* (1860–1861). A funny, touching novel by one of the masters of characterization.

Dunn, Katherine. *Geek Love* (1990). Beautifully drawn characters in a family of circus freaks . . . hugely heartbreaking and blackly comic.

Forster, E. M. *Aspects of the Novel* (1927). Still one of the best texts on how to write fiction by one of the modern masters, with an excellent chapter on characterization.

Nabokov, Vladimir. *Lolita* (1955). One of the finest character investigations of an unbalanced, transgressive, unreliable narrator ever written.

O'Connor, Flannery. *A Good Man Is Hard to Find* (1955). A heavenly collection of stories (the title one ranks in my top-five list) about the bizarre, the quirky, and the lovable.

Robbe-Grillet, Alain. *Jealousy* (1959). Engrossing experiment by one of the founders of the French *nouveau roman* where the protagonist in a sense is absent from the plot and thus the narrative universe is described in a neutral style without social or moral gloss.

Shakespeare, William. *Hamlet* (1602). Granted, this isn't a novel, but it does center around a character more complex than almost any other—and one you should meet before you've traveled too far in life.

Stretching & Flexing

1. Take a photograph (maybe from a family album, but even better of a stranger from a collection in the library) or a painting that's always fascinated you, and write the story of that photograph's or painting's protagonist, making sure to develop a fully-rounded character capable of surprising us in the process.

2. Take a dreadfully stereotypical character—the dumb blonde cheerleader, the absent-minded professor, the redneck brash

white trash mobile-home dweller, et al.—and write a short story from his or her point of view that transforms him or her into a sympathetic, fully-rounded character, possibly by giving him or her a crucial memory that no one else knows about, and/or a surprising strength or weakness.

Point of Glue

THE IMPLICATIONS OF PERSPECTIVE

There are no uninteresting stories, just uninteresting *points of view*.

Your game as writer is to find the one that freshens your narrative, opens it up, lets the reader see what, stripped down to its essentials, might be a pretty common core plot and problem (growing up, say, or alienation, or passion) from a strikingly new perspective.

John Gardner retells the tale of *Beowulf* (ca. 800), about the brave overachieving hero's exploits with an awful monster, from the point of view of the monster in *Grendel* (1971), thereby transforming a badly-paced, often dreary Old English epic into an arresting postmodern exploration of how we all feel like freaks and fools in an uncertain topology we can no longer read.

Ron Carlson writes a story called "Bigfoot Stole My Wife" in *The News of the World* (1987) about a schlumpy, unreliable narrator named Rick who tries to convince the reader that his wife didn't really leave him because he's a gambling loser, but that she was kidnapped (along with the family dog and the nice Celica) by the Sasquatch himself. The reader, of course, scoffs at the notion, until he or she turns to the next story in the collection, "I Am Bigfoot," told from the Sasquatch's point of view, and learns the hairy guy is in truth quite the lady's behemoth—the embodiment, really, of the passion most husbands can only hope to offer.

Point of view, then, is all about perspective, and how perspective shapes our understanding of a narrative. It's all about the com-

Q. You've written a number of your surreal pieces from what some might consider strange points of view. Can you tell us a little about them, and talk a bit about the why of your choices?

A. Why do I write the way I write? If only I could do otherwise! If only I could please predictable taste. The problem is, the only stories/texts/ poems I am able to tell tell themselves (with a little prodding, pricking, pruning, after the fact). My writing is "sentence-driven," for lack of a better term. The sentences know which way they want to grow—the way branches and roots know. Nathalie Sarraute speaks of tropisms. Mine are more like "trap-isms"—I follow like some dumb beast and always fall. In the writing which I consider my best, I am an it. To be a pliant it, that is my only real aesthetic.

Q. On a completely different topic, what's the more fulfilling part of being a writer and why? What about the least fulfilling and why?

A. A writer's greatest delight is when it flows. Then time stops and nothing else matters—not even love. The greatest grief is the perpetual hunt for publishers. You lose 'em almost as fast as you find 'em. Long unpublished periods suffocate the sentence-making urge, which turns inwards, constipating, constricting, stifling. But the engine survives.

Q. If you knew at seventeen what you know now about the writer's life, would you have still reached for the pen?

A. At five, I wore a rubber Bowie knife in my belt and two six-shooters for psychic protection. Then in fifth grade, I learned the power of the pen to hoodwink, tease and tantalize. At seventeen, I wrote mostly letters, largely because I didn't know how else to fill up the emptiness. If I could have better filled it with something else I would have. Still, the pen's the most potent intoxicant I've ever tried. I can't see how I would have made it to 45 without it.

Peter Wortsman is the author of A Modern Way to Die, as well as countless other texts of various lengths in journals and anthologies in the U.S. and Europe.

plex relationship among writer, reader, and characters. Point of view is the glue that holds your narrative together and gives it life. But for all the complexity it generates, it distills down into a pretty straightforward quartet of possibilities:

First Person. If you want your character to speak the story, you tell it from his or her point of view. Hence your character becomes your narrator, and the chance opens for you to create a provocative distance between author and creation. Your central character, that is, can either be *reliable* or (because he or she is naive, deceptive, or verbally ironic, or because the author has enlisted the help of dramatic irony) *unreliable*. Your character can be the protagonist of the story, like Scribble in Jeff Noon's postcyberpunk cult classic, *Vurt* (1993), or a peripheral narrator reporting action that happens to a central character, like Marlowe in Joseph Conrad's *Heart of Darkness* (1902). Either way, your narrator will undergo education and hence change by the tale's end, and, either way, you should strive to brew a distinct personal voice for him or her, keeping in mind what I've already said about speech above. It's even possible, though seldom done, to tell your story, not from a first-person singular point of view, but from a first-person plural one, like Faulkner in "A Rose for Emily" (1930), where the *we* represents the collective consciousness of the town in which Emily lives and dies—or even from the point of view of an inanimate object or nonhuman entity.

Third Person. If what's fun about the first-person point of view is that you get to inhabit a frequently unbalanced cheat's mind, seeing it from the inside out, then what's fun about the third-person point of view is that you get to play the role of an omnipotent god. You can conjure up the impression of objectivity in your narrative and glide easily through time and space. If you go with a third-person *omniscient* point of view, you can make up a large cast of characters, and visit the consciousness of each as you see fit, commenting along the highways and byways on what characters look like, where they come from, what the truth is about them. If you go with a third-person *limited-omniscient* point of view, you can invent a single character or three or five and stay close by their sides through the story. If the first-person point of view witnesses the world as it arrives filtered through a particular consciousness, then the third-person point of view sees characters moving through the landscape at some distance from the authorial presence—something like seeing actors moving through a film *out there*.

Second Person. Most writers choose to work within either the first- or third-person point of view. But a number have experimented with the second-person over the years. What's engaging about it, as Carlos Fuentes understood when he cast his novella, *Aura* (1965), in it, is that it produces a readerly tension that both parents a sense of immediacy associated with the first-person form by implicating the reader in the action, *and* keeps drawing metafictional attention to itself as an idiosyncratic technique, and therefore to the text itself as an artificial construct:

> You're reading the advertisement: an offer like this isn't made every day. You read it and reread it. It seems to be addressed to you and nobody else. You don't even notice when the ash from your cigarette falls in the cup of tea you ordered in this cheap, dirty café. You read it again. "Wanted, young historian, conscientious, neat. Perfect knowledge of colloquial French." Youth, knowledge of French, preferably after living in France a while… "Four thousand pesos a month, all meals, comfortable, bedroom-study." All that's missing is your name.

The reader can't help feel an imbalance, an unsteadiness in the discourse. Like Fuentes's narrative as a whole, in which a man named Felipe Montero answers a newspaper ad in a labyrinthian section of Mexico City, only to enter into a gothic domain that inverts all assumptions of mainstream realism, the text calls attention to the very process of reading, and hence interpreting, and hence to the physicality of the text in the reader's hands. The *you* refers to the *you* of the reader, pointing to the notion that the "real" narrator seems to be the reader him- or herself, and the *you* of Felipe's memory or present consciousness-in-action, pointing to the notion that the narrator has become protagonist, that Felipe is both self and other, that he is both producer-of-script and actor-of-script. "Author" becomes a position to be filled by the reader, and the very question of identity goes up for grabs.

Multiple Person. Another, more complex, experimental option is to tell your narrative by alternating between first-, second-, and third-person points of view, or by employing only two of them, or by framing your tale with one (say the third-person) and then having some-

Jonathan Lethem

Q. Can you talk a little about your process of discovering what point of view will work best for you in a particular narrative?

A. For me narrative is always secondary to *voice* in the conception of a given work—and so "point of view" comes as a natural extension of the voice I discover. I look for a character who wants to tell a tale—whether it's in the first person (the majority of my work) or the third. Bingo, point of view. The sense of active engagement and curiosity, of emotional drive and necessity, that comes with the discovery of such a character and his/her voice is more important than any mechanical privilege he/she might or might not have onto the narrative events. I'd take a live narrator or protagonist whose view is occluded over a dead one at the center of events any day.

Q. What should a writer just starting out keep in mind about point of view?

A. The same thing he or she should keep in mind about all technical matters at the start: remember to play, to diversify, to mimic freely, rather than locking down into one sober approach too soon. You're sure to narrow your style eventually—now is the chance to try unexpected, unlikely, even foolhardy points of view, just for the pleasure of seeing what the attempt reveals.

Q. Have you ever written a story or, gulp, novel from one point of view only to find it really should have been told from another?

A. No. What has happened—did happen, recently, as I was writing *Girl in Landscape*—is that the point of view I'd selected (and irreversibly fallen in love with) turned out to be insufficient to shed light on certain moments, certain turns that emerged in the progress of the the narrative. My solution was to introduce another voice into the book: brief passages of "god-like" omniscience that briefly rose above the narrow subjectivity of the protagonist's point of view to shed that absent light.

Jonathan Lethem, who lives in Brooklyn, New York, is author of a collection of short stories and three novels, including As She Climbed Across the Table.

one within that frame recount the central tale (say in the first-person), or by utilizing myriad first-, second-, or third-person points of view. Faulkner in *As I Lay Dying* (1930) chose the last. He took a family called the Bundrens, imagined the worst things that could occur to them, and let those things happen—which turned out to be, among other things, the death of the family's matriarch, Addie, her dying wish to be buried miles and miles away from the homestead in the middle of a hot summer, and the Bundrens's (ultimately selfish, we discover as we read along) quest to do so, which takes them through flood, fire and public ridicule. Faulkner—who, by the way, wrote the first draft in six weeks while working the night shift in a heating plant—chooses to structure the novel into 59 sections, each either an interior monologue or splash of stream-of-consciousness told from someone's private point of view: 16 by non-Bundrens in order to lend the story a slightly objective series of perspectives; 19 from the fairly intelligent and second-sighted perspective of a brother named Darl; 10 from the perspective of a retarded (or very young—it's hard to tell which) boy named Vardaman; 5 from the perspective of a simple-minded brother named Cash; and so on (there's even one from Addie's point of view from beyond the grave). The result is a richly psychological novel influenced by the theories of Freud, the fiction of Joyce and possibly Woolf, the poem by Wallace Stevens entitled "Thirteen Ways of Looking at a Blackbird" (1923), and the physics of Einstein—and one that reminds us that if realist narrative in the nineteenth century attempted to be a photograph, then modernist narrative in the early twentieth century attempted to be an x-ray.

Don't be nervous asking yourself during revision, or even during the actual drafting process: *Could I tell my story to greater effect from another point of view?*

If the answer's yes, go for it.

You might even want to experiment to see what sounds and works better for you—try a few pages one way, then a few another, then show your efforts to a friend.

Once you choose your point of view, or points of view, though, make sure you stay consistent in your use of it or them, or, if you don't, you have a very clear and discernible reason for breaking that consistency. A frequent slip when just starting down the writing road is to tell a story from the limited-omniscient third-person point of view, concentrating on a single character, only somewhere along the

Misha

Q. How, if at all, does your mixed-blood heritage inform the choices you make in terms of point of view?

A. First of all, I absolutely refuse to accept the modern western world view as a substitute for reality. Secondly, my mixed heritage allows me to sit at the fires of many ancestral camps. However, soul flight allows me access to any camps.

Q. What advice would you give a writer approaching this thing called point of view for the first time?

A. Between the writer and the subject stretches a thin membrane. The trick is to penetrate the membrane without rupturing it. For example, if you wish to tell the story from a stone's point of view, become the stone. You cannot simply "imagine" what the stone would say. You must get inside and listen carefully to its innermost thoughts, and (this is the hard part) record them faithfully.

Misha is author of *Prayers of Steel*, *Red Spider, White Web*, and *Ke-Que-Hawk-As*. In addition to writing, Misha raises horses on a small farm in Eastern Oregon.

line to unconsciously sneak in a point-of-view switch out of sloppiness rather than need.

You should control point of view rather than letting it control you. Otherwise, you're just confusing your poor reader to no real end.

That said, though, the sky's the limit, so long as you're flying the right fictive plane.

Now Read This

Burgess, Anthony. *A Clockwork Orange* (1962). Fabulous use of first-person to create a distinct voice (not to mention a new language) in this protocyberpunk British classic.

Conrad, Joseph. *Heart of Darkness* (1902). Classic use of narrative framing to tell the tale of a man who, existentially speaking, begins his story in the nineteenth century and ends it in the twentieth.

Di Filippo, Paul. *Ciphers* (1997). Fantastic exploitation of third-person omniscient point of view in a sprawling, wild conspiracy yarn.

Fuentes, Carlos. *Aura* (1965). Impressive investigation of the possibilities of second-person point of view in an eerie gothic tale.

Faulkner, William. *As I Lay Dying* (1930). Brilliant use of multiple points of view in a southern gothic retelling of *The Odyssey* (ca. 800 B.C.).

Stretching & Flexing

1. Take an apple and describe it from five radically different points of view: 1) objective realist; 2) a young girl just coming to consciousness of the world around her; 3) an old blind man; 4) a psychotic killer; 5) a cat.

2. Find a favorite story and retell it from a minor character's or antagonist's point of view, paying attention to how such a move can reframe and refresh the whole.

Time in Space

SUMMARY, SCENE, DIALOGUE, FLASHBACK, SLO-MO, TENSE

Think of this section as a kind of definitional smorgasbord for various central fictive techniques that haven't been able to find a comfortable dining area in previous sections.

What unites them is that they all have something to do with manipulating the reader's sense of time in narrative:

Summary. When you're writing a story, and want to compress loads of time into a very small space, slip into summary.

Use it as a means of providing caloric information concerning your character (his or her background, say, or motives, or general current situation) on a verbal diet plan. Not only does summary thus supply easy transitions from chapter to chapter or section to section, but it can also quantum the reader back and forth by decades, fill in important data about the world of the story, and just give everyone a break from scene after scene after scene.

"Things then did not delay in turning curious," opens chapter three of Thomas Pynchon's *The Crying of Lot 49* (1966), about a woman's quest into the workings of a gigantic conspiracy:

> If one object behind her discovery of what she was to label the Tristero System or often only The Tristero (as if it might be something's secret title) were to bring to an end her encapsulation in her tower, then that night's infidelity with Metzger [her short-time lover] would logically be the starting point for it; logically. That's what would come to haunt her most,

Q. Your first novel, *Deconstruction Acres*, just appeared. From a technical perspective, what was the most difficult part of writing it?

A. Hacking a narrative trail through the wilderness that defines imagination was grueling. But that was a boy-scout picnic compared to ironing out the sour notes I heard in my sentences when reading over my work. I want my sentences to sound like verses from an upbeat Protestant hymn rung out by an expert bell choir.

Q. During your rewrites, what are some of the most salient facts and features you learned about the creative process?

A. Revision is aided by collaboration. Obtain feedback from whatever source you can—corner spouses, shake down family members, stalk co-workers, bribe friends with drugs and beers. Cumulative corrections I made based on comments from a handful of trusted readers resulted in a more focused manuscript. Also, persuading your immediate circle to read your work is a good rehearsal for when it's time to pitch it to publishers.

Q. What advice might you have for people just finishing their first alternative-novel and/or short-fiction manuscript?

A. Seize the means of production by starting a literary zine in which you publish yourself and your friends. Venture off-campus and join your local writing community by attending readings and taking part in open mics. Don't listen too much to creative writing professors, who are a generation or two removed from yours and usually don't understand what you're trying to say. Above all, persevere—rejection doesn't mean your work is bad, it means you haven't located the right audience.

Tim W. Brown is editor of Tomorrow Magazine.

perhaps: the way it fitted logically together.

Notice we're not in a specific place at a specific time. Instead, the authorial voice has taken over and summarized the state of affairs, then what the woman thinks of them, and then what will happen next.

Notice, too, that it would be extremely difficult to write or read this kind of summary mode for too long.

Why?

Scene. It's probably close to impossible to tell a story wholly through summary simply because summary diminishes detail and gives rise to a sense of timelessness, on the one hand, or time speeded up, on the other.

Yet given our filmic and televisual sensibilities at the turn of the millennium, and our intensely visual awareness, it's no problem at all to tell a story wholly through scene—through, in other words, that slowing down of time which relishes in action, gesture, description, dialogue, and sometimes thought, as does Nabokov in *Lolita* (1955):

> When we stopped at the filling station, [Lolita] scrambled out without a word and was a long time away. Slowly, lovingly, an elderly friend with a broken nose wiped my windshield—they do it differently at every place, from chamois cloth to soapy brush, this fellow used a pink sponge.
>
> She appeared at last. "Look," she said in that neutral voice that hurt me so, "give me some dimes and nickels. I want to call mother in that hospital. What's the number?"
>
> "Get in," I said. "You can't call that number."
>
> "Why?"
>
> "Get in and slam the door."
>
> She got in and slammed the door. The old garage man beamed at her. I swung onto the highway.
>
> "Why can't I call my mother if I want to?"
>
> "Because," I answered, "your mother is dead."

For a story to sail, you need to bask in its important moments and use them to hook your reader into turning the page to the next section of summary or scene—or, if you try to violate this guideline, you need to know exactly what you're doing and why.

Usually, if there's a major or even minor confrontation, go for the scene. If there's a turning point or crisis, ditto. That isn't to say you should spend a paragraph showing a person getting out of bed and walking across the room and opening the door while thinking about nothing in particular along the way, or that Nabokov should have described Humbert turning on the car, putting it into gear, inching through the gas station, and edging onto the highway, gradually accelerating—unless there's an important reason to do so.

In other words, you need to begin to learn to discriminate between what moves plot and character forward, and what doesn't, and always stick with the former.

Ask yourself this as you proceed: Is every act of summary, every scene, every paragraph, every sentence, every word giving the reader new and interesting information that somehow contributes to the progress of the narrative?

If not, cut it out.

Dialogue. One of the most indispensable components of any scene, dialogue is a technique that most people just can't get enough of. It moves quickly down the page, and it's packed with more data about character, situation, and plot than just about any other single component of narrative. If used well, it can be a fictive magic bullet.

You can apply to dialogue most of what I said in the last section about speech. In addition, though, you might want to keep these tidbits tucked in your storage disk for easy retrieval.

One: If you take your notebook or journal to a bar, a grocery store, or a mall, and simply listen to how people speak, you'll soon be inclined to agree with Rebecca West, the British writer who early in the twentieth century called attention to the fact that most people don't so much engage in conversation when they speak with each other as they exchange intersecting monologues. That is, people tend not to play Q&A with each other, or even take the time especially to listen to what other people are saying. Rather, they use a phrase or image another person employs as an excuse to launch into a rambling editorial of their own, which often has no special rhyme or reason.

Two: Since people aren't awfully logical on the day to day, their dialogue isn't either. It's often packed with sentence fragments, um's and er's, ellipses, bad grammar, and the latest slang picked up off last night's sitcom.

Not that you should just glob the stuff down on a page, unfiltered, of course. But you *should* keep in mind that your goal is to *approximate* that very feeling of unmediated spontaneity—an approximation that can only be attained through meticulous crafting.

Three: Dialogue—like scene in general—should do several things at once in narrative, whereas in life it seldom accomplishes even one. A writer with a good ear and good sense of rhythm (and dialogue is nothing if not about these two things) can make dialogue convey information (one character explains to another how this gadget works, why he's doing what he's doing, who this other person is, etc.) at the same time it gives the reader a sense of the speaker's education, personal linguistic ticks, geographical source, and obsessions. Moreover, it can remind him or her about things that have happened, forecast those which will, help fill out a sense of place, and keep the plot clicking forward. All this, and yet written conversations tend to last much less time than their real-world doubles.

Four: People tend to mean more than they say. Some of the most powerful writers know this and use the space between speech and meaning to generate incredible tension.

Five: *Tags* are those words that come after quoted speech: *he said, she screeched, he whimpered.* Establish voices for your characters that are so strong you don't need to use tags often, and allow the rhythms and emphases of their dialogue to inform the reader who's screeching and who's whimpering without having to actually tell her or him.

Six: Avoid using exclamation marks unless you really, really have to! Because they become distracting quickly! And then annoying! And then enraging! Or, as F. Scott Fitzgerald said: "Cut out all those exclamation marks. An exclamation mark is like laughing at your own joke."

With these notions in mind, take a look at a short stretch from Cris Mazza's novel *Dog People* (1997), a book about both people who love dogs and people who live doggy lives. Here a husband and wife, Morgan and Fanny, are talking to a marriage counselor. Fanny thinks *she's* the really unhappy one in the relationship, but she's about to learn differently:

> "Do you love Morgan?" [the counselor asked Fanny.] "Do you feel he loves you? What's changed about *that*?"
> "This isn't accomplishing anything," Morgan said abruptly.
> "Why do you think so, Morgan?"

Q. Many of your fictions take the form of pure, or almost pure, dialogue. Why?

A. In a fundamental way, "unsituated" dialogue probably relates to some schizoid cleft in my consciousness. But it also happens to relate to that culturally-imposed cleft in people's consiousnesses—the ever-widening gulf between their colonized everyday, and their (as-yet) uncolonized dream. Moreover, the unsituated dialogue alludes to and sometimes mocks the influence of electronic media with its emphasis on roboticized talking heads.

Because the technique features people talking about whom the reader usually knows very little, it allows me more leverage to alter, reverse, and morph characterisitics from one speaker to another. That is, I can destabilize the narrative transaction more readily than if I were committed to traditional plot and characterization. And destabilization featuring reversal, ambiguity, and character morphing is one way to interrogate official culture.

Finally, I do it because it appeals to me compositionally; I like the spareness, the open spaces on the page.

Q. What sort of advice do you have for a young writer just beginning to wrestle with writing his or her first rounds of dialogue?

A. As with music, it helps to have a good ear for the vernacular, tonalities, and rhythms of primary sources. But with all the "information" out there, having a good *eye* for pertinent secondary sources is also useful. Keep a keen eye open to how other writers render dialogue, and to how actual dialogue is transcribed in newspapers, on TV, on the Net. When you find something, don't trust your memory; cut it out or copy it into a notebook.

Q. Your sometime use of exclusive dialogue, of course, is a small manifestation of a much larger alternative fictional project. What's the appeal for you of such formal and thematic innovation in a larger socio-literary context that tends to belittle it?

A. The former Soviet Union strongarmed dissenting artists and bulldozed (literally) alternative art exhibitions. The U.S. bulldozes by omission. The dissenting American artist is unpublished (or published with small, poorly distributed presses) and unrepresented. Hence s/he is in effect unseen and unfelt.

If you want something of your work to be felt, educate yourself about contemporary culture, technology and ideology (all of which are largely synonymous). Then find a seam, plant a mine, slip away. The seams I refer to are the rents, or fault lines, in the web of interfacing ideology which prevents us from being ourselves. The mines are counter-ideological and issue from the artist's fundamentally revolutionary imagination, which, like dream, is encroached on, but still pulsing.

My use of unsituated dialogue is a guerrilla tactic; it allows me to turn, torque, slash, burn, exit. And almost no mess.

Harold Jaffe is the author of nine books of fiction, including Beasts, Madonna and Other Spectacles, Eros Anti-Eros, Straight Razor, and Othello Blues. He is editor of Fiction International.

"Because I don't want to do this. I've wasted so much time already. I'm losing *my* career because the fucking management can't see beyond the wallets they're sitting on with their fat asses, and we're lolling here talking about a career *she's* never had the gumption to have in the first place."

"Maybe we'd better talk about how each of you feels about the other's career frustrations and disappointments and how you can support each other."

"No. I've already wasted half of my adult life. I don't know how it happened, I'm not blaming anyone, but for me, time's already running out, and it's not fair—by the time I'm forty, it'll be over, I'll be an inept ex-dancer the rest of my life. Doing *this* is pointless. I don't want it. I just . . . I don't want to be married anymore."

How much dialogue should be in a short fiction or novel? Obviously that's a personal aesthetic choice. There's virtually no dialogue in Gabriel García Márquez's *One Hundred Years of Solitude* (1967) or most stories by Jorge Luis Borges, for example. On the other hand, both Donald Barthelme and Hal Jaffe have written stories, and David Foster Wallace complete scenes in novels, that are nothing *but* dialogue, seldom accompanied by a single tag.

If you examine most conventional fiction, however, you'll discover the ratio regularly works out to something approaching fifty percent dialogue to fifty percent non-dialogue.

Flashback. When you need to take your reader back in narrative time through either summary or scene to material that occurred before the beginning of the work, slide into flashback.

Routinely, you do this by having one of your characters recollect a key event in his or her life that sheds light on the present action—Humbert Humbert, for instance, recalling his time with Annabel Leigh and the profound effect she had on how he perceived sexuality.

You can also create a flashback through characters' reveries and dream sequences. And not infrequently most of a narrative will take the form of a flashback. That is, the story will begin with a key event (funeral, wedding, murder), and then track back to map and explain what led to it. Make sure that your transitions into flashbacks are smooth, that they don't call attention to themselves, and that you only use them when you really need to—keep your focus on *pivotal* events. If you place them too early in your story they have a habit of disturbing your story's momentum.

Remember, too, that often you can dispense exactly the same information through dialogue or summary in a way that doesn't distract from your narrative's propulsion.

Done correctly, though, a flashback is pure magic when it only slowly creeps up on the reader that he or she is no longer in the narrative present, but has entered the great fictive time machine.

Slow Motion. It's also possible to slow down an important moment in your story so your reader can see and feel and smell every detail. In a sense, this is the exact opposite of summary. Instead of moving through vast amounts of time quickly, you move through very small amounts of time at a slug's pace. Why employ this technique? Because many of us experience intense events in our lives just that way—suddenly a clarity descends upon you and you can see every atom move around you as your car slides across the ice toward that ditch with the six-foot drop. So in a story you can either say "He was hanged and died," or, as Ambrose Bierce does in a famous example of slo-mo, "An Occurrence at Owl Creek Bridge" (1890), you can write a ten-page tale about what happens between the second a man named Peyton Farquhar is pushed off a bridge during his execution and the second his neck breaks.

Tense. Most stories are told in the simple past tense: "He walked down the street." While you might logically conclude that this would create a sense of temporal distance between reader and action, in practice it usually doesn't because the technique is so widespread and so deeply part of convention as to have become inconspicuous. Over the last thirty or forty years, however, many writers have adopted the present tense now and then: "He walks down the street." By doing so, they self-consciously emphasize the immediacy of the story's action. A kind of glossy photographic *thereness* settles in over their narrations.

Writing Versus Reading Time. A last observation with respect to narrative time: readers experience it at a very different rate than writers do. It takes most writers days to compose a scene, and it takes most readers minutes to process it. Most writers spend a year or two of their lives—if not much more—cooking up a novel, while readers frequently spend less than a week digesting it. That may seem true but trivial, yet it has immense implications for the writing process. As author, you might find yourself bored after a page of dialogue or a paragraph stuck in someone's point of view simply because you feel you've been there and done that and it's taken you two painfully long days to pull off fairly well. At such moments remind yourself that the reader has, if she or he is really careful, spent perhaps thirty seconds on the very same stretch of dialogue or paragraph. The message, then, is to flip-flop less in narrative than your instinct tells you to, or at least keep in the back of your consciousness the disorienting and maybe unnecessarily frustrating effect your frequent switches in pace, point of view, tense, or other techniques are going to have on your helpless, hapless reader—and that that effect might be quite different from the teeth-gnashingly stimulating one it has on you. At the level of narratological clip, there are few creatures more unmistakably unlike each other than readers and writers.

Now Read This

Bierce, Ambrose. "An Occurrence at Owl Creek Bridge" (1890). Excellent classic example of slo-mo in fiction.

Hemingway, Ernest. *The Sun Also Rises* (1926). Hemingway has been much maligned in recent years as an alcoholic macho jock with lots of gender issues to resolve. All true, but it's also true he wrote some of the most successful dialogue in the twentieth century.

Jaffe, Hal. *Straight Razor* (1995). Several stories in this collection use only dialogue in their telling. See, too, Donald Barthelme's *Forty Stories* (1987).

Wallace, David Foster. *Infinite Jest* (1996). A glorious compendium of narrative techniques, *Infinite Jest* displays a perfect ear for dialogue, as well as superb examples of scene, summary, and flashback—not to mention it's one of the best, most extravagant, and funniest novels written during the last decade of the twentieth century.

Wright, Stephen. *Going Native* (1994). A novel that deftly moves between past and present tense, and a haunting one that appropriates and reforms the serial-killer narrative, focusing on the victims rather than the murderer.

Stretching & Flexing

1. Write a sudden fiction that depends mostly or wholly on summary, or write a longer story told solely through scene.

2. Write a sudden fiction composed completely of untagged dia-
    logue between two or three characters, each of which wants some-
    thing different, and none of which says exactly what he or she
    means.

3. Write a sudden fiction whose first and last paragraphs take place
    in the narrative present, but whose body is a flashback, perhaps
    using as your starting point a significant event such as an acci-
    dent, a kiss, or a moment of abuse.

4. Write a sudden fiction in which an event that in real-time would
    take five or ten seconds to occur in your fictive slo-mo takes five
    pages—a death, a fall, a dazzling realization.

5. While writing one of the above, use an infrequently used
    tense—present, if you're feeling safe, but how about trying
    your hand at future or future perfect? Or how about altering
    mood in your story by telling it in the *subjunctive*, or contrary-
    to-fact construction?

20 Power of the Pen

FLEXING THE MUSCLE OF LANGUAGE

No matter what anyone tells you, language is always your real protagonist.

Without it, there would be no writing for or against the new millennium, no literary marketplace, no possibility of education in or out of the classroom, no genres, no narrative forms, no settings, no characters, no time in space, not one single point of view—no story, nada, zip, zilch.

It's an easy matter to forget, especially if you're a reader, because it's easy to buy into the illusion of character and all the rest perpetrated by the abracadabra of language.

Only fiction is one thing before it is anything else: lots of tricks with phrases on the page . . . the bang-on connotative metaphor, the verb that does more than sit still and wait for commands from adverbs and nouns, the lush line that can take the top of your head clean off.

Or, as critifictionist extraordinaire Roland Barthes more euphonically claimed: "Writing is the science of the various blisses of language."

Some people think that they're reading for emotions, and others that they're reading for plot, and yet others that they're reading for ideas, but in fact everyone's reading—in one way or another—for language, the *bon mot*, the *ne plus ultra*, the song of well-done syntax and rich rhythms and wonderful words that magically muster worlds.

Language is the carrier wave from one consciousness to another.

Staszek

Q. You lovingly build every one of your sentences. Is revision of them an on-going process through the course of writing, or do you write out the whole and then revise?

A. In some ways I do both. I always start from a feeling, a *tone*, that I can't express directly in words. That feeling is the *whole* work. I then do what I can to find my way back to that feeling through an incantation in words evoking story. I revise again and again as I go, honing the words home.

Q. How do you know a story or novel's done?

A. It takes me back to tone.

Q. What advice might you offer a writer just starting out about revision?

A. Take the time to learn who you are. Take the time to understand what calls to you. Open your voice. Revise your work or don't. Revise your process or don't.

Staszek is the existential signature of Stan Henry, a fiction writer who lives in Seattle.

That's why Vladimir Nabokov drafted and crafted almost every sentence of *Lolita* (1955) on an individual index card before he committed it to his edifice, and why Samuel R. Delany did much the same for hundreds of sentences in *Dhalgren* (1975).

It's most of the reason that it took Flaubert more than five years to compose *Madame Bovary* (1857), and Joyce more than seven to get *Ulysses* (1922) right.

And it's the reason you should spend tons of time on every syllable *you* fashion as well. After all, if language isn't the most important thing for you when writing fiction, then why not write scripts for television sitcoms? Why not dance? Why not paint a picture or compose a tune?

Here's twilight cast by a non-writer: "It was, uh, really, um, beautiful. The thing is— Well, um, words just can't do it justice, you know?"

Here's twilight cast by Tom Robbins: "Indigo. Indigoing. Indigone."

Without language, you've got yourself nothing but a big blank screen or another art form.

So:

Show, Don't Tell. All over the world, writers' jaws are actually aching from repeating this so much. I'd thus probably save myself the trouble, except for the fact that it's true. It's more true than true. It's beyond true.

If there's a single rule to learn about writing fiction that flies, it's this: the concrete is everything, the abstract null and void.

Go for the universal from the airy top down, instead of from the gritty bottom up, and chances are you'll construct generic prose that sounds a lot like post-war prefab tract housing looks.

Here's telling, courtesy of that guy down the block you pass every day on the way to work: "Girls sure are neat, aren't they? Cuz, well, they're so cool and all. Huh. Huh-huh. Huh-huh-huh."

Here's showing, courtesy of Robert Coover in "The Baby Sitter" (1969):

> That sweet odor that girls have. The softness of her blouse.
> He catches a glimpse of the gentle shadows amid her thighs,
> as she curls her legs up under her. He stares hard at her. He
> has a lot of meaning packed into that stare, but she's not even
> looking. She's popping her gum and watching television. She's

Kelly Cherry

Q. Your characters are delicious, and their lives continually break my heart, but it's always your finely spun perfect-pitch language that delights me most in your fiction. Can you talk a little about your writing process in terms of sentence crafting?

A. If you are right about what a character would say, you are probably also right about how that character would say it. To know the language, know the character.

Q. Why spend that much time on a sentence that sings if most readers these days aren't interested in listening?

A. A question I ask myself a lot! But the music of language—the Bible, Shakespeare, Melville—swept me up from the beginning, seemed to me, always, an essential beauty. A writer makes sentences sing for the sheer joy of it.

Q. What advice might you offer a writer just starting out about how to love language more fully?

A. I imagine any serious writer is born with a love of language. I've always read my drafts aloud to myself, testing rhythms, inflections, sounds. Not only poems but fiction, including novels, and essays, even book reviews. And if I'm really taken with someone else's language, I'll read the work aloud to myself. I used to buy recordings of plays and listen to the language as if it were music. Well, it is music. Laurence Olivier in *Henry the Fifth*—it was better than opera, because it was more interesting music. Listening to great language is a profound physical pleasure, like looking at art or nature, and the more one listens, the more one hears.

Kelly Cherry's recent publications include Death and Transfiguration, poems, and a reprint of her novel Augusta Played.

sitting right there, inches away, soft, fragrant, and ready: but what's his next move?

That's gorgeous stuff from one of America's supreme stylists.

Look at how that guy down the block reverts to large empty tentative assertions composed of hollow adjectives and calorically deprived linguistic filler that mean something different to everyone who hears them, and hence mean nothing much at all.

Then look at how Coover *never* tells the reader his point, *never* makes a bland assertion, but rather *shows* his point through the use of *significant detail*. That is, he goes for the specific, the definite, the things all of us know but only the real writers among us notice and conjure: the certain scent, the way light falls amid the thighs, the tension between the sexy softness of the blouse and the chintzy popping of gum which instantly generates character and mood.

Coover, in other words, *appeals to the senses* . . . to sight, to smell, to touch, to taste, and to sound—all in just seven short sentences.

And while he never tells us the age of the girl or of the boy who's perceiving her, it's clear enough simply because of those precise details that both are in their teens.

Moreover, he uses images that transcend simple *denotation*, or dictionary definition, and float into the realm of *connotation*, or those emotional implications and associations certain textured words carry, juxtaposing the "sweet odor," which suggests innocence, candy, and so on, with those "gentle shadows amid her thighs," which suggest so, so, so much more.

Last, Coover uses *rhythm*, or the recurrence of specific sounds or kinds of sounds—the soft sensuous slightly sad alliteration of s's that slide through the passage, for instance, the sonic glide from "gentle" to "glimpses" in the third sentence, the abrupt *p* of "popping" to accentuate that gum-chewing in the sixth—to raise his prose toward something like poetry.

And *that's* why so many knock-you-down-with-a-fluff-ball prose composers cut their teeth not only on libraries full of fiction, but also Quonset huts full of poems: reading poetry zeros you in on the worth of words, the phrasal turn, the metaphoric splendor, the rhythm of language done well.

All of those components add up to a sense of personal *voice*, that amalgam of style, characterization and tone that makes each writer different from every other writer.

And they add up to a sense of a fully realized fictive world, a

Carole Maso

Q. Your work is about all sorts of things, especially the geography of desire, but for me it's always been primarily about the musicality of language. What in your mind sets your exploration of language apart from other writers' explorations?

A. Probably that music and not literature is my primary source of inspiration. And this I believe is my major affinity with Beckett, whose sources were similar. Most writers understand music through literature. I understand literature through music.

Q. What connects your exploration of language to other writers' explorations?

A. I believe my relationship to language is basically lyric and visionary and to the degree that this is the project of other writers—Blake, Mallarmé, Apollinaire, Stein, Woolf (I could go on and on), we are connected. Certainly I would say our work overlaps and sings to one another.

Q. What advice might you offer a writer just starting out about how to love language more fully?

A. 1. Hang out around children. Try to remember being a child and the original joy language was then.
2. Learn a foreign language.
3. Think of one person you love or loved and one thing they said and how they said it *exactly*.
4. Listen to silence. Respect everything language will never be able to do and love it anyway.
5. Pray the same prayer over and over and over again.
6. Listen to music.

Carole Maso is the author of Ghost Dance, The Art Lover, The American Woman in the Chinese Hat, Ava, Aureole, and Defiance. She teaches at Brown University.

world readers can believe and live in.

Metaphor and Simile. A metaphor strikes an analogy between two objects in the reader's mind that revitalizes the existence of both.

A simile is a metaphor that uses *like* or *as*.

Chapter 10 of David Foster Wallace's *The Broom of the System* (1987) opens with this metaphor/simile-rich passage:

> The reason Lenore Beadsman's red toy car had a spidery network of scratches in the paint on the right side was that by the driveway of the home of Alvin and Clarice Spaniard, in Cleveland Heights, lived a large, hostile brown shrub, bristling with really thorny branches. The bush hung out practically halfway across the drive, and scratched hell out of whatever or whoever came up. "Scritch," was the noise Lenore heard as the thorns squeaked in their metal grooves in the side of her car, or rather "Scriiiiitch," a sound like fingernails on aluminum siding, a tooth-shiver for Lenore.

"Toy car" is a straightforward metaphor, while "spidery network of scratches" moves toward the elaborate: it connects not two things, but three: a spider's web, an openwork fabric or structure in which cords, threads, or wires cross at regular intervals, and the scratches on poor Lenore's auto.

The shrub that causes those scratches isn't really "hostile," obviously. It's just a plant. So to call it hostile is to create another metaphor that compares it to a bellicose person. This subset of metaphor, which assigns a nonhuman entity human qualities, is called *anthropomorphism.*

The sound its thorns make across the side of Lenore's car is "like fingernails on aluminum siding, a tooth-shiver for Lenore." The first part of that comparison takes the form of a simile that compares the scritch to fingernails raking across siding. The second part moves from simile back to metaphor: teeth don't really shiver, but we know exactly what Lenore feels like when she hears that icky noise.

If Wallace had said "fingernails on a chalkboard" instead of "fingernails on aluminum siding," he would have skidded from fervent living metaphor into *cliché,* or unoriginal uninspired language that allows others to do the thinking for you.

If, on the other hand, he'd spun a *really* elaborate metaphor or simile comparing two things incredibly and startlingly unlike (instead of "fingernails on aluminum siding," say, he'd written "a prostitute's long if slightly fungusoidal toenails on the porthole of the space shuttle in high orbit just after the captain's turned out the lights for the night, but just before everyone's really fallen asleep…"), he would have given life to what's called a *conceit*, a rhetorical trope writers like John Donne embraced with abandon in the late sixteenth and seventeenth centuries, and Tom Robbins, David Foster Wallace, and Mark Leyner embrace even now.

Whatever form they take, metaphors and similes wake language up while calling attention to language *as* language . . . that is, as beautiful breathtaking contrivance.

And usually the more work a reader senses went into a text—the more contrived a given text is—the more aesthetic value he or she assigns it. That's why most of us glance at a line of graffiti in the john, grin, and stroll on, whereas some of us spend our whole lives indulging in the linguistic cathedrals called *Ulysses* (1922), *Lolita* (1955), and *Gravity's Rainbow* (1973).

"Words are loaded pistols," Jean-Paul Sartre said.

"Words are the supreme objects," said William Gass.

Complexity as Intelligence. Many contemporary mainstream realist writers keep their use of metaphor, simile, and other linguistic pyrotechnics to a minimum because they want their language to pretend it's clean clear glass through which the reader can objectively witness the world, or, better, a reflective surface that gives back external reality with complete accuracy.

This theoretical impulse tracks back to the early nineteenth-century realists who, along with Stendhal in *The Red and the Black* (1830), believed art should be "a mirror carried along a high road. At one moment it reflects the blue skies, at another the mud and puddles at your feet."

The irony certainly hasn't been lost on more rhetorically adventurous and sophisticated writers that Stendhal couched his scientistic realist creed in—what else?—a really nice metaphor.

That aside, the last thing those realist writers want to do is call attention to language *as* language, to their linguistic contrivances, since such a move would italicize the sleight-of-hand they're trying to pull off without the reader noticing.

Read Ernest Hemingway, Raymond Carver, or Bret Easton Ellis, and you'll be able to count the verbal splashes you encounter in a fifteen-page story or chapter on one very tiny mutant hand.

Read Tom Robbins, Robert Coover, David Foster Wallace, or this passage from Mark Leyner's Avant-Pop short fiction, "I Was an Infinitely Hot and Dense Dot" in *My Cousin, My Gastroenterologist* (1990), and it's literally a different story altogether:

> So begins the autobiography of a feral child who was raised by huge and lurid puppets. An autobiography written wearing wrist weights. It ends with these words: A car drives through a puddle of sperm, sweat, and contraceptive jelly, splattering the great chopsocky vigilante from Hong Kong. Inside, two acephalic sardines in mustard sauce are asleep in the rank darkness of their tin container. Suddenly, the swinging doors burst open and a mesomorphic cyborg walks in and whips out a 35-lb. phallus made of corrosion-resistant nickel-base alloy and he begins to stroke it sullenly, his eyes half shut.

Using scientific and pseudo-scientific vocabulary, narrative jumpcuts (sometimes within the same sentence), and shocking (not to mention absurd) imagery, Leyner assembles the perfect anti-Carveresque language that tries through its information density and kaleidoscopic speed to capture the feel of life in the new millennium—part fun house, part freak show, part science fiction film, part punk riff played by Pinhead in *Hellraiser*.

Every Leynerian clause competes with the tsunami of all action-adventure movies released last summer, the latest rock'n'roll bands, the chatter from outside your window, car horns and brakes several blocks over, ambulance sirens, the jackhammer down the street, that stupid barking dog, MTV looping in the background right next to the blaring blaster right next to the beeping microwave right next to the whistling phone right next to the paper-thin walls of your apartment on the other side of which that couple is beginning to go at it again—all the hubbub of postmodern "reality," a "reality" that's almost beyond belief.

(Prophetic Philip Roth back in 1961: the "writer in the middle of the 20th century has his hands full in trying to understand, and then describe, and then make credible, much of . . . reality. It stupefies, it sickens, it infuriates, and finally it is even a kind of embarrassment to one's own meager imagination.")

Every clause also becomes a kind of comedian as well, drawing attention to its slapstick schtick as it tumbles across the page.

Michel Foucault once said every act of criticism was a comic display.

The same is true of language.

Leyner siphons much of his disruptive declamatory zeal from the prose of William Burroughs in such novels as *Naked Lunch* (1959), which subscribes to an art of the ugly, a kind of *aesthetics of trash* (that thinks itself back to the urban scenes in Charles Baudelaire's *Les Fleurs du Mal* [1857]) that will entrance such diverse late-twentieth-century writers as Donald Barthelme, Kathy Acker, and Misha:

> Motorcycles [Burroughs writes] careening, jumping, overturning. Spitting, shrieking, shitting baboons fighting hand to hand with the Huntsmen. Riderless cycles scrabbling about in the dust like crippled insects, attacking baboon and Hunstman. . . . .
>
> The Party Leader rides in triumph through yipping crowds. A dignified old man shits at sight of him and tries to sacrifice himself under the wheels of the car.
>
> PARTY LEADER: "Don't sacrifice your old dried up person under the wheels of my brand new Buick Roadmaster Convertible with white-walled tires, hydraulic windows and all the trimming. It's a cheap Arab trick—look to they accent, Ivan—save it for fertilizer.… We refer you to the conservation department to consummate your swell purpose.…"
>
> The washing boards are down, and the sheets are sent to the Laundromat to lose those guilty stains—Emmanuel prophesies a Second Coming.…
>
> There's a boy across the river with an ass like a peach; alas I was no swimmer and lost my Clementine.
>
> The junky sits with needle poised to the message of blood, and the con man palpates the mark with fingers of rotten ectoplasm.

Duck!

Incoming workshop heresy: syntactic complexity, sentential length, metaphorical and pun-full richness, informational compactness, dictional diversity, narrative momentum, and so on are not emblems of cluttered confusion, but pristine intelligence.

Ask any psychologist.

Some of the most influential writers of the twentieth century (Stein and Proust, Beckett and Pynchon, Gass and Gaddis among them) have in a multiplicity of approaches welcomed the alternative linguistic tradition that challenges the simplicity and clarity (though not the sure-crafted beauty) of a sentence written by Hemingway, or Flaubert before him, suggesting that such an easily intelligible version of language doesn't necessarily match our contemporary vision of the protean pluriverse we inhabit.

Here's that boy down the block you pass every day on the way to work describing the demise of an elderly person: "Guy just, like, um, *died*. It was really weird. Huh. Huh-huh. Huh-huh-huh."

Here's James Joyce doing the same at the end of *Finnegans Wake* (1939), the Ur-hypertext megametafiction:

> And it's old and old it's sad and old it's sad and wary I go back to you, my cold father, my cold mad father, my cold mad feary father, till the near sight of the mere size of him, the moyles and moyles of it, moananoaning, makes me seasilt saltsick and I rush, my only, into your arms. I see them rising! Save me from those therrble prongs! Two more. Onetwo moremens more. So. Avelaval. My leaves have drifted from me. All. But one clings still. I'll bear it on me. To remind me of. Lfff! So soft this morning, ours. Yes. Carry me along, taddy, like you done through the toy fair! If I seen him bearing down on me now under whitespread wings like he'd come from Arkangels, I sink I'd die down over his feet, humbly dumbly, only to washup. Yes, tid. There's where. First. We pass through grass behush the bush to. Whish! A gull. Gulls. Far calls. Coming, far! End here. Us then. Finn, again! Take. Bussoftlhee, mememormee! Till thousendsthee. Lps. The keys to. Given! A way a long a last a loved a long the

"Oh bliss, bliss and heaven," says Joycean Alex in Anthony Burgess's *A Clockwork Orange* (1962) when he listens to Beethoven's Ninth on his bed. "I lay all nagoy to the ceiling, my gulliver on my rookers on the pillow, glazzies closed, rot open in bliss, slooshying the sluice of lovely sounds. Oh, it was gorgeousness and gorgeosity made flesh."

"Words," said Samuel Beckett, "are all we have."

Now Read This

Any Poetry Anthology. One of the best ways to focus on the finer
        points of prose, from word choice to rhythm, is to read as

much twentieth-century poetry as you can get your hands on. Always recite it out loud.

Coover, Robert. *Pricksongs & Descants* (1969). Every sentence in this collection of bawdy beautiful short stories is a linguistic education.

Joyce, James. *Ulysses* (1922). A stylistic extravaganza by the twentieth-century father of the meticulously crafted mellifluous sentence.

Nabokov, Vladimir. *Lolita* (1955). One of the most exquisitely written novels in the second half of the twentieth century. Read it and weep.

Stretching & Flexing

Describe an object as carefully as possible for one page without ever naming it. To see if your language works, share your composition with friends and see if they can figure out what you're doing and with what. Make sure not to tell ("It's a kitchen appliance designed to keep food preserved longer by keeping it well below room temperature.") but show ("Someone reached into me and shut off my light and everything went cold.").

21 Heavy Muddle

THEME, ALLEGORY, AND SYMBOLISM

During a Q&A after a public reading one night, someone asked Robert Browning what he meant by a poem he'd just recited. When he wrote it, Browning answered, only God and he knew. "And now," he concluded, "only God knows."

The guy had forgotten his own intent, an instructive lapse for a young writer if ever there was one.

How come?

Because it suggests that technique, language, musicality and structural execution are often more important to the established writer than the heavy muddle of *theme*—that central idea shaping a piece of creative writing, the abstract concept that is made flesh in prose or poetry through significant detail, setting, character, action, image, and the rest.

Another way of conceptualizing this: while the dreamboat of words you use, say, or the fictive atmosphere and people you create, can be employed as a direct measure of your fiction's aesthetic and emotional worth, theme can't. You can, after all, choose one of the most important themes in the galaxy—humanity's intrinsic sense of existential loneliness, for instance, or what it means to be alive and kicking in the new millennium—but if you don't weave that theme into a spectacular fully-realized aesthetic object, it will seem emptier than the gaseous sputter of an almost fuel-less Bic lighter.

That's why it's usually good advice to think about letting your theme evolve out of the specifics of a story and your characters' interactions rather than writing mechanically from some artificially invented Big Idea down, college composition courses to the contrary.

Of course (as with so much in creative writing) that needn't always be the case. Sometimes a really bewitching theme will catch your fancy, and you won't be able to shake off its spell, and pretty soon it will begin to engender a fabulous tale for you. When that happens, by all means stand back and let it. George Orwell wanted to write a warning about the potential dehumanizing effect of totalitarian communism and attentively set about to do so in *1984* (1949) to ecstatic success. William Golding wanted to investigate the effects of nature without nurture or regulation and wrote one of the most unnerving books of the fifties, *Lord of the Flies* (1954).

To let theme guide your composition too unforgivingly, however, always runs the risk of producing a chunk of fiction that takes itself too seriously, strains too scarlet-facedly at Importance, and thus reeks of pretension and pomposity.

The same is true of fiction that flaunts a cumbersome allegorical or symbolic charge.

Allegory suggests a one-to-one relationship between an object in a piece of art and an abstract idea outside it. In John Bunyan's *Pilgrim's Progress* (1678), as a case in point, a man named Christian (an allegory for good Christians everywhere) tries to achieve a godly life by running a faith-challenging obstacle course represented by such physical objects as the Slough of Despond and Vanity Fair (pretty obvious what these stand for, right?).

A *symbol*, on the other hand, is an object in a piece of art that suggests *many* abstract ideas beyond itself. So the mention of a naked person swimming in a pond at night may simply be the realistic description of a naked person swimming in a pond at night . . . but, at the same time, through various emphases and patterns carefully created by the author, that water may slowly come to suggest in the reader's mind amniotic fluid and a sort of return to a nourishing maternal space, or even a baptism, and hence a mode of birth or rebirth, and hence an important turning point in the story, while to others that very same image in that very same story might suggest that character's fluid state of mind, or his or her relationship to nature, or something else completely. What does the symbol of a circle mean in medieval Christian iconography, or that white whale in Herman Melville's *Moby-Dick* (1851)? The answer is that the more you think about them, the more significance will emerge from them.

To put it simply, then, in allegory meaning is always set and the author strives to be straightforward about the relationship of object to idea, whereas a symbol is always pregnant with multiple meanings.

More times than not it's wise to keep your conscious use of both to a minimum. Given even a quarter of a chance, your writing will give life to allegories and symbols without your deliberate manipulation. If they grow organically within your story or novel, they will feel natural to the reader. If you force them to grow with various chemical fertilizers, they will come out looking artificially contrived and unsettling like some of those pumpkins and tomatoes that win contests but look like they've been showered in radioactive broth.

A quick last proposition before leaving this literary suburb: it's always easier to confuse your reader than to present a clear and clearly defined world and belief system to him or her.

Yet because many of us were raised on the modernist canon which houses complex symbolic structures by the likes of Eliot, Joyce, and Yeats, we've come to believe that readerly confusion equals writerly profundity. That simply ain't the case as a rule. Readerly confusion tends to equal writerly carelessness, an inability of the author to express herself or himself articulately and succinctly, or her or his inability to distinguish between writing time, where you can plant a full garden of linguistic, symbolic, and character surprises in every sentence, and reading time, where you can only harvest one or two.

That isn't to say that you shouldn't attempt to make your reader work.

It *is* to say that you shouldn't take malevolent glee in turning up the distortion knob on him or her and riffing on the heavy muddle station just for the sake of turning up the distortion knob on him or her and riffing on the heavy muddle station.

Compose at the level of complexity you'd enjoy reading, not at the one you'd enjoy writing.

Stretching & Flexing

1. How much can abstract idea guide story production? Let's see. Lewis Shiner edited an anthology of short fiction called *When the Music's Over* (1991), in which he asked writers to produce science fiction stories in which conflict resolves without recourse to violence. Think about a political, environmental, or medical-ethics problem that's close to your heart, and then write a story (it doesn't necessarily have to be science fiction) in which you offer a nonviolent solution.

2. Here's an even tougher assignment—probably the toughest in this book—to explore how much an abstract idea can guide story

production. John W. Campbell, famous science-fiction editor of *Astounding Stories* from 1937 to his death in 1971, used to give his stable of writers difficult philosophical quandaries out of which they were supposed to create short stories. Try your hand at one of them: a) write a story about a man who will die in twenty-four hours unless he can answer this question: "How do you know you're sane?" b) write a story about a creature that thinks *as well* as a human but not *like* a human.

Avoid Annoyed

MECHANICAL ERRORS THAT
CAN KILL A MANUSCRIPT

When a younger, more hirsute Sting made one of his first videos with The Police, he allegedly told his director: "Keep the camera on the money."

Meaning, of course, Sting.

When you think about language, it's a good idea to keep your camera on these Great Eight:

Avoid clichés. Cliché is a word that derives from the French verb *clicher*, which literally means *to stereotype* and in English refers figuratively to any expression that's been so overused as to become a linguistic clone—a conventional, formulaic, and oversimplified version of itself: *the tip of the iceberg, it's a crying shame, old as the hills.* Clichés usually enter popular discourse because they're pithy and vibrant, but soon through frequent repetition they slip into grating predictability and hollowness. They think for you. Dodge them at any cost.

Avoid mixed metaphors. Mixed metaphors are sloppy comparisons that the author hasn't really thought through. They begin in San Diego and end in Algeria, by way of Tokyo and Hackensack. David Lloyd George, Prime Minister of Britain at the end of World War I, purportedly said, for example: "I smell a rat. I see it floating in the air. I shall nip it in the bud." Not only did he string together a series of clichés for his fumbled effect, but he strung them together in such a way as to get them wrong, bang them into each other, create—if you think about it—a grotesque image of a hovering rodent being bitten in the protuberance containing an undeveloped shoot, leaf, or flower. If clichés are dull, then mixed metaphors tend to be hysterically inappropriate.

Avoid empty verbal filler. There's no better way to take the plug out of your sentence's whitewater raft than packing it with vacant words that function as the written analog for, *um*, rhythmic pauses that carry no content but tend to shade your tone toward the academically pompous: *rather, as it were, so on and so forth, in a manner of speaking, etc.* You know the culprits. Treat them as carbuncular homunculi.

If possible, use the active voice. You create *active voice* when you have the subject of your sentence act instead of being acted upon: *I throw the Chihuahua* rather than the *passive The Chihuahua is thrown by me.* It's a simple trick to keep your verbs working for you by avoiding *state-of-being* (forms of the verb *to be*) *constructions.* You'll thereby energize your prose and your characters, creating a fiction of *doing* rather than *existing.*

Concentrate your attention on the verb. Most young writers think the muscle of any sentence resides in the adjectives and adverbs, since they're the descriptive mechanisms in language. But the truth is that adjectives and adverbs are the verbal cellulite of your sentences. If you use more than a small saki-cup-full per page, your prose will suddenly blotch purple—it will seem overwritten, thick, and messy as a dorm room on Sunday morning: "The tall skinny slightly stooped white-skinned man with the red pock-marked face and large nobby potato nose in the weather-worn full-length wool coat walked blithely and inattentively down the wide brick-lined street on a particularly sunny blue-skied early spring day with the occasional white fluffy animal-shaped cloud scudding overhead through the lush lime-green foliage of the full-bodied lovely trees along the normal-widthed if uneven sidewalk." The muscle of your sentence is always the verb, the center of the sentence's action. So think long and hard about your verbs. Did that man really just *walk* down the street, or did he perhaps *stroll*? *amble*? *crab*? *skitter*? *saunter*? *blunder*? Each of those verbs carries that man's whole character within it. Hint: if you feel too many adjectives and adverbs piling up in any given sentence, it most likely means that sentence wants to be a fleshed-out paragraph all of its own.

Avoid word echoes. Try not to use the same word twice on any given page, let alone in any given paragraph or sentence, unless you're using it for precise rhetorical emphasis. If the word's rare, you should probably use it only once per story or novel. Readers and fellow writers whose ears are finely tuned to language will hear your redundancy as a kind of unpleasant verbal static, and see it as your inability to control your own language. Listen, too, for unwanted and unnecessary *full rhymes* ("like" and "bike"), *slant rhymes* ("drunkard" and "conquered"), *homonyms* ("bore" and "boar"), and one of the most unattractively named verbal slips in the English language: *homoeoteleutons*—those unsettling and graceless likenesses in endings of consecutive words or words near each other ("emerging moaning becoming discernible").

Vary your sentence structure and length. Here's a homely description of a toy wooden dove taking first flight:

> The bird went up into the air. It was made out of wood. It
> wobbled a little. It steadied. It flew. We all thought it was
> cool. We were very excited.

Not bad, especially for a Hemingway or Carver on a lazy day, but certainly not great either. Notice, for one thing, that all the sentences take the same form: subject + verb + preposition/adjective/adverb. And notice, as well, that they all run about the same distance on the page, ticking right along like a squad of marching ants. The outcome is a kind of prose wooden as that dove—sturdy enough, but flat as an unpainted '66 Ford Mustang. Now listen to the same subject matter filtered through Guy Davenport's extraordinary imagination in his short story, "The Wooden Dove of Archytas," which appeared in *Da Vinci's Bicycle* (1979):

> Into the eye of the wind it flew, lollop and bob as it butted
> rimples and funnels of air until it struck a balance and rode
> the void with brave address. We all cried with delight.

Every phrase is a bite of chocolate cheesecake.

You'd never eat sauceless pasta for dinner thirty nights in a row unless you had a disease or bad gastronomic neurosis or suffered some other form of debilitating poverty.

Or, if you think you would, linguistically speaking, then why not just write and read the newspaper, where you'll seldom find a sentence over eight syllables long or articulated in an even slightly unusual way?

Know your mechanics. Alternative fiction isn't an excuse for unconsciously messy spelling, grammar, and punctuation.

Nothing will tick off an editor faster than the equivalent of a big sign that says: I COULDN'T CARE LESS ABOUT MY CRAFT. And nothing will get that manuscript of yours turned around at the speed of editorial indignation.

It'll feel like it never left your mailbox.

"I was working on the proof of one of my poems all the morning," Oscar Wilde once commented, "and took out a comma. In the afternoon I put it back again."

Spelling, grammar, and punctuation are the base metals of every sentence. If you work them correctly, they'll become beautifully invisible till you need to bend them for a reason; perhaps, for example, you want to write an account of Appalachian life from a ten-year-old boy's point of view, or perhaps, like David Foster Wallace in *Infinite Jest* (1996), an account of someone getting on the wagon from the point of view of a fifty-year-old Irish immigrant in an Alcoholics Anonymous session:

> 'd been a confarmed bowl-spatterer for yars b'yong contin'. 'd been barred from t'facilities at o't' troock strops twixt hair'n Nork for yars. T'wallpaper in de loo a t'ome hoong in t'ese carled sheets froom t'wall, ay till yo. But now woon dey . . . ay'll remaemaber't'always. T'were a wake to t'day ofter ay stewed oop for me ninety-dey chip. Ay were tray moents sobber. Ay were thar on t'throne a't'ome, yo new. No't'put to fain a point'on it, ay prodooced as er uzhal and . . . and ay war soo amazed as to no't'belaven' me yairs. 'Twas a sone so wonefamiliar at t'first ay tought ay'd droped me wallet in t'loo, do yo new. Ay tought ay'd droped me wallet in t'loo as Good is me wetness. So doan ay bend twixt m'knays and'ad a luke in t'dim o't'loo, and odn't belave me'yize. So gud paple ay do then ay drope to m'knays by t'loo an't'ad a *rail* look. A loaver's luke, d'yo new. And friends t'were loavely past me pur poewers t'say. T'were a *tard* in t'loo. A *rail tard.* T'were farm an' teppered an'aiver so jaintly aitched. T'luked *constroocted* instaid've sprayed.... Me friends, this tard'o'mine practically

had a poolse.

Or perhaps, like Samuel Beckett in *How It Is* (1961), you want to drop conventional punctuation completely, and mimic instead the breathing intervals of someone crawling through a seemingly eternal tract of fecal mud nowhere nowhen:

> how it was I quote before Pim with Pim after Pim how it is three parts I say it as I hear it

> voice once without quaqua on all sides then in me when the panting stops tell me again finish telling me invocation

> past moments old dreams back again or fresh like those that pass or things things always and memories I say them as I hear them murmur them in the mud

> in me that were without when the panting stops scraps of an ancient voice in me not mine

> my life last state last version ill-said ill-heard ill-recaptured ill-murmured in the mud brief moments of the lower face losses everywhere

Before you try freestyling at this Olympic level of sentence fabrication, though, make sure you can dog paddle steadily and with a hint of expressive poise.

Far too many young writers take the plunge into the linguistic rapids of such carefully ruptured discourse before they've mastered the mechanics that make a firm clean conventional sentence a firm clean conventional sentence.

Consequently, their sentential life preservers aren't much use, and what happens next is always a sad unpretty sight.

"All my life I've looked at words as though I were seeing them for the first time," Hemingway wrote.

Everyone should be so lucky.

Now Read This
Any Good Dictionary. Always keep a dictionary by your writing desk, and consult it frequently for the exact definition of the

words you're using. Read it on the toilet. Read it before you begin to write. Read it as you stroll past it throughout the day. A strong version of Webster's dictionary is available for free online at: www.m-w.com/netdict.htm

Any Good Thesaurus. You should approach these with caution, but, used sparingly and correctly, they can be beneficial. Hint: after you think you've found the word you want there, make sure to check it against your dictionary to see that it's the one you think it is. *Roget's Thesaurus* is available for free on the Web at: www.thesaurus.com

Strunk, William C. and E. B. White. *The Elements of Style* (1918; regularly updated). Still the best short course in the rules for correct usage. Everyone should read this one at least twice. Available for free on the Web at:
www.columbia.edu/acis/bartleby/strunk/

Stretching & Flexing

Have some devious fun by writing a sudden fiction saturated with as many clichés, mixed metaphors, passive constructions, and other versions of verbal obesity as you can parodically pour into it without sacrificing readerly understanding. Get them all out of your system, every single silly one, and, when you're done, never ever write another.

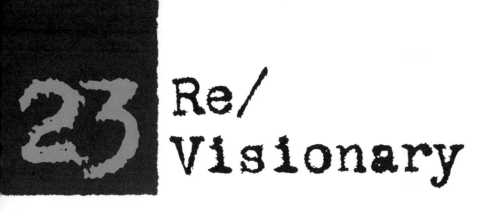

23 Re/ Visionary

TECHNIQUES FOR REVISION

F inishing a book," Truman Capote said, "is just like you took a child out in the yard and shot it."

Many writers will tell you the same about finishing a short story.

Imagine the hours you spend on a good, solid seventeen-page prose parcel—sometimes the weeks, even months.

Then imagine the years you spend writing a good, solid novel. You live in your language and you live with your characters. You watch both grow as your plot commences to shape itself, and by doing so you learn about yourself and the world outside your window and inside your mind's eye. You write hard, you write long, and you write seriously, usually for *way* below minimum wage. You take no prisoners. You often spend as much time in the virtual reality of your own fictive universe as you do interacting with more mundane protoplasmic entities. Simple biological gestation periods sometimes start seeming like slices of pumpkin pie at Thanksgiving dinner compared to those half-decade-plus narratological ones.

No surprise, then, that it's difficult to know when you're done, difficult to admit it, and sometimes even difficult to muster strength enough to shrug on to the next project.

But after a first draft of a story or chapter, you shouldn't sweat it too much.

Many young writers think it's time to pack up the manuscript and send it out in tomorrow's mail. The truth is you're still a good distance from the finish line in the race called fiction.

In a sense, you've really only just begun.

William Gibson wrote twelve drafts of the opening of *Neuromancer* (1984) before he was satisfied, and that's not at all unusual. If anything, many authors run through even more versions of a short story than they do of a novel. And poets? You don't even want to ask.

Nobody ever said writing was going to be a cinch, but loads of authors have said just the opposite.

"Writing doesn't get easier with experience," Tim O'Brien has pointed out. "The more you know, the harder it is to write."

"Writing is easy," Gene Fowler commented. "All you do is sit staring at a blank sheet of paper until the drops of blood form on your forehead."

Overstated? Sure.

Untrue? Never.

And for some it's even more arduous once the revision process gets under way because now you've got to start macheteing your very own prose and people, whereas for others revision is a kind of massive existential sigh and forehead slap of relief because the once-blank pages are finally full and all you have to do now is push the already-created world around on them.

Either way you feel about this stage of the process, though, my advice is to write that first draft of yours as quickly as possible. If you want to use an outline, fine. If you don't, fine. But whatever you do, don't think too much. Don't hesitate.

I know that sounds strange. Write like a subatomic particle in a wicked accelerator, fast as your fingers can carry you into your characters' lives and their plot's plural tangles. *That's* the stuff of inspiration. Go ahead. Contradict yourself. Let your favorite character enter one scene wearing jeans, sneakers, and t-shirt, and exit wearing a three-piece suit, top hat, and tap shoes. Grow a mountain outside a pioneer's forty-acre prairie fence if she suddenly needs to see one. Who cares? Go where your imagination and language take you. Otherwise you'll chance skirting the precipice dubbed Gunking Up, Pondering Plot and Prose Too Much, Scudding into Creative Paralysis.

Now write your second and subsequent drafts as slowly as possible. Write them at the speed of a garden slug on sand at high noon in the Sahara. Once you've got your primary lump of authored clay, take all the time in the cosmos sculpting it. Taste every clause. Rephrase every sentence. Test every punctuation mark for effectiveness. Try an alternative plot twist. Change your point of view and see what happens. Change your setting here, your dialogue there. Compress that swatch of scene into summary, and pitch that patch of summary into scene. Try a different ending and see if it's what you've been intending all along. Is that *really* where your climax should be? Is that *honestly* what your character wants to learn? Is that even what he or she should look like? Act like? Speak like? Take chances, knowing your safety net of a first draft will catch you if you fall.

Ask yourself this: Is everything serving the architectural whole? Is every page moving plot forward or teaching the reader something important about your central characters or fictional galaxy? Because if it isn't, don't bother. Cut it up, print it out, and plop it in a pewter pot for future narrative cannibalization. You can always use it as the basis for your next story or novel. You can always put it in the imagination bank.

Only never, ever, *ever* keep a scene, paragraph, sentence or word just because you like it. That's the easiest way there is to grow unsightly fictive love handles.

As Faulkner reminds us: "Kill your darlings."

If you like a phrase or scene or character *too* much, be suspect. Unsheath that Bowie knife.

Keep it lean. Keep it mean. Life is short and very few readers want to make a career out of slogging through a single dense story or loose baggy novel. If each element doesn't contribute to your overall effect, if it doesn't spin either plot or character forward, ditch that sucker, and ditch it fast. Drop it like a pound of plutonium.

Before you even begin asking yourself such questions, though, stick that first draft of yours in a drawer and take a psychic holiday. Maybe stop writing for a few days. Take a trip you've always wanted to. Spend a day in the park. Go for multiple pints of Ben & Jerry's and a dozen B-flicks, or simply turn your attention to another creative project, or perhaps to all those letters and bills you've let build up on your desk like a miniature Mount Everest while you've been engaged in more pressing business.

Why?

Because you need distance from what you've just created.

If you reread it and it seems like the most brilliant thing you've ever had the pleasure to revere, chances are you haven't let it sit in that drawer long enough. If you can't begin to spot problems from the nanosecond you pick it up, put it down again and walk away for another week, two weeks, six months. You're in no rush, after all. It isn't going anywhere, and you've just invented yourself some time to move on to something else. Let the gremlins of unconscious cre-

Steven J. Frank

Q. Your first novel, *The Uncertainty Principle*, recently appeared. What did you learn about the craft of revision while writing it?

A. Someone once said, "Novels aren't written. They're rewritten." Revisions are essential; nothing is ever right the first time. Yet it's difficult—and painful—to assume the objective viewpoint of a reader. My approach has been to allow a "cooling off" period; before I revise a chapter, I let it smoulder for a month (or more!) in my drawer. It's the only way I'm able to develop critical distance.

Q. If you could begin it all again, what would you do differently?

A. I tend to draw characters ahead of story. Beginning with a more detailed plot summary would have saved me much suffering as I struggled with the story's trajectory . . . but it's suffering that I like.

Q. How do you know, when you showed your novel-in-progress to other people, that the criticism they offered was valid?

A. Good criticism is like pornography—I can't define it, but I know it when I see it. Generally, the more someone evinces understanding of what I'm trying to do, the more compelling will be the critique. You always want to find someone who's predisposed to the kind of material you're writing.

Steven J. Frank writes patents by day and fiction by night. His short stories have appeared in numerous print and electronic journals. The Uncertainty Principle won Permeable Press's Pocket Rocket Prize for Best Novel in 1996.

David Memmott

Q. You not only publish short story collections and novels via Wordcraft of Oregon, but also write them. How can you tell, either from an editor's or writer's point of view, when a piece is really finished?

A. It's something like comparing bells: a brass bell sounds different than a glass bell sounds different than a ceramic bell. Some bells may be poorly cast or have clappers too long or too short or made of the wrong material. The truth is in the tone. If it rings rich, full and clear, it sets off a sort of harmonics of the soul and you know it's right. To tune your ear, you've got to have heard a lot of bells ring.

Q. How do you know you're giving or getting good criticism about a manuscript?

A. Good criticism excites you about the work, brings new energy, makes you want to get at it again. If it leaves you feeling a little sick in the stomach, then it's blocking energy and you have to let it go, no matter how long the critic's resume. You have to trust your own gut reaction. So I think of criticism like energetic healing, it either opens up or blocks the energy. A good critic or reader can stick you with needles but you don't feel any pain, only this energizing warmth spreading throughout your body.

Q. What sort of tricks do you employ during your own revision process?

A. It's interesting that Jacob dreamed of a stairway to heaven with angels ascending and descending, then later wrestled with god until dawn and went off limping with a dislocated hip. That's what the revision process is for me, the dream followed by a struggle to find the right form. There are no tricks. You start again from the beginning and work through. A helpful tool has been Thomas E. Kennedy's checklist for self-editing called "Torturing Your Sentences," including advice such as: less says more, *le mot juste* (finding the right word), use strong verbs, avoid unecessary repetition, etc.

David Memmott is the editor/publisher of Wordcraft of Oregon, a Rhysling Award winner, and author of several books of poetry.

ativity work on it behind your back. When you pick it up again, you'll be surprised at all the damage they've done.

When you're ready to get down to some serious revising, pick that piece up again and read it through from beginning to end to gain a sense of the ensemble. You've been busy during the original writing process with this sentence or that paragraph. You've been standing really close to your narrative canvas. Now it's time to step back and observe the complete painting. You'll probably have the same sensation Claude Monet did when he backed up from those splotches of color on his Impressionist productions and saw the magnificent water lilies for the first time. You'll see the context those sentences and paragraphs exist within. And *that's* the level you want to focus on first.

These are the sorts of questions associated with the first stage of revision: Is my plot working? Is there really a point to it? Have I created enough psychological, linguistic, and action hooks to keep the reader going from one page to the next? How has my character changed? Has he or she changed enough? Are my characters as fully rounded on the page as they are in my imagination? How about my point of view? Is my story told from the best vantage possible? Is my plot paced steadily? Does each part of it occupy the right amount of narrative space? Is every scene necessary? Is each part of each scene logically consistent with every other part? Am I missing any indispensable transitions between scenes? Does time in the story feel like it's moving at the rate it should be moving? Are there any authorial intrusions I can do away with?

Those questions will take you several ages to answer. Let them. They're the big narratological enchiladas. Don't rush. Read your story or novel through, make some notes as you go along about things to recall or possibilities for change, think long and hard, put it down again, read a really good prefessional novel or story and pay careful attention to how the writer structures it, pick up your manuscript a week or three later, read it through again, concentrate on the sections you have real problems with, and don't hesitate to chop, hack, cleave, dismember, rearrange, reconfigure.

When you're finally pretty content with the overall contours, then you can move down to the next level: sentence and paragraph. Again, strike out anything that isn't absolutely essential. Find ways to say with one word what's taken you ten to say before. Ask yourself: is every sentence utterly clear in its intention and execution? Will my reader find each as enjoyable to read as I did to write? Have I oriented her or him sufficiently at this micro-stratum with respect to time, place, character, action?

Now move down to the individual verbs. Is each as active and powerful as possible? What about the adjectives? Are there some you can do away with? Some you can move from more abstract to more concrete? Have you varied sentence length and structure enough to keep things fetching? Is your tone consistent? Are there any verbal tics (certain words or phrases you repeat far more than you thought you did, certain sentence constructions) you need to watch for? If you've written dialogue, is it simply chatty or does it really have a fundamental narrative function? Are your characters' accents and verbal eccentricities consistent? Does your prose feel fresh, or does it still seem flabby with first-draft laziness? What about word echoes? Verbal fillers? Clichés? Mixed metaphors?

When you're done with that, cut some more.

I'm not suggesting you whittle your piece down to a skeleton and leave it for dead by the side of the road, just that you pay keen attention to proportion at every level from overall plot to solitary clause.

You need to be ruthless with your own writing at this stage of the game, and ruthlessly honest. You need to be your own hardest critic. That's how you'll challenge yourself to excel, write more effectively today than you did yesterday.

At the same instant you're looking to trim, however, you should also be keeping your eyes open for places that need to be fleshed out. Because you've written your first draft at a fairly hefty clip, there are bound to be many segments that will now strike you as fairly anorexic. Remember, several things need to be going on in every scene for it to feel fully conceived. Are they? Have you expended the energy necessary to describe your characters' external characteristics, internal states, histories? Have you given them movement and thought and feeling during every scene? Have you detailed your setting so it doesn't seem out of place and time?

If you're pretty comfortable answering yes to all these, your next step is to read your story or novel out loud to yourself, or, better yet, have a friend, colleague, roommate, fellow student, relative, or lover read it back to you. Here's another place where you can pick up on confusion at the level of plot and character, and clunkiness at the level of sentence. If something isn't working, the person reading it is going to stumble over your words. Listen attentively, not to admire your own work, but to be aware of the point where the tripping begins and ends. Afterward, ask your reader a couple of easy objective questions about plot and character. If he or she can't answer them satisfactorily, there's a good possibility the fault lies, not with her or him, but with your ability to make your work accessible.

If you're reading your work to someone, and that someone starts looking bored or (like the time I read several awful pages of an ultimately aborted chapter from an early novel to my wife) falls asleep, you've got yourself a problem with either audience or (more likely) author.

After you've gone back to the drawing board and tidied things once more, you're ready to bring your manuscript up for analysis in your writing community, however you've decided to define it. This is where you can begin to talk about the Big Stuff: your ultimate thematic intentions and world view. But it's also where you can once more get some incredibly helpful feedback on matters ranging from plot and character to punctuation and sentence rhythms.

A bit of advice is worth repeating: don't listen for praise, but for constructive criticism, the kind that you can take home and use to better your manuscript.

That's hard counsel to follow, obviously, since we all want our writing affirmed, and affirmed as quickly as possible after we've struggled weeks, months, or years with a manuscript. We all sooner or later want to hear we're the cat's pajamas, creatively speaking. Except listening for those words too early in the writing process (and your friends, lovers, fellow students, relatives and the rest will almost always be speedy with plaudits) will deafen you to the suggestions that will make you a better writer. Listening for those words too early will plant a sense of false security in you that over the years can grow into a willingness to be content with the average and unexceptional.

So whom should you listen to and how much advice should you take from them in the long run? A good rule of thumb is never buy into a single individual's comments. There are all sorts of reasons why she or he might be biased, unhelpfully abusive or complimentary, or just plain ignorantly wrong. People act, if nothing else, just like people. If you put your manuscript up in a workshop at this point, or maybe feel brave enough to mail it to a magazine, don't worry if it comes under heavy fire from a particular classmate or teacher or editor.

If, on the other hand, a number of people in that workshop start saying the same thing, or a number of editors start sending your piece back, or a number of teachers point to the same problem within several pieces you've done for them, well, then it's time at least to stop and ask yourself why. In the end, you may decide they've got it all botched up, but you may also decide they've got a point. Don't be too hasty in your evaluation of their evaluation. Sleep on it. Think about it for a few days. Give it some time to sink in and take effect. Listen for consensus, even if you in the final go-around don't decide to take that consensual recommendation. Hear before you understand, understand before you choose. Always try to be as open to criticism as you can, even if your reflexive response is the very human one of defensiveness. That criticism may, after all, be hogwash. But it may also be super sound advice you just never thought of before. You don't want to have your earplugs in when it arrives.

Over the years and the workshops and the editors and the writing buddies, you might even be lucky enough to find someone whose opinion you deeply value and who offers suggestions that resonate with something you already feel but somehow forgot to tell yourself about your manuscripts. That doesn't always happen in the course of a lifetime, and seldom in the odd writing group, but it frequently does happen eventually.

And then you've got yourself some gold.

Another caveat in the revision process: know when you're done with it. While there's little of more importance than patience when rewriting, there's nothing sadder than someone who just won't give up on a manuscript.

Sometimes you'll spend months on a piece only to discover it's never going to work the way you want it to. If that happens, simply recall that that sort of thing occurs to all writers, especially young ones, and that even though the manuscript may never match your expectations, the process of writing and rewriting certainly will teach you a world about fictionalizing.

And sometimes you'll find yourself tinkering and tinkering with a manuscript, unable to tell whether you're done or not. How can you know? Well, for one thing, if you haven't rewritten every one of your sentences at least once—if not five or six times—chances are you haven't revised enough. Concomitantly, if you find yourself making smaller and smaller alterations that change the quality of your manuscript less and less, it's probably time to stop. And when you read and reread a sentence or scene, and just don't have any sense of objectivity about it anymore, it's either time to cease and desist or put your manuscript back in that drawer for a little while longer.

In any case, while you're letting it rest, or while you're reworking it and showing it to your friends and reworking it some more, make it your business to start a new project. Don't feel you need to dock one before you set sail on another. Look for fresh ideas. Go somewhere you haven't gone before. Continue work in your journal. Begin outlining another story or novel. Dive into words. Put marks on the page. If you don't, you might start obsessing on your incomplete manuscript, even waiting for it to be accepted by your colleagues or friends or for publication before you press on, and that's simply counterproductive. Think how much time for developing and improving your craft you're going to lose if you do that. Think how many days, weeks, months, even years and decades you'll be sacrificing.

As an undergraduate I wrote a little unpublishable novella for my honors thesis. As a graduate student I wrote two full-fledged novels that never (thank goodness) saw print, though I used parts of all three in later works. John Gardner beat me several times over by writing seven books before his first was accepted.

Why?

Serious authors don't write to publish. They write to write. Take care of the words, and publication will someday (admittedly through some usually huge hard work on your part) take care of itself, and it will almost always take longer than you ever dreamed it would.

Most young writers think they'll send out a story on Tuesday, and the acceptance letter from *The New Yorker* will arrive in Thursday's mail. Once they find an agent, they think the only thing they'll have to worry about is what color yacht to buy on Friday. Actually, most published stories will circulate six, twelve, or even eighteen months before they find a hutch to call home, and landing an agent and thirty-five cents will allow you to make a phone call at most fast-food restaurants.

Meantime, keep growing.

Ask yourself every night: what have I done today that will make me a better writer tomorrow?

Have I taken chances? Have I pushed myself? Have I tried something new and worked on something old and refused to compromise my aesthetics and read another novel by someone I admire?

Frame your life so you can always answer yes, yes, yes.

Now Read This

Madden, David. *Revising Fiction: A Handbook for Fiction Writers* (1988).
   A strong guidebook to the art of revising.

Stretching & Flexing

1. Go back to one of the Stretching & Flexing exercises you decided to try your hand at, and revise it, keeping in mind the suggestions offered in this section.

2. Exchange manuscripts with another writer and read his or her manuscript with an eye toward revision. Pretend you're an editor. Go through it line by line offering suggestions at the sentence level. At the end, summarize your comments in a short paragraph by: a) citing two or three specifics that work very well; and b) citing two or three specifics that, if rethought, would make the manuscript significantly more successful.

Packing Heat

PREPPING YOUR MANUSCRIPT
AND FINDING A PUBLISHER

You've read deeply in your genre, kept your antennae tuned to the world around you, and thrown every sort of creative detritus into your garbage disposal imagination. You've psyched, you've brainstormed, you've got an idea that you think amounts to a solid narrative building, and you've broken figurative ground. You've played with form and point of view, experimenting with how best to tell your tale. You've taken chances. And you've filled out your piece with significant detail, resonant setting, interesting characters in conflict, and language that can knock you down with the cusp of a single chewed fingernail—all while avoiding that tricky trap of heavy muddle.

Finally, you've put your short story or novel on a high shelf and given it a long vacation, then drafted and redrafted it, making sure that every scene has been muscled up while every gram of narrative cellulite has been liposuctioned clear.

You've thought and rethought every sentence to the point where it hurts and you know that if you look at one again, even for a second, you might just go mad.

Plus you're feeling pretty darn happy with it all.

That means you're done, and *that* means it's time to start looking for a publisher if you feel you're ready.

Of course, you may not feel ready. You may feel proud of your labors to this point—and deservedly so—but also that your craft still needs several more years of development before it's fully seasoned and ready to go public.

Or you may simply be uninterested in publishing: the act of writing—of processing your emotions and your universe through a breathtaking aesthetic lens—may be more than sufficient.

You should never push here. Be honest with yourself about your motives and your level of accomplishment.

There's no sense sending out a piece that doesn't feel ready to you, since chances are it won't feel ready to any editor, either. And there's no sense going through the emotional tempest of the submission process if you're just not that interested in the idea.

On the other hand, if you *are* being honest with yourself, and you *do* feel like now's the time, whatever you do, don't stall. Don't hesitate. Don't toe the dirt. Go for it. You have nothing to lose, if you stop to think about it, except for the price of a couple of stamps and envelopes and the possibility of a little piece of paper called a rejection slip. Besides, as most professional writers who have struggled long and hard on a piece of fiction will tell you, there are few finer feelings in the cosmos than seeing your own work presented flawlessly between two gorgeous covers, your sentences marching down the page like a troop of literary soldiers on their way to your contributor's note.

"On the day the young writer corrects his first proof sheet," Baudelaire observed more than a hundred years ago, "he is as proud as a schoolboy who has just gotten his first dose of the pox."

So what do you do now?

How do you go about finding a publisher?

The answer's going to be slightly different for short stories than it is for novels, especially if you're contemplating teaming up with an agent.

Agents seldom handle short story collections, even more rarely individual short stories, unless your name is Stephen King, and they tend to conceptualize poetry as a financial accident waiting to happen.

If you have a novel manuscript, however, you should probably think seriously about whether an agent might be right for you. Agents basically are the ambassadors in the United Nations of publishing. Often based in New York, where most of the major publishing houses are located, agents have their feet in countless editorial doors. They spend decades developing working relationships with the key players at the key venues. Furthermore, they've become over the last ten or fifteen years the first line of defense for major publishers, providing a net to catch and throw back writers they feel aren't ready yet for a bite of the Big Apple. Ask many writers, particularly young ones, and you'll hear that landing an agent today is as difficult (if not more so) as landing a publisher was back in, oh, 1973.

Needless to say, then, there are many benefits to having one. Procure an agent, and you've already leapt the first hurdle on the often unpleasant race track called publishing. Find one who loves your work, and you have a fairly powerful advocate in major publishing circles. Agents know who's buying what kind of fiction where, and thus where best to try to place your novel. They also know the contractual ropes, and so can work on your behalf to secure the strongest deal possible. They know about things like royalties and movie rights, foreign rights and paperback rights, and can labor on your behalf to secure you a healthy economic apportionment, and one perhaps a smidgen higher than you might be able to secure on your own.

There are many potential problems with having an agent as well. Unless you write fiction that is potentially salable to major mainstream New York publishing houses, chances are you're out of luck before you even pass GO. Agents, when all is said and done, are business people first, lit lovers second. (The first thing my first agent said to me wasn't "I love your novel," or, "What a terrific piece of fiction," but "How do you see marketing it?" and "What's your target audience?") Most agents deal with young writers who by definition haven't had time to establish any sort of track record in a less-than-enthusiastic way, taking one on for a short time, sending out some perfunctory feelers, and losing interest within three or six months if no deal manifests. Most ask for about fifteen percent of the deal they cut, to be paid after the author's advance arrives, and many can assert more control over a writer's career than that writer is fully comfortable with.

Some less-than-reputable ones will ask for several hundred dollars to "edit" and "shop" your work, and pocket the money whether or not they make a sale. Never, ever deal with this sort. They're nothing more than a bunch of ugly bottom feeders who can do more damage than good, actually preventing a writer from obtaining success.

If, having weighed the pros and cons, you think an agent is for you, then your next step looks much like the one you'd take to secure a publisher for your novel. First, do your research. Most reputable agents belong to the Association of Authors' Representatives, a group which subscribes to a list of ethical guidelines. Look in most agents listings at the back of such publications as *Writer's Market*, and you'll discover that information quickly. Stick with the members of AAR.

Once you've located someone who looks good to you (and a lot of looking good has to do with a mixture of intuition on your part plus the nature of the other clients on the agent's list, which you should ask to see), you need to put a package together that contains a *cover letter* (more on this soon), a *synopsis* of your book, and a *partial*. Written in present tense, each turning point or crisis should get its own short paragraph in your synopsis, and the whole—seldom more than five or eight pages—should introduce your main characters and summarize your novel in straightforward, pared-down language, while very briefly placing it in the context of one or two novels like it to give the potential publisher a sense of what you're up to and how much you know about the market. Your *partial* consists of the first fifty pages or three chapters of your manuscript (whichever's shorter).

If the agent likes what he or she reads, he or she will ask for more. If he or she likes the aggregate, he or she will write you a letter that will serve as your contract, stating, in essence, that you've agreed to work together and, should that change, you both need to agree in writing that you're going to go your separate ways. If you have a strong publishing record, or if you appear fantastically promising, then an agent may submit your work simultaneously to a number of publishers. In all likelihood, however, if you're just starting out, your agent will send your manuscript to one publisher at a time, each of which will take two or three months to respond. In other words, publishers read agented material just slightly faster than they do agentless material, but they do read it with more interest than what they find in their *slush pile*—that dusty dark corner where unsolicited manuscripts build up. Novels in New York slush piles almost never find their way between two hard covers. If they do, it's news.

It's important to remember that just because you can't find an agent doesn't mean you won't be able to place your novel outside New York. I was lucky enough, after much blind groping, to secure an agent for my first publishable (and more conventional) novel. After nearly three years of hard work, that agent was lucky enough to place my novel with a New York publisher. But when I sent her the manuscript for my second and less-conventional novel, she tried the same publisher, who had *first-reading rights* (i.e., he was entitled by contract to have first dibs on whatever I produced next), and was told it was "too stylistically flashy and psychologically dark." My agent then dropped it and me like we were bombs covered in burning gasoline.

So I began to peddle the book myself while writing a third novel, which I finished in two years and which I also began peddling myself. The third novel found its home first with a wonderful small press (small presses are almost always more caring and concerned about their writers, ready to listen to them, take advice from them, and collaborate with them in the production of an aesthetic object, than New York houses, which tend to think of writers the same way Henry Ford did Model-T's), sold many more copies than my New York novel did, and ultimately became a finalist for the Philip K. Dick Award. A month later I had a contract for my second novel, which had yet to find shelter. Soon thereafter I completed my fourth novel, which ended up at the same small house that brought out my third.

It's a complicated scenario, but not in any way an unusual one. Many writers can and do find homes for their manuscripts after agents have given up hope on them, and many writers will work with agents for some parts of their careers and not work with them for others.

And, again, realize agents probably won't be very useful if you're looking to place a short story, especially an innovative or alternative one.

That calls for some arachnidan legwork of your own.

The first step is to go to the library and hunt down the latest edition of *The International Directory of Little Magazines and Small Presses*. There you will encounter a great resource that lists thousands of zines and journals alphabetically and by genre. Go to the genre section first, and work back from there. Each entry will give you the editor's name, address, and phone number, as well as the date the zine or journal was founded (usually the longer a zine or journal has been in business, the longer it will remain that way) and a quote by the editor about exactly what he or she is looking for, and, equally helpful, *not* looking for. Sometimes you will also be able to learn the names of several authors who have published there, which can give you a sense of whether your fiction will fit in or not. Too, you will discover the publication's circulation, cost of individual copies, length, format, payment method (normally one or two contributor's copies, sometimes a small sum up to $100, very seldom more), copyright information (most publications copyright for the author), and reporting time (customarily editors will tell you it'll take four to six weeks for them to make a decision on your manuscript, though the truth will be closer to four to six months).

Make sure you read all the fine print. Some places only read manuscripts at certain times of year, while others will let you know whether they accept simultaneous and/or electronic submissions.

Make sure, too, that you find an editor's name and then address your cover letter to him or her. This demonstrates you've done your homework.

When you've gotten a list of six or twelve possible venues, go to the library or write away to the publications themselves for sample copies. Look at the layout, check out several stories, get a feel for what the zine or journal is all about in terms of politics, aesthetic taste, and hard copy or electronic organization. There's no reason to send your work to a place that won't be interested in the sort of fiction you write. And don't think you'll be the one in a million to sway a particular editor to like a particular kind of fiction he or she has heretofore shown no love for.

Next you need to deal with the ethical dilemma of *simultaneous submissions*—i.e., sending out the same manuscript to many publishers at once. Obviously if an editor says in his or her entry in *The International Directory of Little Magazines and Small Presses* that he or she doesn't want them, don't send them, and if an editor says he or she will consider them, then do. More and more the latter is turning out to be the case.

But not infrequently editors are plain silent on the subject, and assume you won't submit simultaneously, or, if you do, that you'll let them know in your cover letter. Those who don't advocate simultaneous submissions argue that all they do is clog up multiple publishing pipelines, slow down an already long editorial process, and lead to embarrassing showdowns among editors or between editors and writers, if not even to blacklisting of those writers who get caught. Those who do advocate simultaneous submissions argue that the publishing pipelines are already clogged up, that it isn't fair to a writer to have to wait up to half a year per submission, that the statistical probability of two places accepting the same piece on the same day is almost zilch, and that editors don't remember writers' names long enough to create blacklists (think of how many submissions they receive every day, and multiply that by the years they've been in business), let alone hold grudges.

Either way you decide to play it, my simple advice here is to be up front about what you're doing. Always announce that you're simultaneously submitting, if you go that direction. If you happen to be lucky enough to have your simultaneously submitted piece accepted somewhere, immediately let the other zines and journals you've submitted that piece to know. Never simultaneously submit with the intent to play one zine or journal off another for the most money or highest profile.

Once you've narrowed down your search to a couple of possible venues, it's time to pack up your story or synopsis and partial and send it. Here cleanliness really *is* next to godliness. Editors despise sloppy presentations, which they rightly see as indicative of unprofessional behavior and even writerly disinterest, neither of which will ever endear you to them. Make sure you've run a spell check, make sure you print out your story or synopsis and partial neatly on fresh medium-weight paper using a letter-quality or laser printer, and make sure you use paper clips instead of staples for stories, nothing at all for novel manuscripts except the boxes you're shipping them in. Double-space, and use at least one-inch margins, preferably one-and-a-half. If you're sending a novel, use a title page which, in the center, includes the title of your book and your name, address, phone number, and e-mail. If you're sending a short story, you should forego the title page, but make sure that the title of your fiction and your name appear centered about a fourth of the way down the first page of your piece, and that your address, phone number, and e-mail appear in the upper right-hand or left-hand corner. You really don't need to indicate your story's word count, though a few writers do and a few editors prefer things that way, and you definitely shouldn't type in the copyright symbol or some phrase about copyright, both of which do little more than flag amateurism.

A *cover letter* should accompany your submission (and you should only submit one story or synopsis and partial per package), and it should be short, sweet, and to the point. It should include your name, address, phone number, and e-mail in standard letter format, and it should include at most three short paragraphs, none of which is more than three very short sentences long. The first should give the title of your story, its type in terms of genre, and a sense of its tone and plot while not giving away too much or sounding too Hollywood. The second paragraph should give the highlights of your publication record—that you've published stories here, here, and here, that you've won this or that award, that you have a novel appearing next year, perhaps that you attended such-and-such M.F.A. program. If you don't have a publication record, don't fake one; it simply doesn't

Q. What's the hardest part of editing a zine?

A. Responding to submissions is the most time consuming and taxing element of editing a zine but the hardest is trying to figure out exactly what you want your publication to be and to stick with it. Without direction and a sense of what you want to convey to your readers a zine loses its individuality and can get lost in a sea of generic genre publications.

Q. What can writers thinking of submitting to zines learn from that?

A. Do some research into the publications you want to send your work to. You don't necessarily have to buy sample copies, but writing for guidelines will always help and save time in the long run. Also, there are market news publications out there such as *Scavenger's Newsletter*, *Gila Queen's Guide to Markets* and *Heliocentric Network* that have oodles of guideline information.

Q. If you could offer young writers just thinking of sending out their first work to zines a few words of advice, what would they be?

A. Don't let a tidal wave of rejections bring you down. It's easy to get discouraged after receiving slip after slip of disappointing news. As long as you're writing true to yourself you'll get your message across and sooner or later it will resonate with an editor.

David Rogers publishes *Freezer Burn* and enjoys the Boston Bruins, playing bass guitar and watching Hawaii Five-0.

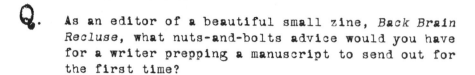

Chris Reed

Q. As an editor of a beautiful small zine, *Back Brain Recluse*, what nuts-and-bolts advice would you have for a writer prepping a manuscript to send out for the first time?

A. Before you submit your story to me, evaluate it as follows:
- Give 5 good reasons why I should buy this story for *BBR*.
- Now give another 5 reasons.

Then, if you're still convinced *BBR* is the best outlet for this story, go ahead and send it to me.

Q. What do you look for in a cover letter? What don't you look for?

A. It's nice to get a cover letter that says, "Hi—hope you like this story, look forward to hearing from you in due course." Anything more is a waste of time.

Q. What sucks in a cover letter?

A.
- Explaining your story.
- Praising my magazine but addressing me as "Dear Sir/Madam" or "Dear Editor"—if you're familiar with *BBR*, then you'll know my name.
- Sending your full list of credits—it's your story I'm buying, not your reputation.

Q. From your point of view, should a writer send out simultaneous submissions?

A. No. 😦

As well as producing Back Brain Recluse since 1984, Chris Reed runs BBR Distribution, a worldwide small press outlet that's ideal for writers researching new markets (www.syspace.co.uk/bbr/catalogue.html).

serve any purpose. In that case, admit you're just starting out, or drop the second paragraph altogether. The last paragraph should consist of a quick, pleasant, non-unctuous sign off. Never try to bully or convince an editor, and never rave about your story's worth. It should be able to do all the raving it needs to by itself.

If you're planning on sending a long partial or even full novel manuscript to an editor, it's always a good idea to send a *query letter* first. That letter should traverse much of the same ground as a cover letter, but should also dwell another paragraph or two on the subject and shape of your project. You might even want to enclose a synopsis with it. The letter, though, shouldn't be longer than a page, and, though it should be tight and energetic, it shouldn't be shrill, clever, or a deliberate jump-up-and-down attention-getting mechanism. If you have any important qualifications for writing about the subject you're writing about, make sure you mention them.

Whenever approaching an editor or publisher for the first time or during follow-ups, include a Self-Addressed Stamped Envelope, or *S.A.S.E.* Bring that and the one everything's going to go into to the post office. The people there will do the weighing and pricing. If you don't enclose an S.A.S.E., you'll probably never hear from an editor or publisher, nor see your manuscript, again.

For short stories, use a manila envelope the size of the manuscript. For novels, use a shipping box you can find at your local copy center or business supply store.

What I've just described is the conventional approach to publication. It represents the way things have been done for most of the twentieth century. With the advent of the World Wide Web, however, all that's changing, and changing in some pretty fascinating directions.

Remember that there are vast numbers of electronic zines and journals cropping up throughout the digital ether, all of which are looking for good material. A simple Web search will turn up thousands. You can design and construct your own Web site where you can make available your own fiction, or you can create your own cyberspatial zine or journal for much less than it would cost to do the same in the hard copy world. If you already edit a hard copy zine or journal, you can put up excerpts. Moreover, the Web offers an exciting zone in which to experiment with form and content. It lends itself to hypertext and mixed-media productions, and it still exists as a fairly uncensored and inexpensive option.

You should also be aware, though, of some real problems with publishing on the Web. Many people feel there's no such thing as real quality control in cyberspace. Anyone can publish there, they say, so it's extremely difficult to sort the aesthetic wheat from the banal chaff. Hence stories that appear on the Web are sometimes valued less than those which appear in hard copy format, or hard copy format first.

This strikes me as a fairly myopic bias. After all, hard copy publication certainly doesn't assure quality any more than electronic publication does, and a quick search of the Web will reveal that more and more serious writers—Richard Kadrey, Bruce Sterling, Kathy Acker, Shelley Jackson, and Brian Evenson among them—are allowing their work to find a virtual room there. As more people disregard the technophobic anti-Web hype in the world and take a surf for themselves, such a bias will gradually disappear.

A greater problem is the question of copyright. Once your work is up in cyberspace, anyone can download it, change your name to theirs, and upload it as their own or submit it to a hard copy zine or journal. The postmodern idea of appropriation is thus enacted in a very tangible form everyday. Currently there's no real way to stop appropriation, if stop it we should, let alone discover it.

And, publishing on the Web often means publishing without payment, much like publishing in many real-world small-press hard copy outlets.

It also means, though, unlimited freedom in terms of what you publish. And it mean tremendous public access. Publish a story in cyberspace, and your potential audience instantaneously increases from a few hundred to millions.

Plus all the middle-people—from agents to printers to bookstore owners—are eliminated. At least theoretically, then, you're dealing with a mode of creativity that travels directly from writer to reader. So even at its most expensive, the Web will reduce production costs drastically and, in some cases, do away with them altogether.

There are plenty of reasons to believe that the Web (or at least those corners still uncolonized by commerce) will continue to offer a larger and larger space for alternative fiction.

We're standing at a tremendously exciting cybercultural intersection.

The lights have changed.

It's time to cross over.

Now Read This

Editors of *Coda. Poets & Writers Newsletter. The Writing Business* (1985). About the practicalities of being a writer, with very good sections on "The Writer As Business Person" and "Adventures in Publishing."

Fulton, Len, editor. *The International Directory of Little Magazines and Small Presses.* (Updated yearly.) Correctly called the Bible of small-press publication, this lists thousands of alternative publishing possibilities.

Hewitt, John. *Writer's Resource Center.* Good guide to writers' organizations and more, plus a writer-friendly search engine: www.azstarnet.com/~poewar/writer/writer.html

Kuroff, Barbara, editor. *Novel and Short Story Writer's Market.* (Updated yearly.) A guide to some of the more commercial publication venues, as well as to writers' conferences and workshops, retreats and colonies, organizations and resources, and publications of interest to writers. For a list of agents, see *Writer's Market*, also published by Writer's Digest Books.

Literary Agents of North America. (Updated regularly.) A good place to start agent-searching. A companion to this book is the one published by Poets & Writers, Inc.: *Literary Agents: A Writer's Guide.*

Writer's Market. (Updated yearly.) A listing of some of the more commercial publishing venues and a strong agents listing.

Stretching & Flexing

1. Visit your campus or local library, and begin to acquaint yourself with both the above publishing references and several issues of some of the zines and journals that sound like they might offer you a berth for your story.

2. Run Web searches to discover electronic publication outlets, and begin to familiarize yourself with some of those that might look appetizing and their submission guidelines.

3. Follow the instructions outlined above, take a deep breath, and, if you feel ready, send out your first story, or synopsis and partial.

In Space No One Can Hear You Scream

COPING WITH REJECTION

Once you've put that manuscript in the snail mail or hit the SEND button on your e-mail program, forget about it instantly and get on with your writing life.

I'd be lying if I didn't say that's extremely tough advice to follow, but follow it you must. Obsessing over a manuscript that's been shot into the Great Beyond isn't going to bring an editor's decision any sooner.

Back when you were revising your piece, you should have begun a new story or novel. If you haven't, do so today. Right now. Put this guide down and do it.

Go on.

Set your mind on other creative endeavors.

It's easy investing a lot of emotional energy in a single story's or novel's fate. Finishing one and sending it out can feel like the most momentous event in your life. At the minute it enters the mails, though, you have to readjust your focus from the short to the long view: "This piece may have taken me a couple of weeks or a couple of years to write," you should admit to yourself, "but now it's done and gone and I can't do anything about it and it's time for me to get going with something else anyway, move in new directions, challenge myself more fully, give myself some reasons and methods to improve as a writer."

Once again return to your journal. Reread it for ideas and continue taking notes on your geographical and imaginative environments.

Brainstorm with friends.

Read an armful of excellent novels you've always meant to read but just never got around to.

Try some of the exercises suggested in this guide and see if they might spark a fresh thought, approach, or even subject for investigation.

Only whatever you do, don't hem and haw.

Do that, and you'll lose months of development as a writer. And what happens if you wait all those months and your story or novel isn't picked up in the end? You can spiral into a deep blue funk that can work some major hoodoo on you and your productivity, and there goes yet more time.

So pack up that manuscript, send it, and then ignore it.

That doesn't mean you should forget where it goes and when. Make sure to buy yourself a notebook and begin a *log* to keep track of your babies' sojourns. Each piece you send out should get its own page or three. At the top of the first, write the title of your story or novel. Under it, create four columns. In the first, record the name of the journal you're sending your fiction to. In the second, record the date your fiction enters the mails. In the third, record the date you hear about its fate. In the fourth, record what happened, its rejection or acceptance. Better, do all this in a simple database program or your word processor.

Early in your career, you'll swear on a stack of Shakespeares that you'll never need to keep a log because you'll always be able to remember where everything is and when you sent it.

Slowly, however, your memory will surprise you. Sometimes you'll feel like your piece went out yesterday only to discover it actually went out half a year ago, and sometimes you'll feel like your piece went out half a year ago only to discover it actually went out yesterday. You'll start wondering if you really sent it to X, or if you just *thought about* sending it to X, but in fact sent it to Y or Q or J.

Best, then, not to trust your fiction's fortune to faulty recall. Keep an eye on your pieces' progress. Establish a regimen in which you check up on every fiction's whereabouts every month or six weeks.

If you don't hear back from an editor within three months, feel free to send him or her a follow-up. Write a very brief, polite letter that: a) gives the title of your story or novel; b) the date you submitted it; and c) asks about its status. Enclose a self-addressed, stamped postcard to make it simple and free for the editor to jot you a reply.

You'll most likely receive a quick slightly guilty-sounding scrawl saying the editor is very busy and will get to your piece just as soon as possible. You may hear nothing at all. In either case, wait another month, then follow up with a phone call or another letter.

The worn adage is that no news is good news. In my experience, no news just means no news. Sometimes it can mean a sloppy editor and a lost story, or a zine or journal that's abruptly gone belly up, or even a gruesome postal mishap.

After six months, write another letter stating that you assume the editor's no longer interested in your work and that you're withdrawing it from his or her consideration. Don't expect to see your manuscript again (one of the many reasons you should always keep several backups)—that editor's a lost cause.

And that's perfectly okay.

You really don't want to work with someone who can't get around to reading and deciding on your manuscript within half a year. Even if he or she then *did* finally accept it, what does that initial delay tell you about how long you'll wait to see it in print (a process which in the best circumstances can take anywhere from an additional three or four months to one or two years, and sometimes, I'm here to tell you, nearly half a decade) and about how disorganized the editor you're dealing with honestly is? So move on to another (there are thousands and thousands to pick from out there) and see if you don't have better luck.

Remember, too, that your manuscript will probably be rejected the first ten or twelve times it's sent out.

That's just the law of the literary jungle.

It usually says less about your story's or novel's quality than it does about the fact that millions of people across the country are writing and submitting their work to thousands of zines and journals, most of which appear once or twice a year, and have only three or five slots open for stories each issue, and to the major New York publishing houses, which accept less than one percent of what's submitted to them.

So merely on a statistical basis, it's going to take some time to find the right match between your piece, an editor who loves it, and a zine or journal that has enough space to publish it.

Still, rejection *might* say something about your fiction's quality, so make sure you listen if an editor takes the time and effort to write you a line about it. That'll be an extraordinary occurrence if he or she does, something to treasure and ponder.

Usually, though, you'll be greeted upon opening your S.A.S.E.

with a small slip of evilly bland paper with a form rejection printed on it that will make you feel your manuscript was never handled by a real live human being.

Often those things aren't even signed.

Don't feel bad. Or at least don't feel alone. It's happening to hundreds of thousands of other people this very second.

Rejection is one of the things that defines a professional writer's life—and separates that life from the ones lived by most of her or his friends and acquaintances. You know more of what you generate will be rejected than accepted. And you know this in advance. You know you're going to take critical hit after critical hit—willingly, no less—frequently from people whose opinions you don't especially admire or respect, and frequently in a manner that will have more to do with economic and space considerations than with your fiction's quality—whatever you finally mean when you say that word. And you know it's going to hurt something fierce.

Yet you also know you're going to keep coming back for more.

How bizarre.

The best way to confront that juggernaut called rejection is head on. When I started receiving my first rejection slips, I wallpapered my refrigerator with them. When the fridge was full, I moved to the bathroom: walls, ceiling, you name it.

Sometimes I got mad, sometimes sad, but more often than not I just got more determined.

After a few years, they started sliding off me like water off an oil-slicked duck's back. My psychic calluses grew into some pretty gnarly looking ornaments. And I found that one acceptance could gird me for twenty of those squares of paper untouched by human hands.

I promised myself that I'd act like a professional since I decided I wanted to be one, and that meant I vowed not to take my frustration out on editors, my family, or my friends.

Rejection, I told myself, was my business, and my business alone, and so I'd just have to learn to deal with it.

I sat down and figured my odds in this crazy game and soon got used to the idea that they weren't especially good.

Don't get me wrong.

I wasn't an angel about it.

I pouted. I raged. I sometimes tore things up.

But I didn't target my sense of personal failure or anger toward other people, and, more to the point, I always pushed on, and pushed on immediately. If, after a dozen rejections, I still had faith in my

Tim W. Brown

Q. It takes some time for a young writer to realize that, at least during the early stages of his or her career, more pieces will be rejected than accepted. What sort of advice should a writer heed to deal with this notion of rejection?

A. There's nothing final about rejection; there are always more outlets to which you can submit. If you receive a rejection in the mail, take a moment and curse the editor, curse all the uncomprehending philistines in the world, curse God, then move on to the next publication that might be interested in what you have to say. Keep the faith, baby, is my best advice.

Tim W. Brown is author of Deconstruction Acres and editor of Tomorrow Magazine.

Janice Eidus

Q. It takes some time for a young writer to realize that, at least during the early stages of his or her career, more pieces will be rejected than accepted. What sort of advice should a writer heed to deal with this notion?

A. Writers—and others in the arts—must learn to develop thick skins because rejection letters come readily and rapidly to most beginners. Still, when you really believe that your story is "finished," that it is as nearly "perfect" as it can be, then you must also find a way to believe that it will eventually find its true home, no matter how many rejections come first. Writing and sending out work for publication both require that you make what is essentially an existential leap of faith. And that faith in yourself and your worth as a writer deserving to be heard are crucial. Perseverence is key: continue to send your work out—again and again and again.

Janice Eidus, novelist, short story writer, and editor, lives in New York City.

piece of fiction, I revised it. If I thought the problem lay with the editorial rather than authorial eye, I packed that puppy up and sent it out a thirteenth time in the next day's mail.

A twenty-four-hour turn-around: this was my guideline, and remains so even now.

Flannery O'Connor used to make a hierarchical list of venues she wanted her fiction to appear in. She'd start by sending her story to her number one choice. If it was rejected, she'd send it to number two, and so on until it finally came to rest, sometimes after a dozen tries.

I've known a lot of good writers who never took that quantum leap into publication because they lacked the tenacity to do so, and I've known some at-best-mediocre writers who got a lot farther than many thought they had any right to simply because they wouldn't give up. They wouldn't take no for an answer. They learned that writing was all about rejection, and rejection was all about learning how to overcome rejection.

Weirdly, almost as wrenching as rejection is acceptance. For starters, you're never ready for it. For another, after all the hardships of rejection, you simply might not feel worthy when that real letter arrives. You might, along with Groucho Marx, believe you don't want to be a part of any club that would take you as a member. Plus, of course, there's that huge swath of time you still have to wait from acceptance to publication, and that can drive any sane author right over the brink.

Then there's the give-and-take dance you have to endure as your editor asks for a change here, a change there, some of which are wonderful and strengthen your story or novel in ways you've never imagined, and some of which are the dumbest things you've ever heard a guy with opposable thumbs utter. If you can't get around these latter, just remember: never sacrifice your vision, but never shoot yourself in the aesthetic foot, either. Think long and hard about an editor's suggestions, and be prepared to counterattack with careful arguments. If that doesn't work, be prepared to withdraw your fiction. If one editor came that close to publishing it, another will eventually go for the gold as well. Publication is nothing if not about learning how to wait with patience and aplomb, how to be still.

After publication of a novel or short story collection, there's yet another kind of rejection you'll have to deal with: negative and/or plain ignorant reviews. To avoid this problem altogether, many writers refuse to read the things. Period. But I do. I read every one. I search them out. I ask my friends and editors to do the same. "What in the world for?" you ask. Well, I believe writing isn't a self-absorbed monologue, but part of a larger conversation across time and space, and I'm always eager to suss out how people have responded to what I've had to say, not to mention flattered that they've had anything to say at all. That leads to loads of frustration when I feel someone's missing my point, isn't even living in the same existential solar system I am, or when I see gobs of factual errors throughout a piece that indicate the less-than-ethical reviewer didn't even take the care to read my book, though I spent weeks, months, or years laboring over it, or when I realize someone's being malicious just to hear his or her own shrill voice approximate wittiness.

But those sorts of reviews and reviewers are few and fairly far between. I can count the negative ones I've bumped into during my career on one hand, and I don't think that's especially uncommon. When I come across the occasional truly insightful, thoughtful review that understands what I'm doing and why, can both place it in the larger literary conversation and pinpoint specifics about my text and how it extends or challenges or meditates upon that conversation, not to mention sometimes even giving me a few pointers to think about the next time I sit down to write—that's the definition of the good life for me: that's the movement from finger exercise to symphony.

For a person with writing in her or his blood, there are only two sure-fire antidotes to rejection in whatever form it shows up at your door or in your e-mail inbox. The first is to start your own zine or journal or publishing company, knowing you can do a better job with a better eye to aesthetics than those schlumps who just turned you down.

The other is to write.

If that story or novel of yours comes back for the twelfth or twentieth or two hundredth time, and you're starting to get the feeling all those editors out there might just be trying to tell you something, do this: commence another story or novel.

Never stop.

Never slow down.

If you fill up your bathroom with rejection slips, just remember: there's always the hall.

Q. Do you simultaneously submit your work to multiple zines or publishers? Why or why not?

A. Publishers are like policemen. They keep a record of your calls and can ignore you for a decade if you fail to deal with them fairly. Play nice with presses if you expect to publish in their precinct.

My short story, "Knives for a Narcoleptic," appeared simultaneously in both *Funeral Party 2* and my collection, *Distorture*. But that was because *FC2* was published a year behind schedule and the editor knew *Distorture*'s publication date before accepting the story. Another piece, "Exterminating the Angels," appeared simultaneously in a few magazines and one anthology—but that was because each editor gave me permission to publish the story anywhere else I liked.

Don't expect mainstream houses to be as flexible as smaller presses.

Q. It takes some time for a young writer to realize that, at least during the early stages of his or her career, more pieces will be rejected than accepted. What sort of advice should a writer heed to deal with this notion of rejection?

A. Pound said, "Seek always to stand in that hard, Sophoclean light and take your wounds from it gladly." On the other hand, a famous eighties pomo author, whom we shall call Mithtreth Eth, once said to me, "All editors are idiots."

(But consider the following circumstances: After one letter of rejection, Mithtreth Eth found crossover acceptance, while Pound had to wait for decades before finding *academic* acceptance. I leave it to you to decide whose writing will survive the longest, Pound's or Eth's. Today, imaginative novels by writers like Colin Raff and Julia Solis await publication, while commercial houses spew the disposable rants of spoken word hacks, and publicists pitch the memoirs of new age narcissists like Sapphire—who seem content to vomit undigested autobiography.)

Submit your manuscripts *reflexively* and don't worry about acceptance. Submit only your best work for publication; be aware of its failings and merits. Think only of your responsibility to your own writing—of your need to improve, to understand copyediting, fact-checking, and all of the clarifying failsafes that go into making a lasting work of fiction.

Q. Your wild collection of stories, *Distorture*, received all manner of critical praise, but how did you deal with the published form of rejection: bad and/or ignorant reviews?

A. Successful or unsuccessful, my published friends all say the same thing: Reviewers just don't get it. Bad and uncomprehending reviews are to be expected, but even good and indifferent reviews are generally misinformed.

Since writing is a solitary occupation, literary excellence demands some measure of self-certainty and self-reliance. To know you've accomplished what you intended—and to be certain of this without resorting to self-justification—is to receive the best possible review. Your book must be submitted to reviewers not because you need their approval, but because reviews are part of the business of publishing. A bad review is far better than no review at all, but good work will outlive the myopia of illiterate critics.

Rob Hardin, short story writer and musician, lives in New York City.

Stretching & Flexing

1. Buy a notebook and start a log of where you're sending your manuscripts. As I mentioned above, each should have a page or three dedicated to it, and each page should have the manuscript's title at the top and be divided into four columns that catalog: a) where the piece was sent; b) when it was sent; c) when it was returned; d) whether it was rejected or accepted.

2. Like Flannery O'Connor, develop a working list of venues in which you want to see your manuscripts published. At the top of the list should appear your dream sites. In the middle should appear those places you think you have a fairly good shot at. At the bottom should appear four or five safeties. All told, there should be in the neighborhood of twenty or twenty-five venues which you can tick down.

3. This is an easy one: if you've just had a manuscript rejected, yet still have faith in it, get it in an envelope with S.A.S.E. and new cover letter, and shoot it out in tomorrow's mail. Don't forget: a twenty-four-hour turn-around, max.

26 Contract Rights and Wrongs

Acceptance should be cause for a major festival in your honor. It will almost always come as a surprise, and for some writers it will come as a surreal anticlimax. They've just put too much work into their manuscripts and struggled too long against rejection to take any honest delight when that acceptance letter finally appears in the S.A.S.E. They feel jaded, burned out, cynical about the process they've gotten themselves mired in. They don't have enough self-confidence to take a moment to celebrate their success, or they expect more to happen to them upon acceptance than actually does. They want fireworks and civic celebrations.

What they'll probably get is a "That's really nice. So what do you want for lunch?" from their partner, friend, or colleague.

Don't be one of those blue souls. By the time your first acceptance arrives, you'll have worked mind- and soul-numbingly long to be a writer. Don't allow yourself to shrug off this amazing day.

Take yourself out for your favorite meal. Eat lots of pepperoni pizza. Jump up and down on your bed. Have a party for your buddies. Take some time to think about just how spectacular this moment really is. Talk about it. Share it with others.

And then, with every subsequent acceptance, throw a similar bash for yourself.

Acceptances don't come every day, or even every month. They may not even come every year. So learn how to savor them when they do arrive. Learn how to take as much pleasure in an acceptance as you do frustration in a rejection.

Enjoy reading and rereading your acceptance letter, enjoy cashing your check if there is one, and enjoy perusing your contract as if it were the most captivating novel you've ever picked up because it spells out a tremendously significant sentence: "You're a professional author now."

Contracts for short stories and contracts for novels will vary greatly in scope and what's at stake economically, so it's a good idea to familiarize yourself with each for a minute or two before one arrives. Be aware from the start that as a beginning writer without a track record you'll have very little if any room for negotiation. Writing stories or novels isn't the same thing as writing screenplays. Usually you can expect that these contracts are pro-forma forms, more a matter of publishing reflex than chance to increase your income or creative control over your work. That may change over time, as your track record strengthens, but it's a good bet it won't. Editors and publishers struggle within horrific fiscal constraints, and, unless your name is Don DeLillo, Toni Morrison, or, better, the latest sitcom or sports personality, they probably have a lot less wiggle room than you think.

For short stories, the acceptance letter often serves as the only contract you'll see—especially if you're dealing with a zine or small journal. Sometimes, however, it will be accompanied by a more formal agreement. Either way, you can expect a very straightforward statement from the editor outlining the terms for the publication of your manuscript. Those terms will articulate how many contributor's copies of the issue in which your piece appears you'll receive (usually one to five), how much you'll be paid (anything from nothing to a couple of hundred dollars—a sum, in any case, that almost certainly won't be negotiable), when your piece will appear (things regularly turn pretty vague here, but the custom is three months to a year after acceptance, along with a clause that you can withdraw your work from the publisher and send it elsewhere if it hasn't appeared within that time), and what sort of rights you and your editor will get (more times than not the editor will purchase one-time rights and then, upon publication, all rights will revert back to you).

The editor will sometimes ask you to grant him or her what are called *First North American Serial Rights*. This simply means that he or she is asking for the right to publish material in his or her zine or journal before it appears in book form in the United States or Canada, and that's a perfectly fair request.

Part of the agreement will also quite possibly ask you to affirm that you're indeed the author of the manuscript under contract and that the manuscript hasn't been published somewhere else before. Again, no sweat.

Things get more complicated with a contract for a novel. While much of the above will apply, there are a number of new areas you need to be thinking about here, and sometimes you're in no mood to do very much of that cerebral stuff at all. You've spent years writing your manuscript. You've probably already sent it out five or ten or fifty times before it's been accepted. All you want to do now is see the darn thing in print. And so you're feeling pretty much like you're ready to sign anything.

At this point, you should realize once more how little bargaining power you really have, but that should be no reason to avoid understanding your contract, asking any questions you might have about it, and at least making a stab at some changes that might benefit you—within reason.

So tell your editor or publisher you'd like a few days to think things over.

Take some time to let all this new information sink in.

And, whatever else you do, make sure to act politely and professionally every second you're in your editor's or publisher's presence.

The sad fact is that editors and publishers are keenly aware that only about one out of ten books they'll produce and launch will ever recover the cost of producing and launching it, a cost of somewhere between $2,000 and $15,000. From their point of view, in other words, there's a good chance they're entering a losing proposition by bringing out your book. Consequently, no matter how much they might value your work on aesthetic grounds, they're going to be less than rabidly itching to invest a bunch of money in it.

They're just not in a position to do a whole lot of compromising, particularly because they know that if they lose you, there'll be a hundred other really good authors right behind you waiting to fill your publishing shoes.

If that weren't bad enough, it's also true that there's only one thing harder than publishing your first novel, and that's publishing your second. This is because first novels tend to do poorly. Publishers don't expect them to win back the cost of production, so they don't put much money into them. Since publishers don't put much money in them, word about them doesn't get out—few reviews appear. Since few reviews appear, few bookstores even know of the novels' existence. Since few bookstores know of their existence, bookstores don't stock them. Since few bookstores stock them, few bookstores talk them up. Since few bookstores talk them up, few readers buy them. Since few readers buy them, first novels tend to do poorly, and hence a self-fulfilling prophecy writ alarmingly large.

Because first novels tend to do poorly, when you present your second novel to an editor, and that editor checks your track record, well, you can figure out the rest.

Small presses tend to be much more accommodating about contractual matters than the large ones, but, ironically, they have many fewer resources at their disposal, so their forms of accommodation will have less to do with money than with other concerns like cover design and execution, layout, post-publication readings, and various low-cost PR.

Here are some topics you should expect to see covered in your contract:

Advance. Your advance is how much your publisher pays you prior to the publication of your novel. This amount is then deducted from future royalties. Sometimes a publisher will pay half the advance on acceptance, and half on receipt of the final manuscript or publication. You need to remember that advances are always smaller than what you hear John Grisham makes. The usual one runs from absolutely nothing to almost nothing at small alternative presses to somewhere in the neighborhood of $6,000 at New York publishers.

Royalty Rates. Your royalties are the percentage of the retail price paid to you for each copy of your novel that sells. Usually this will run 10% of the list price for the first 5,000 copies, 12.5% for the next 5,000, and 15% after that. It's rare that these amounts are negotiable. At the same time, make sure your publisher isn't paying you less than this, at least for the hardcover edition—if there is one. The paperback deal, on the other hand, may be for as little as 6% to 7% of the list price for the first 15,000 to 20,000 sold.

Delivery of Manuscript. Your editor will want your completed manuscript delivered by a specific date and will write that date into the contract. Many authors underestimate how long it will actually take them to complete and/or revise a manuscript, so give yourself plenty of time, and talk to your editor if the date he or she sets doesn't seem realistic.

Acceptable Manuscript. Search for a clause that tells you that your editor has the right to reject your manuscript if you don't revise it to his or her satisfaction. If you find it, make sure to get your editor to clarify what "acceptable" means, and exactly what changes he or she expects *before you sign*.

Editing Control. It's not uncommon to find a clause that states that the editor has the right to edit or alter your novel. Make sure that those words are defined to mean "copyediting"—i.e., that the editor can't materially change the meaning or materially alter the text without your advance approval.

Duty to Publish. There should be a clause stating within how long after acceptance your novel will be published (usually six months to two years), and what will happen if your publisher doesn't meet that deadline (usually the author can terminate the contract 90 days after giving written notice).

Grant of Rights. Your publisher will want exclusive rights to publish, distribute, and sell your novel in North America for a certain number of years (often five) after the date the contract is signed.

Subsidiary Rights. This means all rights besides the initial book publishing rights, including radio, TV, film, dramatic, electronic, foreign, translation, and first serial (i.e., publication of an excerpt in a zine or journal prior to actual novel publication). Unlike most of the other areas of a contract, this is traditionally negotiable terrain. Many contracts automatically divide things in this category 50/50, but you can and should argue for something closer to 75% to 90% for yourself.

Copyright. Copyright, the legal right to exclusive publication, sale, or distribution of a literary work, should always be registered by the publisher in your name. That way sole control of your novel will revert to you after your publisher allows it to go out of print.

Accountings. There should be a clause that explains how often and in what manner your publisher will report to you on sales. Traditionally, publishers are notoriously remiss here. Keep a careful eye on what's written, and make a point to follow up periodically. You might attempt to have a "Right of Inspection" clause written into your contract that will enable you, upon giving written notice, to inspect the publishers' appropriate financial records to verify the accountings.

Payments. Again, make sure you're clear on when and how payment of royalties will be delivered after publication.

Free Copies and Discounts. You should try to get as many free copies of your novel as you can. Asking for a hundred isn't unreasonable. These will help you promote your own work. Try, as well, to finagle it so you can purchase additional copies at a large discount from the retail price. 40% to 50% is standard, and 55% isn't unheard of.

Warranty and Indemnity. This is an uncomfortable clause to deal with, since in essence it defends publishers at your expense against any suits based on libel, obscenity, or plagiarism associated with your novel. Plainly put, if you get sued, your publisher will drop you as fast as a leper's hand.

Termination Clause. This clause gives you the right to retrieve all rights from your publisher should your publisher allow your novel to go out of print. Make sure it's in the contract, and make sure it delineates exactly what constitutes "out of print," and the mechanism by which you can retrieve the rights. Usually, the latter will consist of you writing a letter to your publisher to that effect within a certain number of months (regularly six or twelve) after your novel has been allowed to go out of print.

Option Clause. This gives the publisher the option to read your next book before any other publishers do. Ask the publisher to agree to extend the option only to the next book *in the same genre based on a synopsis and partial*, and to stipulate how long the publisher's reading process will take (sixty days is more than fair).

In addition to the above clauses, it's a good idea to try to have one inserted that explains precisely what the publisher plans to do by way of promoting your novel after publication, though it's frequently difficult to pin a publisher down on this point.

You might also ask about what sort of input you're going to have with respect to your novel's cover art, design, and layout, and when you can expect to see the *proofs* (a typeset version of your manuscript used for correcting errors and making changes) and/or *galleys* (the first typeset version of a manuscript that has not yet been divided into pages), since your editor will expect a rapid turn-around on your part, and, if you know the dates in advance, you can set some time aside for reading and copyediting.

A last point: it's absolutely true that the rigid obfuscated language of contracts can bring tears to any good writer's eyes, but that shouldn't provide you with an excuse not to read them.

Read contracts with care and read them multiple times till they yield up their meaning.

After all, it's your publishing life we're talking about here.

Now Read This

Editors of *Coda: Poets & Writers Newsletter. The Writing Business* (1985).
> Two excellent short sections on contracts which can be supplemented by consulting Tad Crawford's *The Writer's Legal Guide* and Richard Curtis's *How to be Your Own Literary Agent.*

27 Read in the Face

KEEPING ABREAST OF WRITING AND PUBLISHING TRENDS

No one writes in a vacuum.

Rather, as I've emphasized several times already, you write as part of a larger conversation that extends across time and space.

You're attending a literary party, whether you know it or not. And it's to your benefit to understand what the conversation's about, who the people you're talking to are, who's just entered and who's just left the building, and how and why that conversation's always changing, and always changing in richly interesting ways.

It's essential to know what's going on in the contemporary writing and publishing scene, alternative and otherwise.

If you don't, you skirt the precipice of fudging at countless levels, from inadvertently reinventing an anti-narratological wheel that's been around for centuries to sending off your manuscript to a dead editor at a defunct press.

As an intelligent and committed writer, you should be able to answer these questions: What are the current literary trends? How are they developing and why? How does your work position itself with respect to them? What forces are shaping the publishing industry and how, if at all, does that affect what you're composing? Which publishers are publishing what? What new alternative presses or journals or zines have recently entered the field of play? Which have recently folded? Why? What can that tell you concerning your own ideas about starting a press or journal or zine? What can you learn from their successes or failures? What new writers—both mainstream and alternative—are worth taking a look at? Which might help you to continue formulating your own aesthetic or give you hints about shape, theme, character, or language in your own work? What are other writers talking about in interviews, writing about in their short fictions and novels? What are they reading? Which books published in the last six months are worth perusing? The last six years? The last sixty years? The last six hundred? What will the next publishing season look like? How about the one after that? Which zines and journals are worth keeping up with? What's the current state of electronic publishing in general? Internet publishing in particular? How will this effect what you write and how you write over the next five years? Ten? Twenty?

At first these questions probably seem mind-wearyingly difficult to answer.

As the Red Queen said to Alice: "Now *here*, you see, it takes all the running *you* can do, to keep in the same place. If you want to get somewhere else, you need to run at least twice as fast as that!"

But if you begin to drop by the campus or local library once a month for an afternoon or evening, and thumb through some of the following periodicals (and perhaps even think about subscribing to the one or two you find most helpful), you'll discover in six months you'll have begun to get a leg up on the situation.

And that situation will become increasingly captivating to you. The more you know, the more you'll want to know.

Within a year or two, you'll be an old hand at this stuff.

Alt-X. One of the premier Web sites (www.altx.com) for alternative fiction, *Alt-X* is loaded with interviews with some of the most important edge-authors, rants by them, and reviews of their work, and it's all updated about once a month. Although every year the site goes a little more openly commercial, and although it can sometimes have a fairly cliquish quality to it, *Alt-X* still has some heat left, especially in the archives.

American Book Review. A great gauge of what's happening in alternative publishing, this good-looking literary tabloid runs many book reviews and essays on various trends. Each issue also has a special focus: the Avant-Pop, gay and lesbian fiction, British fiction, and so on. Because it only appears six times a year, however, there are some pretty extensive gaps in its coverage.

AWP Chronicle. For a look at what's going on in terms of teaching writing (including listings of M.F.A. programs), and for a sense of what the issues are with respect to creative writing and academia (almost always fairly conservative and 10 or 15 years behind what the issues are in the alternative publishing world), check out this tabloidal magazine, put out six times a year by the Associated Writing Programs. At the back you'll find a call for manuscripts.

Bloomsbury Review. Eclectic and engaging, this tabloid is filled with intelligent reviews, interviews, articles, and special focuses about fiction, poetry, and nonfiction just at the edges of the mainstream, from the alternative writing scene in London to the literature of science and technology. It's published six times a year.

Factsheet Five. Trucks-full of reviews of alternative zines, books, movies, albums, and much, much more. With a good free Web presence at: www.well.com/conf/f5/f5index2.html. This one's an honest-to-goodness pioneer. Published irregularly.

Locus. Here's where to go for monthly news about science fiction, fantasy, and horror: book reviews, interviews, columns, and sometimes market listings. Excellent Web presence at: www.netwiz.net/~locus.

New York Review of Science Fiction. As *Library Journal* says: "A literate review of the SF field, with a good mix of critical reviews, commentary, and the articles are long, discerning, and written by well-known figures in the field." Published monthly. Presence on the Web at: ebbs.english.vt.edu/olp/nyrsf/nyrsf.html.

New York Times Book Review. Frustratingly conservative, usually poorly informed, and often patently snobbish in its literary tastes (not to mention increasingly inclined to run fewer and fewer fiction reviews), this weekly tabloid is nonetheless an excellent guide to what's what in a very small coat closet of mainstream New York publishing—which most Americans think is the whole hotel.

Poets & Writers. Mainstream literary, this cheaply produced magazine is published six times a year and runs interviews with major and not-so-major writers, as well as a host of practical articles on everything from coping with rejection to applying to writing colonies. At the back of each issue there are helpful sections on deadlines for grants and awards and a call for manuscripts for zines and journals.

Publishers Weekly. A once-a-week must for all writers. Not only does it allow you to keep up with publishing trends in and out of New York, the launch of new presses and moves of old editors, but it also provides a host of book reviews in various genres weeks—and sometimes months—before those books actually appear in bookstores. Web presence at: www.bookwire.com/pw/pw.html.

Review of Contemporary Fiction. In addition to focusing on two alternative authors each issue, providing essays on them, interviews with them, and fiction samples by them, this sharp-looking journal also runs many reviews on alternative novels, short story collections, and the occasional academic study that might otherwise be overlooked by larger review venues. *RCF* appears three times a year and is always an education.

Scavenger's Newsletter. If you're interested in alternative science fiction, fantasy, horror, or mystery, this xeroxed and stapled review and continual update of current zine outlets will be your cup of poison.

Science Fiction Chronicle. Monthly news magazine with tons of reviews of science fiction, fantasy, and horror novels, collections, and anthologies—and a market list for fiction.

Science Fiction Eye. Although it appears erratically, this one's a really intelligent gem. The name, however, is misleading. It's less about science fiction than strange slipstream fiction, music, and more, and it's packed with reviews, essays, and columns by some of the most provocative minds on the contemporary scene.

28 Rebel Sell

A QUICK GUIDE TO SELF-PROMOTION

Once an editor has accepted your novel, collection of fiction, or even single short story, and you've finally signed that diamond-spangled contract, it's time to prepare yourself for a long, winding, pot-holed wait.

It can take anywhere from a few months to a few years for your fiction to appear in print.

Along the road, you'll probably receive a set of proofs to copyedit (as a rule, though, you'll be allowed to make exceedingly few substantive changes by this point), and sometimes in the case of a novel or collection of fiction an editor will ask you for your input about obtaining blurbs, sending off review copies, setting up public readings, and generally getting the word out about what's coming.

If you're dealing with a large press, you might even be turned over to the PR people.

But don't bet on it.

Unless that press has a small Alps of financial resources and perceives you as a hot up-and-coming item, it'll invest very little money toward publicizing your work—a few hundred dollars, tops.

More likely, it'll send out a small number of review copies and keep its fingers crossed that a buzz will rev up in the bookselling community. Given the fact that few review organs handle first novels or story collections, of course, there's a good chance a buzz *won't* rev up in the publishing community, and, three months or half a year after your book has arrived in the world, you'll look around and realize the universe has become silence and void.

If you're dealing with a small press, that will invariably be the way things happen because alternative fiction almost never sells as well as mainstream fiction, and because small presses have so many fewer resources at their disposal than large ones—unless you decide things will be different with *your* book.

Unless, that is, you make the effort to take control of your project's future.

Your work as a professional writer is far from over, in other words, if you want to see your fiction have a chance at being read after it appears.

A truism to live by: if you don't care about your novel or short story collection once it's published, your novel or short story collection won't care about you—and no one else will care, either.

It's up to *you* to let the world know it exists.

As unpleasant and self-serving an endeavor as that might seem, it's simply a fundamental law in the world of publishing. By the time your fiction sees print, your editor will have moved on to other ventures. Your press's focus will have splintered in a million new directions. And yet the country's review apparatus will hardly have heard the needle of your novel or collection drop in the haystack of print.

So it's helpful at this juncture to recollect Truman Capote's dictum: "A boy has to peddle his book."

Plain, to the point, and accurate.

For people to enjoy your work, or hate it, or at least think about which they'd rather do, they first need to know it exists. If you don't make it your business to clue them in, they'll happily remain ignorant.

Remember: no one has the same deep vested interest in seeing your book flourish as you.

So it's time to turn your attention to that part of the writing career that many authors cringe from, and cringe from with good reason: promotion.

It smacks of unmediated ego. It smacks of unctuousness and hucksterism. It smacks of pure bad taste. It smacks of all the things in the cosmos that writers recoil from.

Without it, however, your book doesn't have a chance.

So grit your metaphorical teeth, strap on your seat belt, and try to find the sport in this mess, the part of the process that starts feeling like something resembling a good time.

Take it as a challenge.

Have fun with the run.

To begin, you need to embrace three key notions. First comes DIYSOP, or Do-It-Yourself Standard Operating Procedure. Assume that no one's as interested in seeing your book succeed as you, that virtually no one else will help you or fight as hard on your book's behalf as you, and that to accomplish anything at all you'll need to be the motivated captain of a motivated team of one: yourself. At best, you may be pleasantly surprised—your friends and/or editor may rally around you and chip in. But they'll do so only at your prompting—if they'll do so at all.

Second, you need to embrace the notion of a GE, or Grassroots Effort. Start locally and establish your neighborhood-, town- or city-wide base of operations, then move out regionally, and finally turn your attention to the nation at large. If you attempt doing things backwards, working from the top down, you'll discover that, since no one's heard of you or your book in that wide crowded terminal, no one will be very piqued to hear about it. If, however, you move into the regional realm with some strong local reviews under your arm ("Hometown boy or girl does good!"), and the national scene with some strong regional ones ("Here's someone to pay attention to!"), people will be more likely to sit up and take notice of you and your work.

Third, you need to embrace the notion of a DETE, or Do Everything Twice Ethic. Be efficient. Follow up on every query. Check to see if so-and-so got the review copy you mailed last week. Otherwise, sad but true, things just won't get done. People just won't notice.

DIYSOP.

GE.

DETE.

And boundless energy.

Never forget about the boundless energy.

Here are some things you can and should think about to start the promotional brushfire:

Blurbs. Those bits of usually overblown sound-bite praise on the cover of books, blurbs are designed to get your novel or short story collection reviewed and read. Usually they're the job of your editor to secure: he or she will send out galleys to prospective blurbers several months before publication after consulting with you.

The problem with blurbs is that everyone knows they're a little like insider trading. An author or editor asks writer friends to provide them, and soon the result is a Medusa's head of reciprocated favors. So-and-so owes Such-and-such who in turn owes So-and-so who once did a kindness for Whatshername.

That said, there's very little to be done to damp those suckers down in this hyper-consumer age of exaggerated acclaim.

More important, the act of blurbing isn't necessarily as evil as some make it out to be. After all, what's wrong with one talented writer trying to encourage the career of another? And what's wrong with a more established author trying to help a less established author make her or his debut in this difficult profession? Or with an author who's more well known trying to garner some attention for an author who's less well known . . . or who has even been unjustly neglected for years, if not decades?

Many will argue that those questions are ultimately moot, since it's really the novel's jacket design that catches the reader's eye. I'm not so sure. It seems to me the more literate a reader is, the more likely he or she is to first look at the jacket, then read the cover material (including blurbs), and then take a quick dip into the book before deciding whether or not to buy. So you want to cover your bases.

Suggest to your editor the names of a few established writers whose work you admire, but who you don't know personally. They probably won't decide to blurb your work, given the number of blurb requests that wash up on their doorsteps every day, but, if they do, their blurbs will carry a military transport of weight.

Next, if you happen to know a writer or two—perhaps a published friend, perhaps a former creative writing teacher, perhaps someone you were introduced to at a conference—don't be chary about approaching them. This is just part of the writing business, and all writers know it. Explain the situation, and tell them that you'll more than understand if they decide to pass if they discover your book's not for them.

Last, make sure similar authors blurb similar authors. If you've written a Cyberpunk novel, try to get a Cyberpunk writer to blurb it. Use the blurb to make a statement about the kind of book you've written. That will help your potential readers understand what they're holding in their hands.

Mailing Lists. Use your computer to start a mailing list. You might want to use a simple word-processing program, or, if you can afford it, purchase one especially designed for sorting and printing labels. (For Windows these are free or shareware.) Such lists are indispensable for letting people know about your book's publication and the readings you'll do on its behalf.

Include your friends' names and addresses, naturally. But also include the names of acquaintances, local newspapers and magazines and journals, television and radio stations, regional and national review organs, bookstores, and major distributors. Always try to be as specific as possible—don't just generate an address for a magazine, for instance, but for the review editor there, or, better yet, a particular reviewer who tends to write about the kind of book you've written. Search down the names and addresses of your favorite writers through such reference guides as *A Directory of American Poets and Fiction Writers* (Poets & Writers, Inc., updated regularly), and of community colleges, colleges and universities in your area or which you once attended in such reference guides as *The PMLA Directory* (Modern Language Association, updated yearly).

Trade your lists with writer friends who have come up with their own.

As you set a date for reading in a new city, make sure to do a little research on interview and review outlets and add those.

At your reading, you might even want to leave a sign-up sheet near the exit so you can later notify those listeners interested in your work of future readings and publications.

Review Copies. Most editors will send out a certain number of review copies—always, doubtless, fewer than you'd expect—several months before the actual publication date. Some of those copies might take the form of galleys.

Make sure you know how many he or she's mailing, where they're going, when they're going (the sooner the better, and at least three months prior to publication is preferable), and when he or she plans to follow up to make sure they've arrived at their destinations and are being read by those who should read them.

Suggest some places you'd like to see them go, as well, and be as precise as possible. Consult your mailing list for names and addresses.

As author, you'll receive a number of free copies of your book from your publisher. Try to secure as many of these as you can . . . you should get this number written into your contract. After you've dispensed the necessary few to friends and family, use the remainder to target or retarget several review, interview, or reading venues from your mailing list. Accompany your book with a cover letter that politely states who you are and what your book is about, and quotes from blurbs or—better yet—from some early favorable reviews or reviews of your previous work. Follow up on these after a week or two.

If you do some reviewing, you should always lend your writer friends a hand in getting their books reviewed, and you should expect them to do the same for you. If you love a book you come across, do everything you can to get the word out about it. Again, don't think of this part of the publishing process any differently than you would any other: collaboration counts here as much as it does during, say, brainstorming or critiquing.

And a word to the wise and humane: *never review a book you don't like.*

What's the point?

Books have enough working against them.

If you don't like a book, the easiest way to kill it is simply to remain mute about it.

Brochures, flyers, postcards. Mailing announcements of your book's publication and your reading itinerary is a great way to get the word out about them.

If you can't afford a fancy brochure designed and run off by a professional printer, go for a good-looking Do-It-Yourself flyer or postcard. You can design these on your own computer, or use a friend's who has a simple page-design program. Even a regular word-processing program can do in a crunch—or a pair of scissors, paste, and some press-down type available at most art- or any graphic-supply store.

Stop by your local copy center and run your announcements off on brightly colored paper. For postcards, simply use heavier weight paper and print four or six to a page, then cut them out.

Use eye-catching graphics. If you don't want to or can't produce your own, then create collages garnered from zines, album covers, any snazzy thing. If at all possible, though, include a cover shot of your book. Keep your design open and readable. You need to get the essential info across, but keep in mind that if you put *too* much on a page the reader just won't take the time to sort through it all.

If you're announcing the publication of your book, be sure to include the title, ISBN, price, publisher's snail-mail and/or e-mail address, a Web site if you or your publisher has created one (and you should—there are freeware programs that enable you to do so easily and quickly), a list of distributors, and a blurb or two that gives a sense of what your fiction's about.

If you're doing a brochure, and hence have a little more room to play with, you might also include a note about yourself, any awards you've won, and a list of other works you've published.

These shouldn't go out until you're sure your book is available.

If you're announcing a reading, or even a series of readings, a flyer or small postcard will easily suffice. You might also want to create some simple posters to hang around town. Include the date, time, and location of the reading, and, if you can fit it, a blurb or two about the nature of your book. These should go out about three weeks before the actual event—close enough to the date so your audience won't forget it, and far enough away so they won't already have made other plans. Send copies to the local media up to a month in advance.

Readings. Every reading you give should be an excuse to see old friends and acquaintances, make new ones, possibly take you somewhere you haven't gone before, introduce a few strangers to your fiction, and celebrate the sheer fact of its existence in the world.

If you don't like performing, avoid these things. After all, you'll probably reach a wider audience through reviews.

But if you do like performing, plan on having a really good time, and:

• *Be creative about where to read.* If you've published a book or two, you might want to approach local or regional junior colleges, colleges and universities. If not, check into traditional community reading locations in your town or city. Does the YMCA have a series? Is there an art gallery, writers' group, library, church, bar, bookstore, or café that usually sponsors them? Don't feel constrained by what you discover. Invent your own locale, and create a party around the event itself. If you make your reading feel like something special, others will be inclined to start thinking it *is* something special.

• *Start planning early.* Up to a year before publication isn't an outrageous idea, and certainly no fewer than six months. Ask your editor or publisher for help. He or she will probably say no because of economic considerations, but it sure won't hurt to give it a try. In any case, let him or her know at least six weeks in advance of a specific reading so he or she can make sure to get your books into local bookstores or make them available for you to sell. It's also a good idea to let him or her know so he or she can see how hard you're working to support your book. On another front, think about trying to team up with one or two local writers for a group reading. It'll be more enjoyable that way, since you'll get to meet and talk to some other authors, and you'll most likely draw a larger crowd than if you read alone.

• *Lay extensive groundwork.* You can't do too much to let people in the area know you're going to read, and you can't do too much to find out about where you're reading and under what conditions. Send announcements to local papers and radio stations in addition to mailing postcards to friends and acquaintances and posting posters in nearby libraries, restaurants, co-ops, and bookstores. While you need to remain flexible, you should try to find out what the reading room will be like. Large or small? Will there be a table, a chair, a podium, a microphone, a glass of water for you? How large will the audience be? Why will they be there? Are they coming primarily to hear you, have a beer or espresso and talk to friends, or do an assignment for their professor? What you find out should influence the sort of work you read and length of time you read. Just in case the reality doesn't match what you've been told when you show up, however, bring alternate material. Be prepared to improvise. When you're first starting out, you probably won't be paid for your reading, but it's always worthwhile to ask if there will be an honorarium. Fifty dollars or more, and you should feel like royalty.

• *Practice.* There's nothing more embarrassing for an audience than to realize the reader, thumbing aimlessly through his or her book for a passage, or stumbling over the very words he or she has written, isn't prepared and isn't professional. Decide on a number of possible passages that work as fairly self-contained units, rehearse by reading and rereading them out loud (in front of a mirror, if you think it might help), until they become second nature, and spice them up with accents and interesting inflections. Time them to the minute. Develop some anecdotes around them.

• *Reading is entertainment.* In Europe, contemporary readings grew out of a nineteenth-century salon tradition where people gathered to discuss ideas. Consequently, a reading there tends to form a short (five to 15-minute) prelude to an extended, intelligent question-and-answer session. In America, on the other hand, contemporary readings grew out of a nineteenth-century saloon tradition where people gathered to be entertained and pass time. Consequently, a reading here tends to be heavy on performance and anecdote, and light on in-depth discussion. It will never hurt to remember that as you prepare your material. Attend many readings yourself, not only to meet new and hear favorite authors, but also to see how readings are done. Use what you discover—either by positive or negative example—to shape your own. Everyone individualizes his or her performance, but more often than not you'll find you should keep it short (no matter how many people are participating, readings seldom run more than 50 or 60 minutes, never more than 90—an audience just can't concentrate any longer) and keep it funny—at least in part (it's effective to vary the tone of the pieces you're reading, but you'll never miss if you close with something that leaves your audience laughing). Read more slowly than you think sounds right—this will counteract the tendency by most nervous presenters to read too quickly. Read with energy. Think of your reading as a dramatic performance rather than simple recitation of your prose. Engage with your audience during the reading by looking at them occasionally, smiling, telling stories about the genesis of the pieces you're reading and succinctly explaining their intent, and generally being friendly. It's always a good idea to leave five or 10 minutes at the end of your reading to answer any questions the audience might have for you. Don't be afraid of silence at this point: it will take a moment for those listening to switch gears from passive to active mode. More often than not, they'll appreciate the interaction.

• *You're not done yet.* Be prepared to stick around for a while after the reading to talk one-on-one with audience members, answer more questions, and autograph books or zines. Always bring along copies of your novel, story collection, or even journal or zine you've been published in, just in case the bookstore you contacted and recontacted never quite got around to getting them in, or didn't order enough. Once during your reading mention that those books, zines, or journals will be available for purchase afterwards and if possible enlist the help of a friend to make change and oversee sales. Take your time with each person who approaches you. Enjoy yourself. Enjoy others. And enjoy the moment.

Media. Don't wait for newspapers, magazines, radio stations and television stations to come to you. Go to them instead. Compose letters that introduce yourself, your work, and provide blurbs and reviews to give editors and program directors a sense of what you and your work is about. Tell them that you'd be happy to make yourself available for an interview at their convenience. Send them copies of your book. And then, per usual, follow up. Wait two or three weeks, then phone. Say you just wanted to make sure So-and-so received your package, and that you'd be happy to answer any questions she or he might have for you. This is no time to be shy, though such a phone call inevitably flies in the face of everything a writer believes about interacting with the world. Worse, most of these forays won't lead to anything. Still, some will . . . and one well-placed review or interview will reach hundreds—if not thousands or tens of thousands—more people than a single reading will, with its standard audience of anywhere from three people to over a hundred.

Interviews. If a newspaper, magazine, radio station, or television station does decide to interview you, make it your business to prepare. Always:

• *Know your audience and situation.* Find out what sort of people you'll be addressing and for how long, since both might give you an idea for what you'll want to emphasize and what sort of questions you might be asked. If you've written a novel about—among, say, many, many other things—government conspiracies in the West, and you're interviewed in Portland, you already know the nature of the first questions you'll hear. If you're being interviewed on an alternative radio station on a show about horror, you know you'll need to say a few words about your sense of the genre. Try to imagine what the likely questions will be, and spend some time getting ready to answer them in as few words as possible.

• *Know in advance what you want to say.* Interviews tend to be incredibly short. From your point of view, they'll be over before they start. So it's not a bad idea to approach each with several topics you'd like to see discussed and to guide the interviewer toward them. Sometimes the interviewer will ask you beforehand what you'll want to talk about. Sometimes she or he won't. In either case, if you come armed with some strong anecdotes about your past and your fiction, perspectives on what you're doing and why, and points about your recently published book you'd like to get across, you'll be able to lead rather than follow, and there'll be many fewer uncomfortable dead spaces between questions and answers.

• *Stay alert and affable.* Often you won't be able to do two takes of an interview, so make sure you're on your toes, and make sure to think before you speak. Even if you find yourself confronted by an aggressive interviewer, stay relaxed and friendly. Some interviewers thrive on conflict, but that's not why you're there, so just steer around it back to those topics you want to discuss. Some interviewers don't do *their* homework. Don't be surprised to learn the person asking you questions hasn't read your book, or hasn't read it carefully. Again, be ready to take control of the shape and direction of the interview to get across the information you feel is important. Answer the questions you want asked rather than those the interviewer in fact poses—rephrase or even change his or her questions into the ones you'd prefer, and answer those. Don't reveal the fact that you've already answered the same questions a hundred times before. Keep in mind that, even though that might be the case, your listeners, viewers, or readers won't have heard what you have to say.

• *Keep it brief.* It's easy to go on and on about your favorite topics—yourself and your book—in an interview, yet remember that your interview will seldom last more than twenty or thirty minutes, and usually only three or five. So keep your responses short, pithy, and information-rich. Thirty seconds or a minute is frequently as long as you'll get for an answer before an interviewer cuts in with another question. That's not a problem, as long as you expect it. Don't work against this framework. It's simply one of the conventions of the interview situation.

• *Once again, follow up.* Make a point of tracking down a copy of the interview if it's in print, or a video or cassette of it if it's been broadcast. Interviews are wonderful items to include in future PR packets, since they give sturdy, compact profiles of you that will help future interviewers, reviewers, and reading sponsors get a sense of who you are, where you came from, what you believe, and what your work is about. Also, writers can learn by listening or looking at themselves about how they can improve next time by, say, being more concise, or looking at the camera, or dropping verbal tics.

No doubt we've come a very, very long way by now from discussing the science of the various blisses of language and the sweetness and light of the aesthetic object itself . . . let alone how best to compose for the new millennial moment.

No wonder this is the part of the profession that few writers like to talk about, and even fewer like to participate in.

But it's there, and, short of having a major New York publishing house behind you with a tall stack of dollar bills and a snazzy PR machine, it's utterly necessary to know about these things and use them to your advantage if you want more than a small handful of friends to find out about what you're creating and how to find a copy of it.

So don't fall for the quasi-self-righteous (and usually well-financed) voices that tell you this is all crass commercialism to be avoided like some bucktoothed, drooling, limp-left-legged plague.

You'll never get rich doing any of this, but there's a great chance more people will hear about you and your fiction.

And, short of writing in a closet, that's most likely what you're after.

"If a writer proclaims himself as isolated, uninfluenced and responsible to no one," critic Charles Newman once said, "he should not be surprised if he is ignored, uninfluential, and perceived as irresponsible."

In the new millennium, then, a writer needs not only to collaborate, read widely and deeply, spend long and hard hours imagining and then drafting and then redrafting his or her fiction, and give over months (if not years, if not decades) of his or her life to finding it a good home.

A writer needs to peddle it, too.

Index

Lance Olsen is author of more than a dozen books of and about postmodern fiction, including *Tonguing the Zeitgeist*, 1995 Philip K. Dick Finalist, and the first full-length study of William Gibson. A Pushcart Prize recipient, he teaches creative writing and contemporary fiction in the MFA program at the University of Idaho and resides digitally at Café Zeitgeist <www.uidaho.edu/~lolsen>.